French Manners

Colette closed her eyes and stroked the hand
of her lover. He'd been eager, pushing into her
with a force she was unused to. Then she
looked up and saw the dark figure of the curé
bending over Victor. 'Was that enough for you,
my darling?' he asked. She was shocked to see
that it was Victor he was talking to. 'Now you
understand you do not need her. I told you
she was a whore; your father's whore.' Colette
was paralysed, unable to understand what
was occurring. What a fool she had been!

French Manners
Olivia Christie

BLACK LACE

Black Lace books contain sexual fantasies.
In real life, always practise safe sex.

3
This edition published in 2005 by
Black Lace
Thames Wharf Studios
Rainville Road
London W6 9HA

Originally published 1997

Typeset by SetSystems Ltd, Saffron Walden, Essex

ISBN 978 0 352 33214 1

The Random House Group Limited supports The Forest Stewardship
Council® (FSC®), the leading international forest certification organisation.
All our titles that are printed on Greenpeace approved FSC® certified paper
carry the FSC® logo. Our paper procurement policy can be found at
www.randomhouse.co.uk/environment

Printed and bound in Great Britain by
CPI Antony Rowe, Chippenham, Wiltshire

Chapter One

Colette lay naked on her back, letting the flow of the river wash over her tired body. The clear, brown water swirled round her limbs, cooling and softening her skin after a week in the fields.

She had been given time off to make herself beautiful for Gaston. As if she cared! Gaston already followed her around like a lap dog, and would marry her as soon as she said yes.

She shivered, and swam towards the rocks where she had left her clothes, feeling the May sunshine warm her skin as soon as she clambered out on to the hot stone. Colette stood up and stared at her reflection in the water below her. She put her hands round her waist as Gaston had done at the dance last week. He had wanted her then, and she had felt her body start to respond to his, but when he pressed his hips against hers, and she felt his hot, winey breath on her lips, she had told him to wait. The thought of spending the rest of her life with him frightened her, but she knew she must agree soon.

1

Her hands dropped to cover her flat belly. Below her, on the smooth surface of the water, she could see the tips of her fingers dipping over the thick bush of dark hair covering her mound. Slowly, she reached further between her thighs, and gently parted her soft sex lips.

If she did as her mother wanted, and promised to marry Gaston, he would have the right to know her body better than she did herself. He wanted her already; she had felt him swell beneath his rough breeches when he held her close. Clumsy, ignorant Gaston would put his hands over the place she stroked now, and then he would drive his thick shaft deep inside her. She shivered with excitement at the thought. Gaston was dull and ugly, but she could not deny the feelings he aroused in her. If Victor had not come home, she would have given Gaston his answer today.

For a moment, poised on the rock, she remembered Victor standing here. This was where they used to swim when they were children. It was on the rocks high above here that Victor used to stand beautifully naked, his skin gleaming in the sunlight before he soared into the air and dropped into the murky depths of the river like a golden hawk. Everything about him was bright and glowing, so different from most of the men in this village, especially Gaston.

Now Victor had returned to Argnon. Last night his father had ridden past their orchard, and had stopped to talk to her parents. Colette had hidden at the top of her ladder, leaning against a branch of the peach tree, and stared at him. The Count looked nothing like his son. He was not tall, shorter than Victor, and his skin was olive, not the kind of

2

golden tan that Victor seemed to have all year round. He looked as though he spent his life shut up in rooms, not in the open air of Argnon where he had been born.

It seemed a long time since she had last seen him, four years ago, when he had visited the village school, and looked round the class, before asking the master who was the brightest pupil. The master had pointed her out, a plain, awkward little girl, who enjoyed reading. Monsieur had patted her on the head, and she had wanted to hit out at him for making an exhibition of her. This was the man who had taken Victor away from her. She hated him. But Victor was back now, and she would see him again. And he would learn that she was no longer a child.

She looked down at her bare breasts, with her nipples stiffened by the chilly river, and laughed. She felt proud of the way her body had developed. Below, the deep pool beckoned her. Colette stretched up and felt a thrill of fear as she plunged into the water below.

She swam to the bank and rubbed herself dry with her petticoat, shaking her head so that the water flew off her dripping hair. Her thick, black curls dried quickly in the hot sun, and she brushed them furiously until they gleamed, then ran up the rocky hillside to her family's cottage. In an hour, she would put on her faded Sunday dress and sit in church with the family, waiting for the chance to see Victor.

'Sit still,' her mother hissed.

Colette could not. There was a rustle of excitement from the back of the packed church, and she had to look round. Victor must have arrived. In another moment she would see him.

She felt her mother's elbow poke her sharply in the ribs. 'It's not Victor you should be thinking about. Gaston will want to talk to you after the service. Make sure you give him the right answer.'

How could she think of anyone else but Victor? Colette shifted uncomfortably on the hard wood of the bench, feeling her river-washed skin still tingling under the thin cotton of her dress. She would do what her mother wanted; she would agree to marry Gaston, but not today. For the moment she could only think of one man, even though she knew that her mother's angry words were true. 'You were friends with Victor when you were children simply because of your lessons with the curé. You must not expect him to notice you now. Maintain your dignity.'

Colette turned her head slightly, met her mother's warning glance, and stared straight ahead of her. It didn't matter. Victor would have to pass close to her when he walked up to the family pew. She gazed down at her prayer-book, greedily glancing sideways when she heard the footsteps draw level. Victor looked taller, more broad-shouldered now; she could not see his face, but the golden hair curled as brightly on his head and his tawny skin glowed in the shaft of light from the window above the altar. The window that his family had given to the village, as everything else of beauty came from them.

Victor gave no sign that he had seen her. Colette took a deep breath as if preparing for the hymn, aware that her bodice was too tight over her breasts. She had been promised a new dress after the

4

harvest, but that was months away, and there would be no new clothes until the fruit was in. Why couldn't Victor have returned then? It was all very well for her mother to look at her with satisfaction; because the laces of the faded, red cotton strained over her breasts and the sight kept all the village boys awake at night. She would have no trouble making sure that Gaston married her, but Victor would be used to elegant ladies. Her clothes would make her seem even more beneath him. Would he even notice how the men in the village admired her now?

Risking another glance towards Victor, she was disappointed that he was still looking straight in front of him as though intent upon the service. She was a fool to think he might consider her worth looking at; he must have seen so many beautiful women in Paris. While he had been away in the fashionable world, she had stayed in the village and seen nothing. Even the lessons with the curé had become less interesting. Although Gilles de la Trave had continued to pay for them, the curé took less trouble with her. And without Victor, it had been hard to learn on her own.

Colette smoothed her skirt over her hips. It would not do to look too eager, she knew. But what if her mother were wrong? What if he had come back for her?

Her mother nudged her. 'Gaston is watching you. Smile at him.'

She saw Gaston staring at her eagerly, and she smiled back, surprising him. She raised her head, letting her freshly-washed, black hair ripple over her shoulders. If Victor would only look round now, surely he would feel jealous?

After the service Gaston would want to walk her home, and he would ask her again when she would marry him. She saw him beam at her and flush deep scarlet beneath his sun-dark skin, and she smiled again.

Her mother was right; she had to marry. Already several of the girls of her age were married, and none of them attracted the men as she did. Gaston was a good catch; he had the biggest farm in the village. Colette looked across at her friend Jeanne who had married last month. She looked smug now and satisfied, as if she knew something that Colette did not. And her husband was as rough as Gaston.

If she could just feel Victor's hands on her body, if he could be the first for her, that would be enough. She knew he couldn't marry her, but if he would take her once, she would do what her mother wanted and settle down with Gaston. But first she had to get the thoughts of Victor out of her mind once and for all.

She sang well and clearly. The curé seemed pleased, as well he might with such a full church. She hoped that, after the service, Victor would stop outside the church to talk to her. Colette prayed that the curé would not talk too long.

As the choir filed out of the church, she risked another glance at the pew in front of her. Victor was rising from his knees; in another moment he would look her full in the face. But the eyes that slowly undressed her, staring at her as if she stood naked in the cold nave of the church – those cool, grey eyes belonged to his father.

For a moment she stared back, fascinated. It was an ugly face, dark and frightening, and she remembered the stories she had heard as a child, about

6

how he had deserted his wife and child. Victor's mother had hardly ever been seen in the village although the château was always full of her friends from Paris. Victor had chosen to spend most of his time with her, and had seemed happier then. Now, with Gilles' gaze full on her, she refused to look away. Why should she not be pleased to see Victor, her friend whom she had not seen for so long. Was it forbidden?

And Monsieur's expression changed. The sinister sneer softened. The curled, sardonic lip curved up at one corner; the cold eyes swept over her again, as if assessing her, and only when he passed by the end of her pew did either of them drop their gaze.

Gilles de la Trave obviously did not approve of her friendship with his son. He must consider her beneath contempt, just a peasant girl, but perhaps dangerous now that she had grown up. Well, that was flattering and gave her some hope. And it was his fault that she had an education. He was the one who had paid for her lessons. He had picked her out.

She would do as her mother advised and marry Gaston in the autumn. But before that she wanted Victor to make love to her. She had always dreamt that he would be the one to awaken her body. Of course he would not marry her, but he could be her first lover.

Most of the villagers waited in the square outside the church. It was usual for them to gossip at this time, and today they lingered for another chance to stare at Gilles de la Trave. Colette leaned against the trunk of a plane tree, and tried to appear unconcerned. Gaston would come over in a moment; she could not put him off any longer, and Victor had still not spoken to her.

Now her father was standing with his hat in one hand, nervous and embarrassed, as Gilles walked towards them. She saw Victor standing outside the church, blinking in the bright sunlight, and forced herself to remain where she was. Let him come to her! He was talking to the curé, shaking hands. At any moment he must look in her direction.

What could he have to say to the curé that took so long? Colette struggled to contain her impatience. Finally Victor moved away from the priest, looked vaguely around him, saw her and gave a brief smile before stepping up into a waiting carriage.

Was it possible that he had nothing to say to her after four years away? They had been friends, how could he ignore her like this now? No doubt Monsieur disapproved of his son's childhood friendship with a peasant girl from the village, but Victor was a man now. He should make his own decisions.

She stepped backwards as Gilles shook her father by the hand, and almost bumped into Gaston who stood behind her, waiting for her. She turned to him. 'You may walk me home,' she said, but his quick beam of delight irritated her and the heavy pressure of his arm round her waist disturbed her.

She did not pull away. If Victor chose to ignore her here, she would let him see that other men found her attractive. She almost laughed out loud. Victor's father had not disguised his appreciation. Perhaps that would goad him into action.

Gaston led her into a narrow lane between dusty hedges edging the orchards, taking the long way back to her home. His pace quickened until they were out of sight of the last villager, then she felt the heat of his body burning against her as he pulled her against him. Her legs parted instinctively over the hard curve of his thigh, and she reached up for him as his body shuddered in response. Both his hands gripped her now, cradling her hips with his fingers.

'Colette, there is no need to wait. Say that you'll marry me.' His voice was harsh and husky, pleading with her. He dipped his head and pressed his hot lips on the curve of her breast. She had never let him touch her like this before, now she seemed powerless to prevent him. She felt the rough pads of his thumbs brush over her skin as he loosened the strained laces over her breasts, and she made no move to stop him as his callused fingers rasped over her rigid nipples.

He pushed her back against the thick trunk of an oak tree. 'I can't wait any longer,' he said, stroking her stiffened nipple. 'You want me too. Let me take you now.'

Gaston had the right. They were almost promised. All the village expected them to name a date for the wedding. His hands circled her breasts; he felt hot, and her skin tingled at his touch. If she let him go any further, all her resistance would end. She knew that he could sense her need.

She pulled away and retied the laces on her bodice, covering her breasts. 'Let me go home now, Gaston. Mother will be waiting for me. I have to help serve our lunch.'

He looked away, but she knew he would understand the priority of her family. 'Let me come with you,' he said. 'Let me ask your father now.'

She must have a couple of days, time to see

Victor and to let him know how she felt. She shook her head. 'No, not today, my father rests on Sundays. But I will speak to him soon. Come on Wednesday.'

His face lit up. 'I may ask him on Wednesday?'

'Don't press me now,' she shouted as she sped down the lane. 'I'll see you tomorrow, we'll talk then.' She blew him a kiss and ran faster. She really was late, and she knew that if she stayed close to Gaston any longer her resistance would break down.

The sweat was running down her face as she reached the end of the narrow track. She slowed down as she saw a shadow crossing the dusty earth of the path, and looked up to see a stranger on a chestnut horse blocking her way. He must have seen her with Gaston. She blushed, and tried to straighten her rumpled clothes.

'I'm to take you to the château,' he said.

So Victor had not forgotten her. She had been right to refuse Gaston. She wished she had not run so hard or so fast. All the care she had taken with her appearance that morning was wasted. This man must have seen the way Gaston had touched her, perhaps even her bare breasts beneath the loosened bodice; his eyes were insolent, and he stared hard at her.

He bent down, put his arms around her waist and lifted her easily on to the saddle in front of him. 'My name is Jean-Pierre,' he told her. 'I work for Monsieur.'

Colette was shocked by the intimacy of their posture; she had never nestled so close to a man before, not since she had left her father's knee. Even at the village dances she had kept her distance. This felt more intimate. Now, pressed between the leather pommel of the saddle and the man's thighs, she could feel the outline of his body through the thin folds of her skirt, and she realised immediately that the sensation was arousing for him, too. A large, firm shape pressed between her buttocks, stirring with the rhythm of the horse's movement. She dared not look round, but her face burned with shame as they progressed.

If he had said one word to her, she would have leapt off and run home, but they rode in silence and the rocky path beneath the horse's hooves seemed far down and jagged, so that she dared not jump. She hoped there would be time to tidy herself when they reached the château, before she saw Victor.

The thought calmed her a little. She allowed herself to relax and enjoy the ride, thankful that they had not taken the road through the village so that everyone could see her disorder. She flushed again. It was impossible to hide her reaction to the man's body pressing against her; it was better that no one could see.

When they reached the gates of the château, she turned to face him. 'Set me down here,' she said. 'I'll walk the rest of the way.' She needed time to compose herself.

Jean-Pierre said nothing, simply swung his leg over the horse's rump and slid lightly to the ground. He looked up at her, his face alight with amusement as he saw her glance involuntarily at the obvious bulge in his tight riding breeches. The corners of his mouth twitched and he stared at her impudently before he turned away and led her on the horse up the cool, tree-lined drive round one

11

side of the lake to the château. So he knew why she had asked to be set down!

When they stopped, Colette waited upright on the horse, uncertain what was expected of her. She looked up at the honey-coloured façade of the building. She had only seen this place from a distance, and it seemed impossible to believe that this was just a home for people to live in. It was many times larger than the church, and far more beautiful, with turrets and spires of pale, pierced stone making a lacy pattern against the sky. The crisp outline of its rooftops was reflected in the lake, shimmering in the afternoon sun. Victor's lake, where she had never been allowed to swim.

She looked up uncertainly. When would she see Victor? She felt Jean-Pierre's hand on her waist, lifting her down, and she jerked forward, trying to hold her head up.

As she walked towards the wide, stone staircase, she saw the massive front door swing open. A figure at the top of the stairs was at first hidden in shadow, and then she saw Gilles de la Trave standing between the stone pillars of the entrance to the château. She felt Jean-Pierre's eyes watching her, and she straightened her back so that he would not see the cold fear that gripped her. 'Oh, Victor, where are you?' she breathed as she stepped forward over the pale, carefully raked gravel.

Gilles reached the bottom of the steps just as she put her foot on the hard stone. He held out both hands to her. His skin felt dry and cool on her hot fingers; she prayed that he could not feel her trembling.

'Monsieur.' She lowered her head, and let her knees bend in a bare suggestion of a curtsey.

12

'I am delighted to make your acquaintance at last,' he said. 'Victor has often spoken of the child who shared his lessons.'

'It was kind of you to pay for them, Monsieur.'

He smiled. 'My son needed stimulation, and you showed intelligence. I believed you were good for him.'

Colette thought of the long, hard look he had given her in the church. If the count were the judge of women she had always heard, she should be flattered.

But where was Victor now? Monsieur was leading her up the stairs and there was still no sign of his son. She could only follow. A footman held the door open, a man she had never seen before, not a villager. The interior of the château was gloomy, and her eyes struggled to become accustomed to the darkness after the bright light outside.

She stepped on the hard, black and white diamonds of the marble floor of the hall, looking around her. Glossy mahogany doors rose above her on either side, but this massive space led right through to the other side of the house and the wall ahead of her seemed to consist only of square panes of glass, open to a private park she had never even glimpsed before. The hills rose behind the château, dark and forbidding, blocking out the light so that an extraordinary darkness loomed over the woods at the back of the garden.

'You never played here together, did you?' he asked as they walked through the wide, cool hall. 'It would give me pleasure to show you around my house later.' It felt strange to be in the mansion she had only glimpsed before. 'Victor is waiting for you in the pavilion. Will you allow me to take you to

13

him?' Gilles led her towards the glass doors where another footman stood waiting. As they approached, he held the doors wide open.

She turned toward Gilles. He stood like a shadow against the darkness of the walls, looking out towards the summer house where he said Victor waited for her. He gave no hint of his feelings. Was he giving them his approval?

The pavilion was the same honey-coloured stone as the château, but it stood in the shadow of the trees and its walls were covered with ivy. She could see Victor in the dim interior, waiting for her. The smooth lawn seemed endless beneath her feet and she clenched her hands until her fingernails bit into her palms.

Her mother was wrong. Victor thought of her as she had dreamt of him. And Monsieur? Was it possible he accepted her? Her steps quickened until she was running across the velvet stretch of soft grass towards the golden figure of the boy she adored.

Why had he chosen to meet her here instead of one of the places they used to play together, the river or the wood where no one would see them? She looked back to see if his father was still watching her, but the glass doors had closed behind him and she could see nothing.

Victor was not alone; the curé was with him. Colette bent her head in acknowledgement of his presence, and to hide her burning face. Surely Victor could do better than this! He must know that she wanted to be alone with him.

She looked around her. The garden was laid out in a series of formal paths, separated by high yew hedges. They were dark and private. 'Will you show me round the gardens?' she said quickly.

Victor turned to the curé, who bowed. 'I must leave now, Victor. It would do you good to take some exercise. Of course Colette must be interested. I don't believe she has been here before.'

She smiled innocently. 'You're right, father. I do want Victor to show me everything.'

'You will come back?' Victor looked at the curé anxiously.

'I was here last night. I don't want to intrude.' Colette watched his slim, black-robed figure turn and walk away through the woods to the village.

So the chaperone Monsieur had provided was prepared to leave them alone. Colette held out both her hands to Victor and stretched towards him so that the tips of their fingers touched. He looked at her with his beautiful, amber eyes, warm and glowing in the sunlight.

'Have I changed, Victor?' she demanded.

The golden eyes clouded. 'You are beautiful, Colette, as I always knew you would be.' He stroked the gleaming fall of black hair that rippled down over her shoulder blades. She could feel the warmth of his hand through the thin cotton of her dress. She turned and reached up for him, to press her lips on his, that touch she had dreamed of for so long. But he pulled back and his lips merely brushed her cheek, a dry touch, scarcely a kiss at all. He turned away abruptly, and gave a short, embarrassed laugh before he took her hand again. 'Walk round the garden with me, Colette. Talk to me about our lessons when we were children. Do you still visit the curé?'

'He takes little interest in me now that you are not there.'

She pointed to a long walk between two lines of

tall yew hedges, as far out of sight of the château as possible. 'Will you take me down there, Victor?'

He placed her arm on his and patted her hand. 'Of course. Come with me.'

He was so close! She could feel the heat of his body. She was conscious of her nakedness beneath her thin dress, and the fabric straining over her breasts seemed tighter now. Surely he, too, must be aware of her body? When they reached the privacy of the yew walk, she waited for him to take her in his arms. Now that they were out of sight of the château, away from the brooding presence of his father, she wanted him to seize his opportunity.

When they reached a heated glasshouse at the far end of the walk, Victor turned as if to go back. Desperate to keep him longer, Colette entered the steamy enclosure and stretched up for an early apricot. She took her time, choosing the highest she could reach to show off her newly-developed figure to advantage. Gaston would have been driven mad by now.

Casually Victor reached up and twisted the fruit off the stalk for her. 'If you eat it now the juice may stain your dress. My father hopes that you will dine with us. I will have it prepared for you.'

Colette frowned, surprised. 'Eat here, Victor? I can't.' She would have more time with Victor, it was true, and it was an honour, but the thought frightened her. His father intimidated her, and the curé's lessons had taught her nothing of how to behave in a situation like this. What would they eat? Surely something very different from the bread and soup that was her family's evening meal?

Victor's hand pressed hard on hers. 'He wants it,

Colette. Say you agree. Jean-Pierre will tell your parents, and take you home later.'

So he had a plan. That was why he was so cool to her now. He knew they had more time together. There was an intensity in his voice that convinced her it was important for her to stay, but the thought of eating dinner with the count alarmed her.

'Will you show me what to do, Victor?' she asked. 'Will you help me?'

'There will be no difficulty, Colette. My father will make every effort to ensure that you enjoy your evening.'

'And you, Victor, will you be pleased if I stay?'

'Of course. We are old friends, are we not?' And he gripped her hand tightly as she climbed a stone staircase beside a fountain.

At the top, she stood on the step above him, looking at him as the sunlight glinted on his golden brown hair and turned the warm amber of his eyes to gleaming gold. She wanted to reach out and stroke him, to press her mouth on his full, red lips and to feel his body hard against hers. But he made no move towards her, standing beneath her at the length of their outstretched arms for a long time until he climbed up beside her, took her arm in his and led her past the ornamental ponds, across the parterre to the open, glass doors of the salon.

She felt her body tremble at the thought of what they would do later. Victor had a plan, she was sure of it, and she would give herself to him willingly. It need only be this once. All she wanted was for him to be the first. Until then, she would do her best not to disgrace him in front of his father.

* * *

Monsieur, rising from a deep, leather armchair in a corner of the salon, came across the room like a smooth, grey shadow and she felt a chill as he advanced towards her. The touch of his cool hands made her shiver and she struggled to understand his purpose in inviting her to stay for the evening. Surely Victor could have arranged to meet her somewhere other than here? Did it excite the count to see them together? He seemed to understand all her deepest thoughts. Was it for the pleasure of tormenting her that he wanted to watch her in Victor's company, unable to touch him?

When Jean-Pierre announced dinner, Colette followed the men through a high doorway into a dimly-lit room where black and gold brocade curtains shut out all daylight. Candles flickered on the polished oak of the dining table, but their light failed to brighten the drab tapestries lining the walls. Despite the heat of the day, a fire burned in the massive stone fireplace of this cold room.

Jean-Pierre stood behind a chair in the middle of one side of the table. Gilles gestured to Colette to sit down; he and Victor sat at the far ends of the table. In front of her, she saw rows of bright silver cutlery ranged on either side of a gilded plate.

Jean-Pierre held out a tray of glasses. She took one; it was heavy and deeply-cut, full of a dark red wine. She waited until the men raised their glasses to her and then she sipped.

'The claret is not to your taste, Colette?'

Once more, Gilles seemed aware of what she was thinking. She ran the pad of her finger over the sharp edges of the crystal before replying. His question was not only about her wine. She sipped again, and smiled. 'I'm perfectly content, Monsieur. You are too kind.'

Victor was frowning. Did he hate his father so much? It was as though he was frightened of him. What was it between these two?

She wanted to reassure him. Later, when they were alone, she would let him see how just being near him aroused her. Beneath her dress she could feel her nipples enlarging, rubbing against her rough cotton bodice. Her breasts seemed to swell as she looked at him, as his penis had grown while they took their lessons with the curé. She understood now how he had felt; she had been too young then. Perhaps he had been disappointed in her; tonight she would show him how she had changed.

A shallow cup of soup was placed in front of her. She watched carefully as Gilles lifted one of the spoons at his right hand and then she copied him. She was hungry.

In the centre of the table the flickering light from a heavy silver candelabra dazzled her. She stared at it, fascinated, until she realised that each shining column rising from its base was formed in the shape of a vibrantly erect penis over which the dripping wax of the candles was melting like cream. She looked away hurriedly and studied the tapestries on the wall.

'Do they interest you, Colette?' Gilles' voice broke through her concentration. 'Our tapestries are famous.'

'I know very little,' she said. 'Our lessons did not include embroidery.'

She saw him frown and rise to his feet. He took her hand, and led her over to the hangings on the wall. 'Look.' He lifted her hand up to the dull

19

fabric. 'See how the figures seem to live and breathe.'

She touched the silk stitches with the tips of her fingers, tracing the outline of a peacock's out-stretched plumage. Gilles picked up one of the candles and held it between them, and she saw the pale colours leap into jewelled life, illuminated by the flame. The vivid blues and greens of the feathered tail were echoed in the glistening leaves of the trees and the glowing gowns of the ladies resting beneath them.

'You see there is more than you realise at first? But don't let me spoil your meal.' Colette felt his hand cover hers once more as they returned to the table. He caught her eye. 'Of course you must understand that everything here belongs to my wife.' He paused. 'Victor's mother. She used to spend a great deal of time here. Now she prefers Italy, doesn't she, Victor?'

Victor looked sullen. 'She seems happier there.'

Colette wanted to know more about Victor's life in Italy, but Monsieur had already changed the subject. Why had he shown her all these things? Did it amuse him to see how the pictures aroused her? He must know how she felt about Victor, but was he simply teasing her? Did he intend to make sure that she had no time alone with his son?

A mound of crayfish lay curled on a plate in front of her. She had often caught them in the river and eaten the sweet flesh straight from the shells. She was sure that was not what Victor and his father would do.

She saw Gilles glance towards Jean-Pierre, who took a crisp, white napkin from the sideboard and placed it round her neck. Gilles took his own, tucked it into his shirt, and picked up one of the crayfish in his fingers. Encouraged, she broke the brittle shell and sucked out the juicy meat.

When she had finished, the count pushed back his chair. Relieved, Colette thought that now she would be alone with Victor. He would take her home and they would have time together. But the count came to stand behind her chair and took her hand. 'Let me show you our paintings,' he said. 'Perhaps you will find them more to your taste than the tapestries.' She waited for Victor to intervene. She was here as his friend; surely he could offer to show her the paintings himself. Or say that it was time they went home. She was sure it was dark outside, although from this enclosed room she could see nothing.

Victor did not stop her, he simply turned away as his father led her out of the room. She found herself in a long gallery, where the walls were covered with paintings in heavy gilt frames. 'Tell me what you think of this,' the count asked. 'And this.' She saw his eyes narrow. 'And this one.'

She almost laughed out loud. Did he think she was a fool? It was easy enough to read in his eyes which ones he thought were good. And they were hung in the best positions, so that the light fell on them better than the others. Then again, the curé had taught her how to look at paintings. She had stared for hours at those in the church until she could see them with her eyes shut. She ran her fingers over the heavily laid paint of a Madonna. 'The flesh tones are magnificent,' she said, and held his gaze. He had paid for her education and now he wanted to know how much she had learnt. Well she would show him all she knew. She would prove that she was worthy of Victor.

'See Monsieur,' she said, 'how the colour of the robes echoes the clarity of her eyes.' She touched the blue edge of the Madonna's cloak, where it fell open to reveal the breast of a nursing mother. The count appreciated women, she could tell. She had brains, and it excited her to show off to this man, who was so sophisticated. She had never had the chance to talk to anyone about the things the curé taught her. Not even Victor had been as interested as she was. And the paintings were very beautiful. It was not simply to shock him that she stroked one of the milky nipples on the rough-textured canvas with the tip of her finger.

She refused to let Monsieur intimidate her. She would have time to be with Victor before she went home, she was sure. But later, when she expected that he would offer to ride back with her, Monsieur intervened. 'We hope you will spend the night here,' he said. 'Jean-Pierre has informed your parents.'

A maid led Colette up a wide, marble staircase to the first floor. She turned to the left, walked a few paces along a wide corridor and opened a tall, mahogany door. Colette saw a bedroom dominated by the four gilded columns of a massive four-poster bed, draped in the same scarlet brocade that lined the walls.

Laid out on the bed was a white, silk negligée, delicately edged with lace. 'This is for you,' the girl said. 'My name is Marie. Will you let me assist you?'

Colette nodded. The maid seemed friendly, but she felt tired and confused. What was she doing here? Why had Victor not taken her home as she had expected? He must plan to come to her here tonight, but Colette felt embarrassed that it was to be made so obvious, and she felt ill at ease in these strange surroundings.

She turned to Marie in a panic. Perhaps, even now, it was not too late to go home. But Marie was busy rearranging the delicate silks, and was obviously waiting for her to remove her clothes.

Colette was embarrassed at the poor quality of her dress, but Marie took it without a murmur and laid it over a chair. Grateful for a few more moments when she could keep on her thin petticoat, Colette sat in front of a gilt mirror at the dressing table. Marie picked up a blue, enamel-backed hair-brush and started to stroke Colette's long curls of silky, black hair, taking her time, smoothing the tresses carefully. She slipped the straps of Colette's bodice down over her shoulders, loosened the lace fastening, and let it fall back on the chair.

Colette stared at herself in the mirror. Her hair fell over her chest, but her large breasts showed clearly through the black strands. Her nipples were pink and swollen, unfamiliar to her as a stranger's. At home she had one small piece of glass and no time to look in it privately.

Marie pressed her arm in a friendly fashion. 'I'll be back in a moment with some hot water,' she murmured. 'Will you slip off the rest of your things now, please?'

Unused to any help, Colette quickly stepped out of her petticoat. She stood naked in front of the mirror. In contrast to her face and arms, her body was pale, and the black triangle of crisp curls between her legs seemed prominent and provocative, as if

23

her body was designed to draw attention to her private parts.

The door opened and Marie slipped in quickly with a porcelain pitcher and basin. 'Beautiful,' she murmured, and held out a soapy sponge. 'Now if you'll just step on to the towel here – ' she laid it out on the carpet ' – I'll have you washed in a moment. Hold up your hair for me, will you?'

Horribly embarrassed, Colette raised her arms, and piled her hair on top of her head. Her breasts stuck out even more prominently now and she was sure that Marie was staring at them. She looked away from the maid's busy fingers. Was this how ladies were treated? She could perfectly well have washed herself. She felt a wave of anger at the thought that Victor might have asked Marie to make sure she was clean for him. Did he think she was a dirty peasant?

Her anger helped her to ignore the scented, soapy water trickling over her breasts and belly as Marie carefully sponged her skin. Then the girl's hands started to stroke the soap over her buttocks and legs, parting her thighs with a small murmur of appreciation as she continued her work, apparently unconcerned. Colette looked into the mirror, desperate not to show her embarrassment.

She saw the stiffened, rosy peaks of her breasts jutting out as the water cooled on her skin. Marie knelt with her back to the mirror, intent on her work, as her fingers delved between Colette's thighs. To her surprise, Colette realised that the sensation was pleasurable, more exciting than when she touched herself there, yet soothing. She saw a deep rose flush colouring her skin. Marie looked up and smiled, dabbing at her body with a soft towel.

She dried her all over and held out the sheer nightgown, slipping it down over Colette's shoulders. 'Beautiful,' she murmured again. 'Do you like it?'

The fine silk skimmed over her body like a transparent cloud, hiding little of her body. Marie gathered up the washing materials in her arms, moved towards the door and paused. 'If you want anything, please ring. Sleep well.' And she closed the door behind her.

What now? Would Victor come soon? Colette wished that she could have asked Marie, but what would she have said?

The room was hot and stifling. Before climbing into bed, Colette crossed to the window and drew back the heavy curtains. The windows were stiff and hard to open; she tried to push up with both her hands, and then stopped. There were lights in the pavilion, and she could see two figures. Victor and his father faced one another, with raised arms as though they were arguing. So that was why Victor was not able to come to her yet. Was his father angry with him? About her? Behind them, in the shadows between the yew hedges, there was another figure, dark and thin. The curé stood hidden and waiting.

Colette closed the curtain hastily, without opening the window, afraid they might hear a noise and see her light from outside. As she extinguished the candles, and slid between the soft sheets of the bed, she wondered how long it would be before Victor was free to come. And how would she feel when he made love to her?

* * *

Marie walked out of the room, carrying the damp towels and Colette's old clothes. She had enjoyed her task; now her day's work was nearly at an end. She felt a pair of hands catch her round the waist, and she gasped.

'You feel hot,' Jean-Pierre said, 'and a bit wet.' He pulled her close to him so that the pile she was carrying fell to the floor. She bent down to pick them up, and felt Jean-Pierre lift her skirts.

Angrily she pushed him away and collected the wet things together. He was too free with her, and too sure of himself. She didn't want him to have everything his own way. Not until they were married. She had quite a lot of money saved, and Monsieur was very generous to his valet. It was time for Jean-Pierre to settle down.

'Here, let me carry that. The sooner you're finished, the more time you'll have for me. And I want to hear all about the young lady.'

'I thought you had plenty of time to check her out when you brought her here,' Marie said, unloading her burden into his arms. It would serve him right to have his hands occupied for the moment. She had seen his condition when he brought the horse back to the yard earlier.

'You can't think I stopped to take her clothes off,' he protested, following her down the back staircase.

'You would have done if you had the chance!'

'Which you did.'

'And very pretty she is, too.'

'And hot. When I picked her up she'd come straight from her young man. She hadn't even had time to put her clothes straight.' He grabbed at Marie's skirt, but his hands were full and she slipped away.

'I bet you waited to have a good look at them together. Shame on you Jean-Pierre. Can't a young girl have a bit of a cuddle without you leering at her?'

'She didn't let him get very far,' he said, dumping the clothes down in the wash-house. 'If I'd been him I'd not have let her get away with no more than a kiss. She was ready for it all right. I could see that.' He pressed his hand over the lace of Marie's bodice and loosened it.

She giggled. 'She was ready for it when I put her to bed, too. Her nipples were leaping right through that tight old dress of hers, and she came upstairs quite pink with excitement.'

'Monsieur had been showing her his pictures.'

Marie sighed. 'He has a way with women,' she said quietly, 'but it's not him that young lady wants tonight.' She felt Jean-Pierre's hot breath on her breasts and let him part her laces fully. She thought about Colette lying alone in that big bed and took Jean-Pierre firmly by the hand. 'Not here,' she said, 'come upstairs with me.'

She had a room at the top of the house, larger than the one she had in Monsieur's house in Paris. Last night it had been fun to have sex in the new surroundings. Now she wanted Jean-Pierre again. Washing Colette's body had made her itch to feel a man inside her. The girl had made it quite obvious she was expecting Victor to come to her bed tonight.

Marie pushed her breasts out, wanting Jean-Pierre to put his hands round them again. 'How was she when you went to fetch her?' she asked. 'Did she want to come?'

Jean-Pierre laughed. 'She wanted to come all right. I almost had to pull her off her boyfriend.'

Marie grinned. 'Hadn't she had enough with her young man?'

'I told you. He got no further than the top of her breasts.' He pushed Marie's dress further down over her shoulders so that she was bare to her waist. She wriggled, and let it fall to the floor.

Colette's naked body had been a pleasure to touch. She looked at Jean-Pierre's cock coming towards her, and thought about it pressing between Colette's rounded cheeks.

'She's very charming, that girl,' she said, looking at his stiffening penis with a sigh of pleasure.

'You enjoyed helping her?'

Marie nodded vigorously. 'More than she did. She was very nervous. But after a while I think she liked it.' She sat up on the bed and took Jean-Pierre's erect penis in both her hands. 'Did it get hard like this with her, as well?' she asked.

He nodded. 'I made her ride on the horse in front of me, and let her feel how big it is,' he said proudly.

On the wall behind him there was a large mirror, and in it Marie could see Jean-Pierre's buttocks clenched tight. She had never had such a thing in her room before. Why had they put something like that in the servant's quarters? It seemed that everything in the château was meant for sex. She reached out for him and guided his thick shaft towards her thighs, watching the reflection of their two bodies as she did so.

'Tell me what she did when she felt you,' she said.

He laughed. 'She didn't know what to do. Her boyfriend had already got her going, and then there was this big fellow pressing against her.' He poked the base of his penis proudly, and then pressed it harder between her thighs, showing her how he had let Colette feel it. 'Turn over,' he said, 'and I'll show you properly.'

She sat up on the bed, facing the mirror, and looked at the two of them sitting one behind the other with their legs spread wide open. Jean-Pierre was straddling her from behind, as if he was riding her, and she felt the length of his thick shaft push right between her buttocks. In the mirror, she could see his big, red hands slide round, underneath her arms, and grasp her breasts hard. 'You didn't touch her there,' she gasped.

He shook his head. 'No, I didn't, but I would have if I hadn't had my orders,' he said. 'I'd have laid her right down on the grass, and shown her what she'd been missing.'

'What were your orders?'

'To bring her straight here. And no messing about. Monsieur was firm on that point. From the look on her face, I'd say she's never had it before.' He laughed. 'But she's good and ready.'

He pushed harder behind Marie, and they both toppled over. Marie pulled herself up. 'Show me,' she said. 'Show me everything you wanted to do to her.' She lay back on the bed and put her arms above her head.

She saw his tongue poke out of the side of his mouth as he lowered himself on to her. She felt his big cock ride into her, and she started to come. She wanted to hold back a little longer.

'Wait,' she said, pushing him off her, and climbing on top. 'If she gets half a chance with Victor, she'll have to take the lead.' She straddled his hips with her thighs, and lowered herself on to his rock-hard penis. She felt Jean-Pierre push up inside her, and she bent over him, letting her breasts swing over his open mouth until his teeth closed on her pointed nipples. He was rough with her then as if he had waited too long already.

Marie pressed down on Jean-Pierre's thick shaft and squeezed hard, revelling in the hard rod which leapt up inside her. He would not have dared to touch the girl, but every thrust told her how much Colette had excited him. Marie was content for the moment to reap the benefit of his arousal. She took him deeper into her, then paused for a moment. 'She expects Victor to come to her tonight.'

Jean-Pierre nodded. 'I know.'

'She's going to be disappointed.'

'Of course.' Jean-Pierre grasped Marie firmly by the buttocks, and pulled her hard on to him. She gasped, and shuddered as she climaxed. 'It's not our affair, Marie,' he said as he thrust into her, 'but Monsieur's not going to let that girl go in a hurry. I reckon we shall all see more of Colette.'

Marie started to speak, but he placed his hand over her mouth. 'Don't think about it now,' he said, 'just make sure you look after her in the morning.'

Chapter Two

Colette woke to see sunlight stream in as Marie opened her curtains. A fire was already lit in the grate and a pot of coffee steamed on the table beside her bed. The maid must have been in the room a few minutes already, while she was asleep. At home she was up soon after her mother, helping to prepare breakfast for the family and tidy the house. Here, she was being treated like a lady.

Marie was smiling at her. 'It's late,' she said. 'Did you sleep well?' she asked.

Colette shrugged. She had lain awake for hours, expectant and aroused after Marie's attentions, waiting for Victor. And he had not come. She felt as though she had only just fallen asleep. She shook her head and lied. 'It's difficult to get used to a strange room.'

Marie looked surprised. 'You don't find it comfortable?'

'I'm not accustomed to anything like this.'

'Of course not.' Marie grinned and filled a cup

31

with coffee. 'Now drink this and let me show you what you will wear this morning.'

'I only have one dress.' But Colette found that she was talking to herself; Marie was out of the room before the sentence was finished. The door swung shut behind her, and Colette sipped at the strong coffee in its green and gold porcelain cup. Her hands shook a little, she noticed, and she realised how very tired she felt, and how lonely.

When Marie returned, she carried a mound of cream lace petticoats and a dark red, silk gown. Colette watched as the maid piled all the clothes on to a chaise longue and then picked up the dress and held it out. 'What do you think?' Marie asked.

'Why can't I wear my own clothes?'

Marie's arms fell to her sides. She laid out the glowing silk on the end of the bed, and stroked the thick folds of rich material. 'I took it downstairs,' she said. 'Do you really want me to bring it back for you?'

Colette put down her cup and sat up in bed. 'At least it's mine. Who owns this one?'

'It was in the cupboard upstairs, but I'm sure it's never been worn. I heard that Madame de la Trave used to order clothes every season and hardly wore a tenth of them. Such waste. It must be one of hers. Of course it's a little out of fashion.'

Colette looked at the beautiful silk. She had never seen such a dress, not even in the town on a feast day. Out of fashion! What must Marie have thought of her old red frock?

'I chose a red one because I know you like the colour.' Marie's voice was persuasive. 'Won't you try it on? It will suit you so well.'

Reluctantly, Colette pushed back the bedcovers

and stepped into the first petticoat. When Marie lifted the silk dress over her head, the material felt cool against her skin, like the soft water of the river. Was she meant to wear it home? Was it a present from Victor? She felt confused. How long was she expected to be here?

Marie's fingers were busy at her back, fastening a row of tiny, fiddly buttons. When she had finished, she held out a pair of red, kid boots. Colette slipped them on; they felt soft and sleek on her feet and the colour enchanted her. She held them out in front of her, twisting her legs so that she could admire them from all angles.

'Please sit here, Mademoiselle.' Marie held out a chair in front of the mirror and brandished a silver-backed brush. Colette felt the unfamiliar strokes of stiff bristles pulling through her thick curls and remembered how her mother used to let her sit on the step outside their cottage sometimes, when she was very young, before her sisters were born, and had brushed out her hair like this. She relaxed, closed her eyes, and let the steady rhythm of the maid's hands soothe her. She was almost asleep when she felt the girl's hands round her waist, raising her to her feet and pushing her towards a cheval mirror in the corner of the room. 'Take a look at yourself,' Marie urged.

Colette saw the silk clinging to her figure. She thought she looked like one of the ladies in the portraits that Gilles had shown her in the long gallery.

'Now.' At last Marie seemed satisfied, and walked to the door. 'It's time to go downstairs. Your parents are waiting.'

'My parents?' Colette felt bewildered. If they had

33

come to take her home now, why was she wearing this dress? Was it Victor? Had he asked them to come? Perhaps he wanted her to stay with him and was asking her parents' permission. 'Do you know why they are here?' she asked.

'No one's told me anything, but you'll find out soon enough. Now follow me, Mademoiselle, and I'll take you down to them so you can ask all the questions you want yourself.'

Without another word Marie hurried off down the stairs. Colette followed obediently. Jean-Pierre was waiting in the hall. 'Good morning,' he said, bowing low before he quickly straightened up and swung open the mahogany doors to the drawing room. Colette was dazzled by sunlight streaming in through the tall windows. At the far end of the room she saw her parents standing in front of a pale yellow satin sofa, as though they thought they might dirty it by sitting down.

Monsieur stood near them, leaning against the marble mantelpiece. He smiled when he saw her come in. 'Your father and I will talk about the crops,' he said, opening the glass door on to the terrace. 'Will you listen to what your mother has to say?'

Colette felt confused and saw that her mother, too, looked awkward and made no move towards her. From their opposite ends of the room they watched the two men walk across the formal parterre, away towards the wood.

And then she saw her mother cross the room towards her. She expected a morning kiss, but although her mother held her arms out, Colette barely felt the tips of her mother's fingers on her shoulders. It must be the dress, she thought; her mother was frightened of spoiling the fine silk. She felt an awkwardness run through her, too. What was happening to them all?

'Monsieur says you have something to tell me.' Please let it be what she wanted to hear. If she was invited to stay here, however uncomfortable she felt, she could spend a few days with Victor, and she was sure they would regain their old closeness. Why was her mother hesitating?

Her mother finally sat down on the yellow sofa. She patted the seat beside her. 'Come and sit here.' she said. 'Monsieur has talked to me about you, Colette.'

'About Victor?'

Her mother stared hard into her eyes. 'No . . . no. It is not that.' She grasped Colette's hand. 'He is offering you a year in Paris.'

Colette felt a surge of excitement.

'As his mistress.'

She did not understand. Her mother continued hurriedly. 'The count has asked you to be his mistress for a year. Colette, you must think about it.'

'Monsieur? How could I consider such a thing? How could you?' There was nothing to think about.

Her mother stroked her hair. 'You look lovely today, Colette. That dress suits you.' She hesitated. 'You have taken your time about marrying Gaston. Is it what you really want?'

'What else is there for me? You have told me that often enough.'

'You are young and fresh, and you make yourself attractive to men. Gaston wants you, and his father has a good farm. At the moment you can have your pick of all the young men. But there are already some you have lost by delaying. You have to make up your mind.'

'I have decided. I told Gaston he could come to see father on Wednesday.'

'Ah. Then we will say no more. I will tell Monsieur that your answer is no.' Colette saw her mother start to rise to her feet. She pressed her back down on the sofa.

'I'm not sure,' she said slowly.

'What about?' her mother asked. 'Are you sure you are content to stay in this village?'

'Content! It is you who have always told me to be content with my life.'

Her mother shrugged. 'You must consider carefully. If you accept the count's offer you will have a year in Paris. At the end of that time you will be educated, sophisticated and still young and beautiful. There will be other men.'

'Who would want me then?'

'There will be many men eager for a beautiful wife with a good dowry.' Her mother looked at her directly and spread her worn, red hands in her lap. 'Monsieur would be generous.'

'What about Gaston?'

'Gaston was the best on offer for you. Now you have a choice.'

And Victor? What did he think of this? He must know of his father's plan. That must be why he had not touched her, why he had been so awkward with her last night. Why had he not warned her? Surely he must know that she could never accept such an offer? She turned to her mother. 'Gilles is an old man.'

Her mother laughed softly. 'He is 42, Colette. It

is not so very old. An experienced man can teach a woman so much.'

Yes, there would be books, paintings. But to be the mistress of an old man! She could not consider it. She saw her mother look down; there was something she had not been told. 'What do you mean when you say the count will be generous. Is there something else?'

Her mother slowly raised her head and looked straight in her eyes. Her weather-beaten, lined face was still pretty; her brown eyes were sharp and bright, but there was a glitter in them now, like the time when she had succeeded in persuading the grocer to let them have credit one month when the harvest was late. 'He would give us our farm.'

Colette was stunned. Only a few families in the district owned the land they worked on. Gaston's father was respected as a wealthy man in the village. She felt a moment's pride that Monsieur thought she was worth so much.

'And money, Colette. There would be enough for a dowry for your sister.'

To own their own farm, and to have a little money. They had worked all their lives without any hope of such riches. And she could earn all that in one year. But she could not do it; surely her mother could not expect her to. Through the windows of the salon, she could see her father, his cap clutched in his hands, walking beside Gilles de la Trave. She expected that her father would want to accept the offer. But her mother?

'What should I do?' she asked quietly.

'He has made you an offer, Colette, but you do not have to make your mind up now. Go with him

37

to Paris for one week. He will try to persuade you but he will not touch you unless you wish it.'

'And you believe that?' Colette remembered the cool depths of the count's gaze, and the way he had looked at her during dinner.

'Your father says he is an honourable man, Colette. There is no reason to doubt his word. If his need is too great there will be other women. What has he to gain by forcing you?'

If she went to Paris for a week she could see for herself what it was like. Then she could come home and marry Gaston. At least she would learn something of the world. And Victor would not let her come to any harm. Victor would be there to protect her.

Why not go to Paris? At least she could do something with her life before settling down with Gaston. And if she had the chance to be near Victor for a whole week, surely she would be able to explain to him how much she wanted him, and what she was prepared to offer?

If she did not go, what was there waiting for her? Long years of hard work and deprivation. It would not always be as good a harvest as this year. She had known years when there was no money to buy shoes, let alone a new dress. She could not walk away from the chance of such a lot of money without a second thought.

Colette looked out of the window, where she saw the count and her father walking back to the château. Her parents seemed content with the arrangement; they regarded it as no more than a business transaction, as marriage with Gaston would be.

She watched Gilles closely as he stood outside on the stone-flagged terrace. His lean, dark face no

38

longer seemed ugly to her; she had seen the way his features lit up when he talked of art or literature. There was much he could teach her, even in a week. She turned quickly to her mother. 'What will you tell Gaston?' she asked.

'The curé will speak to him, and explain that it is part of your education,' her mother told her. 'He will say that it is an honour.'

So Monsieur had thought of everything. Colette waited until he appeared in the doorway, then she spoke in a clear voice. 'I will come to Paris with you for one week, Monsieur, if you wish it.'

Gilles nodded, and she saw his fingers tighten round the silver knob of his ebony cane. He did not look surprised; she thought he must be used to buying anything he wanted. People did not refuse the requests of Gilles de la Trave. 'I believe you will appreciate the experience,' he said. 'I will leave you to say goodbye to your parents. We will depart in an hour.'

When Colette came down the stone staircase at the front of the château, she saw a black, closed carriage standing in the driveway. Gilles was already mounted on his black stallion; he merely nodded as if her presence was of little interest to him, and rode ahead with Victor. Marie climbed into the carriage and held the door open. The maid had far more luggage than Colette, but reassured her. 'In Monsieur's house in Paris there will be cupboards full of clothes for you. Monsieur will provide everything you could wish for. And soon he will call in the best couturiers for your fittings.'

So Marie did not know that she had only agreed to stay for one week. It did not matter, so long as

Gilles understood, and he was, as her father said, a man of honour. But whose clothes would she be wearing? Who owned the dress she had on now? Its colour was perfect for her and so was the size. Did it really belong to Madame de la Trave, who had not visited the château for years, or was it owned by a woman who had been Gilles' mistress last year?

Colette imagined a girl very different from herself, someone who was used to living with men who paid for her services. But her colouring must have been similar. One needed to be dark to wear this shade. Perhaps a chic Parisienne, well able to take advantage of Gilles' wealth. Where was she now?

When they were about eighteen kilometres from the château, the carriage stopped. There was a shout of farewell from Victor; he rode past their window, waved at them both and spurred on his horse. Gilles sat motionless in his saddle until his son had ridden out of sight.

Colette turned to Marie in a panic. 'Where has he gone?'

'Back to Argnon. Did you think he would come to Paris with his father? The two of them do not choose to spend their time together.'

The maid seemed to be studying her closely. Colette did not want to give herself away. She had come to Paris because she wanted to be with Victor, but it was too late to back out now. And besides, she had to try to gain some money for her family. She could not let Marie know anything of her feelings; she did not know how close the girl was to her master. Was Marie here to spy on her? If so, she was out of luck; she would tell her nothing.

But she felt lonelier than she had ever done in her life.

Marie seemed inclined to be friendly. She chattered on: Paris was her home; she was glad to be returning. But there was no information she could offer about the ladies in Gilles' life, and she talked more of Jean-Pierre than of the count.

'He is mad about me, you know. And he is a fine man; I might just settle for that one.'

It would take them two days to reach Paris. Tonight, Marie had told her, they would stop at an inn at Lisieux, and the next day take the railway to Paris. The afternoon was hot, and it was dry and airless in the carriage. Colette's head ached. She had slept so badly last night, and this morning had been such a shock. She could hardly believe that she was here on this dusty road, on her way to Paris, while Victor remained behind in Argnon.

She was aware that Marie was looking at her anxiously and she closed her eyes. She would have liked to have rested her head on the girl's plump shoulder, but she did not dare. She had no idea how she was supposed to behave towards a maid, and was frightened of offending the girl, or angering Monsieur.

No wonder Marie was happy; Jean-Pierre was only a few feet away from her, driving the carriage, and she had seen the way he looked at her and took every chance he could get to touch her. But Jean-Pierre liked touching women. Colette bit her lip as she thought of the way he had held her as they rode together through the country lanes. He could not have been more intimate if they were lovers. Cautiously, she half-opened her eyelids to steal a glance at Marie. She imagined Jean-Pierre's arrogant masculinity must appeal to her. The maid was dozing now, and her head had lolled forward over her chest, just above the very visible swell of her pretty breasts. Jean-Pierre would enjoy touching those, she thought, just as eager as Gaston was with her. And a lot more besides. Marie had almost decided to take Jean-Pierre as her husband, in which case they must already be lovers. Colette put her hands in her lap and closed her eyes rapidly, but it was too late to prevent a very vivid image of the stiff, male organ which Jean-Pierre had made sure she noticed. She blushed as she thought of it pressing into Marie's body without any of the barriers of clothing that had been between the two of them on the horse. Colette felt even more unhappy as she imagined them together. All last night she had waited for Victor to show her what sex was like, and he had not come. Now she was travelling as fast as she could away from him. And it was all a terrible mistake.

She was hot and tired by the time they reached their first stop. The count apologised for their poor accommodation. Tomorrow night, he assured her, she would be more comfortable in his house. 'For the moment, Marie will attend to your needs,' he announced, and left them alone together.

Their room was dark, but large and airy enough, with a little breeze from the courtyard. There was one large bed in the centre of a polished wooden floor; she would have to share with Marie, but there was no harm in that. She would be glad of the company in these strange surroundings, and if she could learn more about Gilles, so much the better.

Marie was plainly envious, but there was no

malice in her behaviour. 'What wouldn't I give to be in your shoes,' she murmured as she slid into bed after helping Colette with her clothes. 'A year with Monsieur, a whole year.'

Colette felt bad that she had concealed the truth, but it was too late now; besides, Gilles might prefer her to say nothing about the week's trial she had been promised.

'You think it would be a good life?' she questioned carefully.

Marie rolled over on her back and stretched luxuriously. 'A year with such a man in your bed will be heaven.' She was staring openly at Colette's body, covered only by a light cotton nightgown.

Colette felt a tremor of shock, but Marie was babbling on. 'If he offered me the chance, I would not have taken much persuading, I can assure you.'

Colette could feel the other girl's toes curling and uncurling with excitement in the bed beside her. Marie wriggled some more. 'Think of the pleasures ahead of you, little one,' she murmured confidentially, and moved a little closer. She put out her hand and touched Colette's arm. 'Are you a virgin?' she asked gently, looking concerned.

Colette nodded, a little ashamed. As Gaston had said, at her age it was unusual. But Marie was beaming. 'I was sure of it.' She clapped her hands excitedly. 'How wonderful for you to have a man like that as your first lover. He will know how to arouse you to fever-pitch.' She shook her head. 'If only it had been like that for me. My first, Michel, was not bad, you understand, but he was not an expert. Not like Monsieur. He will make your body

43

dance like the willows on the river. You will not believe joy like that to be possible.'

Marie's face was flushed, her hands trembled slightly, and Colette could see the stiff outline of the other girl's full breasts jutting through her nightdress. She was shocked when, without a trace of embarrassment, Marie suddenly lifted it above her head and started to rub her breasts vigorously with both hands. Colette watched as she squeezed her nipples between her fingers, moistening her lips with the tip of her small, pointed tongue as she did so.

'Just to think of him excites me,' she muttered, 'and tonight I am missing my man.' Colette wondered why Jean-Pierre had not taken Marie into his bed tonight, but her question was soon answered. 'Monsieur asked me to stay with you.' Marie took her hand and pressed it with her soft, little fingers. 'Please, Mademoiselle,' she said, 'will you help me? I will never sleep tonight unless I satisfy myself. Not after all the things we have been talking about.' She gave a confidential little smile. 'And then, of course, I will help you.'

Marie seemed to be waiting for her. Colette stared at her helplessly. The maid sat up and squeezed her hand again. 'You know what to do?' she whispered. Colette shook her head.

'Well you must learn.' Marie's hand burrowed between her thighs. She began to stroke herself lightly in the little cleft of her sex. Colette could see the tip of her finger sliding in and out between the rosy lips and felt a sympathetic ache deep inside her. She wondered if it would feel as good as it looked to stroke herself there.

Marie's blue eyes looked soft and large in the

44

dim light and there was a fresh bloom on her cheeks as she pushed her fingers higher up into her moist opening. 'Please, Mademoiselle,' she begged, 'touch me here.' She pointed to the stiff, reddened peak of her breast, and pressed one of Colette's hands over it. Colette could feel the firm nipple rubbing against her palm; she began to move her hand steadily over it, unsure what Marie wanted her to do. What would she like herself, she wondered, and then she pressed harder as she thought about it, giving Marie's pretty breast the firm squeeze she felt would bring most pleasure.

Marie gave a soft moan and opened her mouth to reveal a delicate row of white teeth. The small, pointed tongue darted out once more. Colette could not resist bending down and giving her a little kiss. She looked so pretty lying on the bed, with her flushed cheeks and glowing eyes. The moist lips felt cool against her mouth and tasted deliciously sweet and fresh, and they responded so charmingly to Colette's touch.

She felt herself aroused by the heat of the warm bud between her fingers and the small tremors that rippled through Marie's body. She stroked her own breast through her thin cotton nightdress, feeling her nipple spring into life beneath her fingers. She wanted to lift the gown and touch the delicate area between her legs, to see if it would give her as much pleasure as it did Marie, but she did not dare, and she quickly replaced her hand on Marie's breast and continued to squeeze encouragingly.

Marie gave a soft cry and her body arched with a little jerking movement before she sank back on to the mattress with a contented sigh. She reached out her hand to stroke Colette's thigh and smiled sleepily up at her. 'I can do the same for you if you wish, Mademoiselle,' she murmured. 'Would you like me to show you how?'

Did she want that? Colette felt her breasts ache for the touch of another hand. Marie's clever fingers could teach her a great deal, she was sure.

But if she allowed that to happen, would it be harder to resist Gilles? She knew how she had felt when Gaston had touched her. If Gilles was as expert a lover as Marie believed, how would she keep her promise to herself to return home at the end of her week? She remembered her mother's words. 'Once you permit a man to take you, it will become harder to say no the next time.' Was it the same with a woman? Her mother had said nothing at all about that.

She shook her head and kissed the sleepy face next to her so as not to give offence. But she need not have worried; Marie was almost asleep. She reached down and slipped her finger between her thighs; the skin there was so soft and silky that it felt comforting. She stroked the moist padded lips surrounding her litttle slit and tentatively felt inside. She had never dared touch herself like this before. She shared a bedroom with her sister, and she would not have known how to explain what she was doing. And she had always expected that a man would tell her what to do and give her pleasure there.

It wasn't making her feel any better! Each time she pushed her finger into the hole, she wanted to feel it rising further, and her finger simply wasn't long enough or thick enough. She tried inserting two at once and it felt a little better. Then she had a sudden memory of Victor's naked body in the river, and the satisfying solid penis that she had seen, and she knew exactly what she wanted to feel. For a very brief moment, she wondered what Gilles de la Trave would look like naked. If Marie said that he was such a wonderful lover, he must be reasonably well-equipped, mustn't he? She didn't want to think about it, and she pulled her nightgown firmly down to her knees and tried to sleep.

She lay awake for hours, disturbed by the unfamiliar sounds of activity from the inn all around her. She thought of Victor alone in the château, and let her fingers slide once more into the soft little hole that ached for him. It felt moist and tender, but her light touch brought her no satisfaction and she dared not make any rapid movements in case she woke Marie.

She was a fool to have come here. If she had remained in Argnon, she was sure Victor would have wanted her. Then she would have been satisfied and agreed to marry Gaston. And she would not be lying here feeling quite so uncomfortable!

But there was a week in Paris to think about. It would be a thrill to see the city she had heard so much about. That was almost more alluring. Already she had travelled farther than she had done in her whole life. If she was going to settle down to life with Gaston, she needed to see something of life outside Argnon before she did so. And Monsieur would keep his word; nothing Marie had said caused her to believe otherwise.

She ran her tongue over her dry lips, remembering the faint taste of the girl's sweat and the delicious sensation of her soft tongue on her lips. She closed her eyes and tried to sleep. In Paris there would be books to read, paintings to see, avenues to walk down. She was going to Paris simply for the experience, simply to learn. And she would have to learn to control the demands of her body. She was sure that would be easy, if only she were less tired.

Chapter Three

Colette had not expected Paris to look so new or so bright, with such wide avenues leading to the magnificent buildings. Gilles' coachman, Robert, met them at the station and drove her round the city with Marie, while Jean-Pierre and the count went straight to his house.

All the fatigue of the journey left her as they turned into the broad expanse of the Champs Élysées and she saw the wide pavements bordered with flowers. She was almost disappointed when Robert took a turning off to the right, and pulled up inside the gilded iron gates of a great mansion. She could not believe that Gilles had another enormous house.

Marie took her inside, leaving Robert and Jean-Pierre to deal with their luggage. 'See, this is where you will stay.' The maid flung open a door. Colette saw a room with large windows letting in the sunshine, and a bed bordered with pale wood and draped with bright citron silk. There were paintings on the walls, and a glass-fronted cabinet filled with books. A small sitting-room led off it, and a bath-room and a dressing-room. She had never imagined anything as fine as this.

Marie was occupied in the dressing-room, and already the cupboard doors were open. 'Quickly, Mademoiselle, you must choose something to wear. Monsieur will expect you to be ready soon.'

'Whose clothes are these?'

'They are yours. These are all for you. Look at this. It is glorious, isn't it?'

The dress filled Marie's arms. The skirt alone was so vast that Colette could hardly see her maid past it.

'I don't know how to wear that. Isn't there something smaller?' Colette sifted through the racks of clothes herself. She found one with a slightly less exaggerated skirt, in cherry-red satin with cream lace at the neck and sleeves.

'This will do. Show me how to put it on.'

When she was ready she looked in the mirror and saw a tall young woman with a slim waist, a large billowing skirt and a tight bodice with lace frills scarcely concealing her full breasts, who was holding a delicate, cherry-red parasol, edged with the same lace. When she lifted the skirt she saw her feet shod in elegant red boots. She wriggled her toes. Who would ever have thought she could look so good?

'Please, Mademoiselle, hurry. Monsieur will be waiting.'

'What for?'

Colette saw Marie look away. 'He is taking you out, Mademoiselle. He did not tell me where. Now come, please.'

Colette stopped at the top of the staircase. Her

skirt was swinging wildly from side to side over the hooped petticoat. What would happen when she tried to walk down the staircase? 'Slowly, Mademoiselle,' Marie advised. Colette placed one hand on the white marble balustrade. Below her in the hall, she saw Gilles standing, arms folded, watching her.

She took a deep breath and tried to ignore him for the moment. Very slowly, she walked down the steps. If he had thought her pretty enough to want to make her his mistress, he must think her very fine now, in these clothes. The cherry satin was so clear and bright, and it made her lips look so red that he must be pleased. She bit her bottom lip hard to make sure it looked as inviting as possible.

At the foot of the stairs she waited for him to come over to her. Did he think she wasn't used to attracting men? She was satisfied when he bowed and came forward to take her arm.

A different carriage waited outside. This one was low and open, and had room for her full skirt. Gilles sat opposite her. 'We shall drive through the Bois de Boulogne,' he told her, 'on our way to visit a friend of mine.'

She was delighted. He was taking her to meet his friends already! 'Will I disgrace you, Monsieur?' she asked coquettishly.

Gilles gave a half-smile. 'I don't think so. You learn fast, and you will improve after you have had some lessons.'

Colette nearly snapped the ivory handle of her parasol in her anger. She had one week in Paris. There was no time to waste learning things that would never be of any use to her. If Gilles thought she was just an ignorant peasant why had he

51

brought her here? And why was he taking her to see some woods, when she had lived amongst trees all her life?

But the Bois de Boulogne was nothing like the forested hillsides around Argnon. Here there were wide paths, bustling with carriages, and ladies dressed in gowns that left no space for their gentlemen, who rode on horseback beside them. Waterfalls gushed down artificial rocks into smooth, clear lakes, smartly dressed soldiers played music from bandstands and pavilions overflowed with flowers. Colette stared at it all, entranced, wishing that they could spend longer here and did not have to hurry past all the excitement.

Their carriage stopped outside a large house overlooking the Bois. When Gilles rang a small, gilt bell, the door was opened by a maid dressed in a neat, black dress with a frilled lace apron. They followed her upstairs into a pale blue salon, where gilded mirrors on every wall reflected sunlight from the tall windows.

A tall, blonde woman in a dress of Sèvres-blue satin rose from a small chair upholstered in the same colour.

Gilles bowed. 'Anne, may I introduce Colette, a young friend of mine?'

The lady extended her hand. 'Madame Anne de Lessay,' Gilles said, 'one of my greatest friends.'

Colette thought Anne was beautiful, even compared to the fashionable ladies she had seen driving around in the park. Her silver-blonde hair was swept up into a heavy, curled chignon, and delicate wisps framed a face of pale loveliness.

She was not young, but her perfect complexion was smooth and unlined; around her neck four strands of luminous pearls were secured with a cluster of sparkling diamonds. Her hand was soft and small, her slim fingers heavy with jewels.

'Anne will look after you for a few hours,' Gilles said.

Did he think she was a child to be taken care of! 'You are leaving?' Colette asked coldly.

'You will do better without me.'

Colette saw the doors close behind him. She looked round the salon. It was more elegantly decorated than the château, but perhaps not quite as fashionable as Gilles' Paris mansion. Did Anne de Lessay live here alone? Who was this woman he so obviously admired? And what lessons did Anne have to teach her?

'Gilles says you are intelligent and quick to learn. Is that true?'

'I did well at school. It is why Monsieur paid for me to have lessons with Victor.' Colette saw Anne turn to look carefully at her, and no longer felt so confident, or so sure of the correctness of her beautiful dress.

'You have already eaten lunch?' Anne asked.

Marie had made sure she ate before they left. 'Yes,' she answered.

'Then we shall simply play with the cutlery. Please sit here.'

Colette sat at a table laid with an alarming amount of silver and an empty plate.

A selection of fine wines was ranged on the rosewood sideboard, with an array of different shaped glasses. Anne poured a little from one of the bottles into a tulip-shaped glass.

'Please tell me what you think of this.'

Colette was thirsty. 'It's delicious, quite fruity.'

'Good. You have a clear palate. Now we shall talk, and a little later you will sip again and this time you will think carefully of all the flavours you are aware of at the back of your mouth.'

Colette ran her tongue around the back of her teeth. 'I can still taste that one,' she said, 'like strawberries.'

Anne raised an eyebrow. 'Good, now we shall talk of other things. Let me show you which implement you would use to eat a lobster.'

Colette felt tired. Two days ago she had been in Argnon, with nothing but a spoon to eat a poor meal. But she had managed well enough at the château and she had no wish to waste her time here.

She stood up. 'I don't want to learn this. Did Monsieur not tell you that I am only here for a week?'

Anne placed her beautiful hand on the diamond clasp at her neck. 'Are you so very foolish?' she said.

'There is a man at home who will marry me.'

'Then why are you here?'

'I wanted to see Paris. I want experience.'

'Experience?' Anne stared hard at her and her fine, blue eyes were cold.

'I want something good in my life before I submit.' Colette drank the rest of the wine in her glass.

'Never let me see you drink like that again. A lady merely sips, and she is always aware of the wine she tastes.' Anne sat down elegantly on a tiny gilt chair. 'You must think carefully before you throw away such an opportunity. What will your

54

life be like if you return to your village? Judging by your hands, you work in the fields.'

Colette nodded. Marie had oiled them each morning and evening, and Colette thought they had never looked so good. Now beside Anne's beautiful hands, she realised how raw they looked.

'It is good that the summer has only just begun. Otherwise your complexion would be even worse.'

Anne stretched out her beautiful hands on the silk skirt of her dress. 'Tell me what you see,' she said.

'Your hands are lovely.' Colette was reluctant to admit it, but it was the truth.

'Is that what you noticed first?'

'No, I looked at your rings. They must be worth a lot.'

'At least you are honest.' One by one, Anne removed them. 'This was given to me by a prince, and this by a duke. I have boxes more, so many that when I sell a few to pay my rent I hardly notice the loss. There are some I would never part with because the memory still gives me pleasure. And you say you are reluctant to "submit" to a man. Try on the rings, Colette.'

'No, they are yours. I cannot.' But when Anne pushed them towards her, she could not resist. She placed the heavy sapphires and diamonds on her fingers and watched them sparkle.

Colette hardly noticed how late it had become until Anne rose to her feet. It was nearly dusk. 'I shall take you home in my carriage,' she said, 'and on the way we will call to see Monsieur Worth. You will need some clothes even if you intend your visit to be short.'

On the first floor of 7, Rue de la Paix, the most

successful couturier in Paris lived and worked. Anne sat drinking tea while Colette stood and let the great man survey her from every angle. She felt more awkward in this borrowed gown than in her own clothes from Argnon, and both Anne and Monsieur Worth seemed to discuss what would be made for her without once asking for her opinion. Eventually they seemed satisfied.

Anne rose from her seat. 'That is all we need to do for today. Your gowns will be delivered to you when they are ready. Robert is waiting to take you home. I will see you tomorrow afternoon.'

'Tomorrow? Do you mean that I must come to you again?'

'Do you think you have learnt all there is to know? Gilles intends to take you to the theatre tomorrow night. I have asked him to wait until you are ready, but he refused my advice. He said he did not have enough time.'

Anne turned away when Colette stepped into the carriage and did not say goodbye as she drove away.

Colette was glad of the dull lessons when she sat in a box at the theatre with Gilles, above a crowd of jewelled and feathered women who stared at her through little, pearl-handled opera glasses. Anne was right; the dress which she had thought so magnificent looked horribly dull in this company. She should have waited until her gowns from Worth were ready. She leant out to look at all the magnificent jewels which sparkled round the ladies' necks, and wished she had something like that. Her hand went to her bare neck. Gilles reached into his pocket. 'Would you feel more comfortable wearing this?' he asked, holding out a glittering, pearl and diamond necklace. She nodded, and felt his fingers fasten the clasp at the back of her neck, lingering over the bare skin of her shoulders. She was delighted.

She saw a flash of light reflected from a pair of opera-glasses, and looked up. Across the auditorium, sitting in a box facing theirs, a girl had just turned her head towards the stage. Colette was sure that a moment earlier, she had been the focus of the girl's attention. She raised her own glasses and stared back.

The girl was exquisite. Her hair fell in golden ringlets over perfect, porcelain shoulders, rising from a cloud of cream tulle. Diamonds flashed at her wrists and throat, and coiled through her beautiful hair. And the man who sat beside her clearly adored her. He looked quite old, probably as old as Gilles, and not quite so chic. He was heavier, and his dark hair was rather too sleek, but he had a charming smile and his eyes sparkled with fun, and he was treating the girl like a princess. Perhaps he had given her all those wonderful jewels. Colette turned her head slightly, so that her necklace would flash too, and enjoyed the way she caught the eye of the man sitting opposite. She was having at least as much fun as he was.

In the interval the beautiful girl drifted towards Gilles and held out her elegantly gloved hand for him to kiss. She inclined her head. 'I had heard you were back in Paris, *chéri*. Why have you not called on me?' Her voice was light, but Colette could see a sullen glint in her eyes.

Gilles bent low over the woman's hand, but he did not let go of Colette's. 'Éloise, you look as lovely as ever. I am flattered that you find time in your life to miss me.'

The woman's eyes swept over Colette's dress. Even with alterations made by Anne's dressmaker, Colette could see the difference between the cut of her gown and the creation this woman was wearing. She stared at the diamonds which sparkled in the candlelight, feeling young and gauche. Gilles did not introduce her. Was he ashamed of her? Did he hope that she would go back to Argnon on Saturday as she intended, so that this girl could be her replacement?

The older man laid his hand possessively on Éloise's pale shoulders. His fingers were slightly spread, taking pleasure in squeezing the girl's creamy flesh, but his eyes were fixed on Colette, greedily examining every inch of her body. She stared back at him and pouted her lips, pleased to see his swift reaction. So Éloise's lover was not so critical of her, she thought. How very interesting.

For the rest of the performance she noticed the man glancing towards their box, and felt a glow of triumph. Anne was wrong – she had enjoyed the evening.

Robert drove them back to the Boulevard Haussmann where Gilles took her to the door of the mansion, and waited for Marie to come to her. Then he bowed and took his place again in the carriage. Colette felt dismayed. Was he going to see Éloise? Was that why he was in such a hurry?

Anne de Lessay waited for Gilles to arrive. He was making a mistake over this girl, but she would not be the one to tell him. As always, she would be there for him if he was hurt. She sat in her blue and

58

gold salon and watched the candles flickering in their ormolu holders. It was the light she preferred for receiving visitors at night, especially now that she was older and her only lover had such a weakness for young girls.

She wondered whether Colette would return to her home at the end of a week, and shook her head. It was impossible. When Gilles wished to be charming, no woman could resist him, least of all an impressionable young girl. No, the mystery was why he had chosen her in the first place. The girl had charm, of course, and with a little effort she could be made to look presentable. A beauty, even, if she worked at it. There was a vivacity in her looks that was definitely attractive. But at the moment she thought that Gilles was probably interested in the challenge. Colette must be one of the few girls who had shown no interest either in his money or his sexuality.

The little porcelain clock on her mantelpiece chimed the hour and Anne knew that Gilles would be with her in a few moments. She would not ask whether his evening had been a success, and Gilles would not tell her. She was prepared to train his mistresses for him, but not to discuss them with him in bed. Colette would be chastened tomorrow, less sure of herself after she had seen the most beautiful women in Paris dressed in their finest clothes. No doubt their interest in Gilles would surprise the girl. She still had no idea just what a catch he was.

Anne walked over to the mirror above the clock and checked her appearance. She was glad that her skin was still youthful and her lips full and desirable. It was Gilles' kisses that kept them so fresh.

There was nothing so good for a woman's appearance as a lover who could assure her of her attraction. And no one did that so well as Gilles.

She turned to welcome him as she heard the salon doors open, and ran into his arms. He held her tightly to him, and she knew without any doubt that Colette had aroused him. She could not believe he felt so strongly this soon. He kissed her with far more enthusiasm than usual, and led the way straight to her bedroom, instead of sitting with her and drinking a brandy. He was far too impatient for that tonight.

Not by the faintest sign did Gilles betray the fact that his eagerness was due to anything other than his desire for her. She would have been shocked if he had done so. But she knew him far too well to be fooled. He took out the diamond pins securing her blonde hair and let it fall over her shoulders as he loved it to do, and she felt his hands stroking it with the sensual delight of a connoisseur. Only the fast beating of his pulse and a slight quickening in his breathing alerted her to his state. That, and the passion with which he caressed the bare skin above her gown, and the tenderness of his lips on her throat. She felt her own response match his and allowed her robe to fall open so that he could see the milky-white beauty of her breasts fully exposed.

As always, he made her believe that no other woman in the world had a figure of such splendour or a face of such perfect beauty. Whenever he was with her, she was convinced that this was the truth and, as he had been her passionate lover for nearly twenty years, she had no reason to doubt that he meant what he said. The years had brought no dull ease to their relationship. She still craved Gilles' body with a wild desire, and tonight, as he took her breasts into his hands and caressed them, she knew that his passion matched her own. For the rest of the world, she was the cool, elegant Anne de la Trave. For Gilles she would have behaved like the most abandoned slut if that had pleased him. She would do anything for him.

There had never been a moment when she would not have left any one of her rich protectors, even a prince, if Gilles had wished it, and the knowledge of the power over her which her love gave him, intoxicated him. She could not bear him to touch her any longer without a deeper union. Anne slid her fingers inside the waistband of his evening suit, and held his swollen manhood in her hand. Gilles stared at her. Undaunted, she freed him of all constraint, and led him, naked, to her bed. Tonight, she felt like a young girl again, a young girl with her first lover. For her, Gilles would always be that.

Colette wanted to climb into bed and sleep all night. She was exhausted. And it felt so strange to need help to undress herself, although it would be impossible for her to unfasten the complicated arrangements of hooks and eyes that ran all the way down the back of the gown. And no doubt Marie was instructed to make sure that the necklace Gilles had lent her was safely returned. She took it off first.

'Why didn't Victor come back to Paris with his father?' she asked.

Marie shrugged. 'They don't spend much time together. Victor has been living with his mother in Italy. And now . . .'

'Now?'

61

Marie placed the necklace in a little blue satin jewel box and put it away in her drawer. 'Now he prefers to stay in Argnon,' she said.

Colette felt a rush of pleasure. If Victor wanted to stay in the village, it must be because he wanted to see more of her. There was no one else he had been friendly with. It did not matter what Anne said; she was going home as soon as she could, even without the money.

'Then I shall go back to see him.'

'It's not a good idea. Maybe he is not so interested as you think. And it would make Monsieur very angry.'

'He said I was free to do as I pleased.'

Marie looked upset. 'Please don't ask me any more,' she said.

Colette's tiredness disappeared. She sat up in the bed when Marie had left her and hugged her knees. In six days she could be back home. Marie would know whether she would be allowed to keep any of the things that Gilles had bought for her. Not that they would be any use in Argnon, but she could sell them. The money would not pay for the farm but it would help a little. If she could buy new clothes for her sister, it would help her to get a good husband. Why had Marie shut up so suddenly? Was it because she felt she was a servant? Perhaps she would talk more freely in her own room. If she hurried, Marie might not be asleep, and she could go upstairs and ask her about it. She wanted to sit on the end of the girl's bed and tell her how she felt, as she used to do with her sister. This huge room was very beautiful, but it felt big and lonely.

Marie had said that she slept at the back of the

house, and Colette had seen her disappear through a door at the end of the corridor. She went out and found it easily. Behind it was a small, dark staircase and she climbed up two flights of stairs. Marie's room must be near here. She could hear her voice, but it was coming from the next room, behind the curtain. Marie was not alone. She turned to go, but then realised they were talking about her. She recognised Jean-Pierre's voice. He mentioned Victor and she stopped dead. She might learn the truth now.

'He's already got his hands full. Poor young lady.'

'Poor young lady? Just look at what Monsieur has bought her already. The boxes just keep on coming, every day. He is spending money on this one all right.'

'But it's Victor she wants. She's set her heart on him.'

'Well, then she'll be unlucky. He's too busy with the other one.'

Colette moved closer. There was a dark corner just beside the curtain, and she pressed back against the wall there. She felt sick. So Victor loved someone else. But there was no one in Argnon. She had to hear more. She peeked through a tiny crack where the curtain did not quite reach the wall.

She saw Jean-Pierre lunge at Marie, and heard her giggle. The gap in the curtain widened, but they weren't looking at her. Jean-Pierre had Marie's clothes off and he was starting to unbuckle his belt. In another moment he would have his trousers off. She knew that she should go, but it was impossible for her to leave without them hearing her. And it

63

was too late for that already. She pressed further back into the shadows.

'Here, let me do that.' She saw Marie grasp the buckle and deftly loosen Jean-Pierre's belt.

He laughed. 'Can't wait for me to take it off myself, huh? All right then, I'll leave it all to you. Come and help yourself.'

Colette no longer wanted to move. She was too interested in seeing what they would do. Marie had bent forward and reached inside the open flap of Jean-Pierre's breeches. She seemed to like what she found in there, because she gave a little squeal and started to stroke him. He was standing over her now, his breeches had slipped down, but his shirt was covering him. Then Marie reached up and undid the buttons of his shirt, so that it fell off over his shoulders. Colette could see a thick growth of black hair on his chest and below, where the hair came to a thick V over his flat belly, his skin was paler and a massive column of purplish flesh rose up between his thighs. She shivered. It was that which she had felt pressed against her, and that which gave Marie so much pleasure. The room was cold and she only wore a thin nightgown, but it was the sight of that huge penis that made her nervous.

She watched Marie bend down and press her lips on to the huge shaft. Jean-Pierre quivered as if he was enjoying this. Then Marie's mouth opened wide and her tongue flicked over the ridged flesh. She pushed her head right over the swollen column. Colette stared in amazement. She would not have thought that Marie's delicate, rosebud mouth could take in anything so huge. She could see Jean-Pierre's buttocks start to ride forwards, pressing

Marie back on to the bed, as he grunted his pleasure.

His breeches, which had fallen below his knees, were restricting him now. He pulled back, exposing himself fully, and swung his legs down over the side of the bed, shaking the breeches on to the floor. Marie fell back on to the pillows, moaning, and opened her legs wide. Colette could see the dark shadow of the opening she had stroked at the inn and remembered the creamy dew which had come so quickly there. She felt her own sex moisten with her juices as it had done that night, and the familiar ache.

Marie had taken hold of Jean-Pierre's penis with both hands now and was firmly guiding it into the warm nest of her sex. Jean-Pierre pinched one of her nipples, and Colette saw the girl's hips shudder as he did so. The head was just touching her sex lips now; in another moment it would disappear just as it had done into her mouth. Colette could feel the cream gathering between her legs, and a melting sensation as though her body was preparing itself to accept that massive column. She bit her lip to prevent herself from crying out, but the couple on the bed took no such precautions.

As Jean-Pierre lowered his penis over Marie's pretty mound, he clenched his buttocks and rammed himself into her, giving a shout of delight. '*Dieu*, what a climb,' he said. 'You're beautiful up there, Marie.'

And the girl opened her legs wider, and called out, 'Harder, Jean-Pierre. Don't hold back. Oh yes, yes, that's it. Don't stop, Jean-Pierre, I'm coming, I'm coming.'

Colette felt ashamed to be watching. They would

not notice her if she left now. They were too busy to be aware of anything except each other. But she could not take her eyes off them. She wanted to learn exactly what a man did to a woman and imagine how good it felt.

They were both moving together in a frenzy now, their hips locked together as Jean-Pierre jerked into her. He cried out, reared up and then fell heavily on top of Marie's shuddering body. Marie's hands were stroking his back gently, fluttering over him in a sort of helpless caress, and then she, too, closed her dreamy eyes and sank into his arms.

Colette stared for a moment longer at the two bodies on the bed. So that was what it was like. She felt damp and sticky between her thighs. That was what Gilles wanted to do to her. That was what he was prepared to spend so much money to do to her. It looked wonderful.

She crept out of the room. So Victor loved another woman. He had never wanted her. And everyone else here knew all about it. No doubt everyone at Argnon knew too, now. She could not go back there, not even for Gaston.

She wanted to feel a man take her like Jean-Pierre, she wanted to know everything that Marie had felt. And Gilles was prepared to pay her for the privilege. She would make sure he was not disappointed.

Chapter Four

Colette's week sped past. This evening she would have to give Gilles her answer. She had hardly thought about it. There had been so little time with all the excitement that Paris had to offer; a year would not be enough to see it all. But she didn't have a year – tonight she must tell Gilles she was going home.

He had shown her so much in the last few days: the theatre, grand restaurants, paintings at the Louvre, and had taken her racing at Longchamps. And always, each day, Gilles left her with Anne for her lessons, as though they had both of them assumed that she would stay. Their assurance irritated her.

She was angry with both of them! They were all the same. Even Victor was in love with another woman, although she could not blame him for that. There was no reason why he should even tell her; he didn't even know she loved him. And Gilles! He had asked her to become his mistress, had brought

67

her to Paris, and then spent every night with another woman. Or half Paris for all she knew. Life with Gaston would be much safer, if he would still have her.

Colette stood for dress fittings until her whole body ached, struggled each day with her cutlery, and learnt more about wine. Today only one bottle stood on Anne's rosewood sideboard. 'Why do you never offer me champagne to taste?' she asked.

'Gilles believes that it is a wine for lovers. If you choose to stay, you may learn from him.'

'I only came for one week, remember?'

'That was what you said.' Anne gazed out of the window at the Bois. 'Are you sure you can bear to leave?'

To go home to Argnon seemed a dreary prospect. But Victor had not followed her to Paris. Women far more beautiful than she had shown their interest in Gilles, and he had made no effort to seduce her. He had obviously taken her at her word. And of course he had promised her father he would not touch her unless she chose.

Imagine what it would be like to live here. To dress like this each evening before going out to some pleasure. To come home with Gilles, to sleep in his arms. Colette put that thought quickly out of her mind. 'Gilles has been out with other women every night,' she said.

'What do you expect? That he should live like a monk for a week while he is taking a schoolgirl on her first tour of Paris?'

'He invited me here.'

'And made you an offer which you obviously do not appreciate. You would be a fool to refuse him. I shall never forget my year with him.'

68

Colette looked up in surprise. 'Gilles was your lover?'

'Of course. My best. And like most of his women I'm still in love with him. He has the power to make you believe you are the only one in the world for him. When your year is over, he will leave you with your dignity. And Gilles is very generous, Colette; do not underestimate that.'

In love with him. No wonder Anne had been so cold to her. But she was kind now. How could she bear to prepare someone else for Gilles if she still loved him? 'Do you hate me very much?' she asked.

'No, no. I have learnt patience over the years. And it was not Gilles who left me. I had five years of Gilles' love. It was his wife who separated us.'

'Madame de la Trave?'

Anne nodded. 'Antoinette. You are lucky you have not met her.' She made it clear that this particular conversation was at an end.

Colette had almost decided to return home. But Anne had a point. Could she really leave all this? She had to make a decision tonight. If she went home to Argnon, Gaston would still marry her. She had been away six days. She could make him take her – after all, she was still a virgin. She wondered whether he would be able to tell if she did decide to have just one night with Gilles before coming home.

So would it be Gaston – or Gilles? If she chose life as a farmer's wife, she would be better off than her mother, but she would never wear anything like this again. She stroked the thick silk of her skirt. And there was the question of her virginity. Marie had told her how wonderful it would be to have a man like Gilles as her first lover. The girl had gone all misty-eyed. And that was what she had wanted, wasn't it? Could she really settle down with Gaston after that? If she married Gaston, her parents would never own their farm. If she stayed with Gilles, her parents would own their farm, and her sisters would have their dowries. Everyone would be happy.

And she would know how an experienced man made love. She wondered if it was so very different from what she had seen with Jean-Pierre, or from Gaston's clumsy approaches. It was true that Gaston was clumsy, and Marie had told her that made a big difference. And she wanted so very badly to know how it would be with Gilles.

If Gilles was as good a lover as Anne said, then maybe he could give her the experience she craved. She would tell him that she was determined to return to Argnon and marry Gaston, but that she was willing to spend a night with him. Tonight, when he had promised to take her out to dinner.

Should she confide in Anne? The older woman would laugh at her if she told her that she planned to have only one night with Gilles. Colette felt frightened. What if Gaston did not want her back?

Anne hesitated. 'This afternoon I shall prepare you for your final dinner with Gilles. Whatever decision you may make is up to you, but I intend to ensure that if you choose to accept Gilles' offer, you will be ready for him.' She held out her hand. 'Come with me. We have much to do.'

Colette followed Anne across the spacious hall to her bedroom. Sabine and Chloë, two of Anne's maids, were waiting for them, wearing crisp, white aprons over their black uniforms. There was a pungent smell in the room, and Sabine was stirring something in a small copper pan over a flame.

'Take your clothes off, please, Colette,' Anne ordered. 'All of them, quickly, while the wax is still hot. Monsieur prefers his ladies smooth, and without body hair.' Anne's gentle, blue eyes reflected the eggshell tones of her silk-lined boudoir. 'Other men, of course,' she murmured, 'have different tastes.'

Chloë unlaced Colette's dress while Sabine put down her pan and placed a plain sheet over a satin-cushioned chaise longue. Colette lay down on her back with her arms raised above her head. She felt Chloë's gentle fingers cup her breast while Sabine wiped a cold, sharp-smelling liquid over the soft hairs beneath her arms, before smearing them with a thick layer of warm wax. When it had cooled, Sabine pulled at the edge of the set wax and stripped it away in one quick movement. Colette jerked forward, her eyes pricking with tears, while Chloë smoothed soothing cream over her stinging flesh.

'It is not easy to be beautiful,' Anne said, filling a small glass with a shot of vivid green crème de menthe, and handing it to Colette. 'Sip this.'

Colette had not yet tasted liqueurs. The sweet, sticky liquid coated her tongue and teeth with cloying peppermint, but it was delicious. She sipped again and sank back on to the cool sheet as the powerful fumes drifted round her brain.

The second underarm seemed less painful, and Chloë massaged cream not only on to the tender patch but over her shoulders and stomach, caressing her body with a firm, gentle touch as Sabine continued to pour the wax on to Colette's legs, beginning at her ankles, alternately smearing and stripping all the hairs from her lower legs.

She felt Chloë's fingers massaging the aromatic creams into her feet and between her toes, and it felt so good that Colette started to relax, sipping the sweet crème de menthe until she realised with a shock that Sabine had not yet finished with her. The girl was combing the curls of black hair at the base of her belly and snipping at them with a pair of scissors. Colette was not sure what her fleece would look like cut short. Suddenly a hot stream of wax flooded over the base of her belly, coating her pubic hair.

She gasped. 'Surely not there!' she cried out loud.

Anne smiled, and refilled her glass. 'Monsieur insists,' she said, nodding to Sabine to strip away the wax.

Colette clutched Chloë's hand as Sabine stripped off the hardened wax. She had never felt such pain. And she was sure she would look hideous. What had they done to her? She tried to peer down, but could only see Sabine's cluster of red-gold curls as the girl bent over her and carefully removed a few stray hairs with a tiny pair of tweezers.

And then it was all over. Colette's poor, bare mound was soothed by Chloë's soft touch, and she was covered with a warm eiderdown.

'Sleep a little,' Anne said. 'We will wake you in good time to help you dress'

Colette wanted to jump up and look at herself in the mirror, but she was frightened that the pain would start again. Chloë's clever fingers had calmed the stinging, and the powerful mint liqueur clouded her thoughts, so that she closed her eyes and slept until Anne woke her with a cup of herb tisane.

'First look at yourself in the mirror,' Anne said, 'and see how pretty you are.'

The two maids stood back and waited, holding Colette's stockings and lace suspenders while she studied herself in the cheval mirror. She could see everything clearly as Anne gently pushed her thighs apart, exposing the smooth, creamy labia covering her rosy core and the pale swell of her mound, slightly pink still from the heat of the wax and clearly showing a pronounced pad of soft flesh below the virginal hollow of her belly and the delicate line of her hip bones. Anne's fingers trailed over those bones. 'Perhaps just a little more weight,' she said thoughtfully. 'A pound or two more.' She lifted her hands to Colette's full breasts, letting them gently rest against the palms of her hands. She laughed as Colette's nipples immediately responded to her touch and shook her head. 'But no, Gilles will be satisfied with what he sees now. Here there is softness enough for him to enjoy and the little belly below is a charming contrast.'

Briskly Anne stepped back and signalled to the maids to continue dressing Colette. Instead of the tight corsets she wore under most of her gowns, Anne selected a light silk basque which left her breasts completely bare. 'You will need to accustom yourself to this,' she announced, watching the girls fasten the narrow satin band round Colette's waist and straighten the lace straps of her suspenders over her thighs.

'Perfect.' Anne looked pleased with her pupil. 'It is enough for today. Cover yourself with your cloak while Robert drives you home. Marie will help you with your dress this evening. And then you will wait for Gilles. He will come soon.'

The gown that Monsieur Worth delivered for her to wear that evening thrilled her, and she understood why Anne had insisted that she wore only the lightest of corsets and that her breasts were left bare. Marie lifted it over her shoulders and, as a cloud of creamy tulle settled over her petticoats, the maid tightened the silk cords down the back of the bodice. It was almost a copy of the peasant blouse and skirt in which she felt most alluring at home but, instead of coarse linen, there were layers of the finest lace resting lightly on the tips of her shoulders and skimming over her bare breasts. A full skirt swung out like a bell below a sash of dark burgundy satin, with ribbons which trailed behind her like the reins of a chariot.

The effect was almost demure; certainly most of the women she had seen in evening dress wore gowns with far more revealing fronts. But the lace felt so insubstantial compared to the tight basque separating her breasts that she felt quite naked, and Colette was sure that Gilles understood this perfectly and that he had chosen the dress for precisely that reason.

He came into her room while Marie was fastening her necklace. Colette could feel the cold gems resting on her collarbones. If she went home now she would never wear anything like them again, or even see jewels like these. She dreaded the thought of parting with them.

Gilles signalled to Marie to leave and took the maid's place, taking the glittering necklace between his fingers. But instead of securing the diamond clasp, he let the jewels fall into his hand. 'You won't need these tonight,' he murmured. 'And your throat is perfect undecorated.' Colette heard the heavy stones drop on to the marble-topped table and stared at her bare neck in the mirror.

The dismay on her face was so clear that she struggled to lift the corners of her mouth into a smile when she saw Gilles' reflection bending over her, his black eyes gleaming with amusement as he held out her velvet cape.

'Do not worry. Marie will keep them safe for you,' he told her as he led her down the staircase.

But she had grown so used to the weight of the pretty necklace and the restriction of the whalebone corsets she wore with all her other dresses that she felt strangely free and insecure as she stepped into the carriage and allowed Robert to settle her into the satin-cushioned seat.

She knew the reputation of the restaurant where they were to dine tonight and her choice for their final evening had surprised Gilles. Anne had refused to talk about it. 'Gilles is not the sort of man to be seduced by a virgin,' was all she would say. Colette was determined to prove her wrong.

Marie had told her that this was the place where men like Gilles took their mistresses. The Café Anglais had a rabbit warren of private rooms above the main hall, and each was fitted with an alcove where other desires could be satisfied after the extravagant food and wine had been enjoyed.

Their carriage stopped in a narrow road to the left of the great restaurant. Gilles rang a bell at the side of a plain wooden door and they were ushered inside. A waiter led them up a dark staircase and held open the door of a room on the first floor.

A table was laid for two in the centre of a rich Persian carpet. Candles glowed softly in gilt brackets on the silk-lined walls. Deep in the core of the building, there were no windows, but thick velvet was draped around an alcove set into one wall. Marie had told her that behind these curtains she would find a bed.

So this was what it was all about. Food, wine and silks. She felt aware of the new nakedness of her body, of the skilled preparation that had taken place. She knew that tonight she was beautiful all over.

'You are aware that this is the finest food in Paris?' Gilles asked.

She nodded. Anne had devoted a whole hour to demonstrating the intricacies of eating *écrevisses à la bordelaise*, and now Colette took a sharp silver knife and sliced firmly through the thin papery shell of the belly, lifting out the meat and swirling it in the sauce before she raised it to her mouth on the end of a small fork. She caught the sweet flesh she had exposed between her teeth; slowly she dragged it out from its shell and drew it into her mouth. It was delicious, delicate and firm and drenched in a savoury sauce. She ate them greedily. She was so hungry. It was delicious, as was the *croustade a l'impératrice*. She sucked a chilled sorbet from a silver spoon and waited for the tiny roast birds resting on a bed of wild mushrooms which were to follow. Gilles filled her glass.

She sipped. 'Château-Lafite 1848. I am honoured.'

'Your palate is exquisite. And you learn fast. It is a pleasure to watch you, Colette.'

She shifted slightly in her seat. The creamy lace rested on her shoulders and she was aware of the

76

full curve of her breasts rising above the sheer layers. It was not her palate she wanted Gilles to admire. She glanced towards the heavy curtains, while the waiter placed a dish of roasted ortolans in front of her.

She drank the wine. Tonight it seemed merely to heighten the clarity of her mind. She felt quite clear about what she had to do.

She looked at Gilles, at the smooth skin of his face, smooth – like a woman's. She remembered the way he had held her hand over the Madonna's breast at the château. She wanted to feel those long, sensitive fingers on her own breast. It felt almost naked beneath the creamy tulle. The layer covering her breasts was so sheer, so insubstantial. If Gilles raised one finger and touched the light frills, the fabric would fall away and her nakedness would be exposed. She felt a thrill run through her, and knew that her nipples had stiffened above the soft basque. Gilles' eyes were warm; his features were impassive, but she was sure he knew how she felt. His face showed nothing. She wanted the meal to be over. Her breasts were on fire. Did he feel nothing?

She no longer noticed the delicate flavours of the exquisite food; her mind was filled with images of what lay behind the velvet drapes. How much longer would it be before she lay in there with Gilles?

She was sure that he was waiting for her to speak, but the words would not come into her mouth. She stumbled through this course and the next, and still felt unsure. A scoop of Grand Marnier soufflé trembled untasted on a silver teaspoon when she saw Gilles take two long, slim, red leather boxes out of his pocket and lay them on the table.

She must tell him now that she wanted only this one night, but still she could not find the words. Yet she wasn't going to be like the others, thrown out at the end of a year. She would take what she wanted – one night with this man whom women never forgot. And if Gaston did not want her, she would find someone else to support her. The man she had seen with Éloise at the opera would help her to stay in Paris, she was sure. And he would be a man whom she could control.

She looked greedily at the two boxes on the table. They at least would be hers if she spent this night with Gilles.

'What have you decided?'

She put down her spoon. 'I want you to make love to me.'

'How very direct.' Gilles put one box back into his pocket. 'But I notice that you have not said that you accept my offer.'

He frowned for a moment, then rose from his seat and came to stand behind her chair. He placed his hands gently round her waist, lifting her to her feet. Just the lightest touch, scarcely pressing on her flesh, his fingers covering the small of her back and his two thumbs poised over her belly. He made no further movement and yet the blood sang through her body in a wild burst of energy, colouring her throat and face and bringing a surge of moisture between her thighs.

What was it Anne had said? 'For the moment you must do nothing when he touches you. Let him teach you everything. Later, when he has tired of this game, it will be for you to take the initiative.'

The initiative. The idea made her tremble. For a moment she obeyed Anne and remained motionless, with only the trembling of her body and the heightened colour of her skin to betray her desire.

Gilles, his head bent over the low front of her bodice, caressed the exposed curve of her breasts. She could feel the warmth and tenderness of his lips brushing over her bare flesh.

She had to say more; she had to tell him that after this one night she would return home. Only she could not think clearly. The dark curtains terrified her. She had to see the bed behind them, the place where she would lie with Gilles, the place where he would take her.

She pulled away from him and moved towards the alcove. She put out her hand to draw the curtain aside. It would be easier to tell him later, tomorrow.

'Colette, are you trying to seduce me?' She turned back to see Gilles still standing by the table, his face dark with anger.

She knew at once that she had made a mistake. Anne had been right.

'You refuse to become my mistress, and yet you expect me to take you here? You are so desperate to lose your virginity that you want to lie on a couch in a corner of a restaurant?'

'I thought that was what people did here.'

'Come with me.' He took her almost roughly by the hand and pushed her towards the door. He nodded as a waiter hurried forward with her cape, and led her out into the street before she had time to fasten it properly.

Their carriage was just starting to move towards them. Robert's jacket was half undone as if he, too, was unprepared for the haste of their departure. They rode in silence back to the villa.

Colette felt his hand hard on hers as he climbed fast up the grand stairs. Instead of taking her to his bedroom or hers, Gilles led her up a second staircase and a third, until they stood at the foot of a circular flight of iron steps, spiralling almost into the eaves of the house. Only then did he hesitate. He let go of her hand.

'Are you sure of your decision?'

She nodded. She would not back out now. He waved her forward, and she climbed round and round until she reached the top of one of the turrets high up on the roof of the house.

A door to her left led into a domed space covering the whole length of the house, with glass doors opening on to a wide, stone terrace. The room was in darkness, the only light coming through the uncurtained windows from the stars in the clear night sky and the faint glow from the streetlights of Paris beneath them.

Gilles stood behind her as she stared out at the unsleeping city which bustled beneath them like a nest of glow-worms. As she gazed, Colette felt Gilles' lips brush softly on the top of her spine and his fingers lift the single layer of delicate lace on her shoulder. His touch felt as light as the faint breath of warm night air drifting in through the open windows. She stepped forward on to the terrace on the roof of the villa and leant against the rough stone balustrade. Far below her lay the shimmering strand of the Seine with its ribbons of bridges.

She turned to see Gilles, no more than a shadow in the dark interior of the room, twist the cork from a bottle of champagne and fill a glass with foaming pink bubbles. His arm pressed on her collar bone as he lifted the glass to her lips.

He was closer now, and her skirt lifted slightly behind her as the length of his body pressed against hers. She dared not move, unsure of herself, unwilling to lose the delicious sense of his presence.

He took the glass from her lips and placed it on the parapet. He opened one of the red leather boxes and took out a single strand of rosy pearls. Slipping it over her head, he let it fall on to her skin. She felt his cool fingers slide deeper inside the loose folds of lace and stroke the curve of her breasts. She wanted him to uncover her completely, to peel away all the flimsy layers until his fingers circled her aching nipples. He did nothing except allow the pads of his fingers to gently stroke the very top of her lifted breasts.

She shivered. Maybe he would think she was cold and take her inside. Surely there he would unlace her dress and relieve her eager body. He moved only to press his lips on the base of her throat, letting his warm breath drift over her skin. She stretched her back like an animal in the height of pleasure, feeling his lips part over her flesh and the rough, moist tip of his tongue sip lightly at her skin as if to taste her.

Slowly his hands slid down over her breasts and round behind her waist, to the tiny cords lacing her bodice. She felt her breathing quicken as he loosened the first threads and steadily freed each intricate hook until the dress rested lightly on her shoulders. Still she dared not move.

His hands pressed against the light tension of her basque, releasing the laces until her breasts sprang free from all restrictions, falling against the thick mounds of creamy lace which rested precariously over them. Those sure hands curled round her waist, increasing their pressure until the gown fell from her shoulders, exposing her nakedness except for the band of lace securing her stockings, the high satin slippers she had been so proud to wear and the heavy strand of pearls at her throat. She saw that his shirt was open to the waist, loosely tucked into his black trousers.

For a moment she watched him stare at her as she stood naked in the pale moonlight, then he lifted her in his arms and carried her to the bed.

Spread out on the covers was a cloak of rich burgundy velvet, edged with sable. He laid her down on it so that her skin seemed to rest on the silky velvet pile as on a cushion of air. He lifted her hair in his hands and let it fall over the pale sheets above the thick fur border which nestled into the back of her neck and caressed her ears.

She felt his fingers stroking the smooth mound of bare flesh over her sex and lay helpless beneath him, shivering at his touch as his hands moved down towards the padded lips that shielded her core, sliding inwards to the hot passage that now pulsed unbearably in anticipation.

She cried out as she felt him stroke her there. She wanted him to continue to do exactly this, to taunt and tease her until her mind and body pounded with her need for satisfaction.

He pulled back, laughing at her cry of loss, and knelt over her, the muscles of his thighs hard against her hips. Then she rose instinctively to take him as the swollen head of his penis pressed on the lips that his fingers had merely tantalised.

She felt his hands covering her buttocks, curving over their soft flesh as he lifted her higher, letting her take him deeper into her until her sex lips circled the base of his shaft.

His lips caressed first one breast and then the other as he lay over her, his manhood throbbing inside her, pulsing with a life force that threatened to explode into her at any moment. He groaned, and his breath came hot on her breast, his light touch strengthening over her nipple until his teeth enclosed her eager buds and he thrust again with greater force. All his gentleness was gone now as his hips rose and fell over her, pushing the silky head of his penis back and forth over her engorged bud. She moaned as the first wave of her climax surged through her, cried out as she felt him thrust faster into her. She felt sure she was losing consciousness now, melting into him, unsure whether his flesh pulsing inside her was part of her own body, her own desire or his, until she lay motionless beneath him, moulded around his sated flesh.

So this was how it felt. Her head was comfortable, secure, resting on his chest. She had no wish to leave him now. As her eyes closed, she wondered what was in the second red leather box.

Chapter Five

Victor opened the gilded doors of his mother's suite on the west corner of the château, and paused for a moment to breathe in the mingled scents of freesia and pine that still drifted through the air. Even if his mother could not be with him, he loved her room more than any other in the château. The gold damask-lined walls reflected the full blaze of sunlight that poured in through windows on two sides of the corner room. And from here, with a clear view of the avenue of chestnut trees leading up to the drive, he would be sure to catch the first glimpse of the curé arriving.

As a child, Victor had loved to curl up quietly in a dark corner behind an embroidered screen, watching his mother sit at her rosewood dressing-table while her maid arranged her beautiful hair into elaborate curls. First the glorious, red-gold mass was allowed to cascade over her white back while it was stroked a hundred times with a brush made of gold, encrusted with opals, before the maid's deft fingers twisted and coiled the gleaming strands and threaded them through with jewels. The same maid whom he had seen his father fondle vigorously in the dark corridors. Victor hated watching the girl's hands on his mother's soft skin, but he still chose to sit here every moment he was permitted. Which was often: his mother liked an appreciative audience, and his father paid her little attention. Her portrait still dominated one wall of the room, framed in white and gold like the lavish furniture that had been ordered from a craftsman in Paris.

Behind the screen, a narrow arch led through to his mother's dressing-room, where the clothes she had left behind hung beneath layers of loose, linen sheeting. Victor picked up one corner of the light cover and ran his fingers over the familiar textures of heavy satin, rich brocade and delicate, fine lace. He buried his face in one gown that he remembered his mother wearing the week before she left. Its stiffly-boned bodice was torn in a jagged rip down to the waist, so that the lace fichu hung in rags, but no one had dared to throw it out. Her personal scent, created for her by a master perfumer in Grasse, still clung to its silk lining. The heavy tones of ambergris and musk drifted from the depths of the closet, escaping from the tightly-packed racks of garments that reminded him of how she had looked when she lived here.

His mother wore nothing like this now. Last summer, in Italy, she dressed in deceptively simple white, draped silk, which skimmed lightly over her beautiful body, hinting at the colours of her skin beneath its sheer folds and enhancing the illusion that the light silk was transparent. Occasionally a few drops of champagne would fall on to the thin material, rendering it as translucent as glass; sometimes she would pass slightly too close to a fountain and let herself be sprinkled by the flying spray that gushed from a stone seagod's open lips. Often, she sat in the shadow of the olive trees, where only a few, faint rays of dappled sunshine, falling on her white covering, showed the clear outlines of her body beneath her moistened robe. After that purity, these clothes reminded him of the harsher life she had led here, with his father.

Victor shivered, and walked through the corridor to her salon. He sat on a small gilt chair in the alcove of the window and watched the bright sunlight reflecting off the dry stone of the drive. The curé would be on time, exactly on time, but Victor wanted to make sure that he would not miss the first glimpse of the man emerging from the dark shadows of the tree-lined avenue. He was not due for an hour, but Victor hoped he would be early. He had waited long enough already.

He moved over to one of the white and gold bureaux that were placed in opposite corners of the room and opened a drawer containing writing paper. He had to do something to occupy himself while he waited. He wanted to write to his mother to tell her how he felt about the curé. No one else would understand the emotion that swept through him now. Victor's hands trembled as he took out a single sheet of the thick, cream paper. Black ink splattered from his pen on to the page, and drops fell on the white cuff of his shirt, spreading into an ugly mark and staining his skin. Angered by his clumsiness, he looked again out of the window overlooking the drive. There was still no sign of his friend.

It seemed hours before he saw a dark figure emerge from the shadows. The curé's face was obscured beneath his wide-brimmed hat; a black cassock swirled round his long legs. Victor shivered with delight at the perfection of the austerity. He wanted to rush down and fling open the front doors himself, but he preferred not to let any of the servants see his eagerness. He must wait here until Paul came to tell him of the curé's arrival, and then he could slowly rise from his chair, walk across the room and descend the main staircase. Or he could suggest that his friend came to see him here, upstairs, in his mother's room, with that wonderful draped bed where he had slept last night in anticipation of this moment.

The window was stuck; he tried to force it up so that he could lean out. He waved, but the curé was looking down at the raked gravel, and could not see him. There were too many windows glittering on the façade of the château. Paul had walked down the front steps, and across the terrace to welcome him. Victor leaned back so as not to be seen, while he watched the curé's hand rest on the servant's back.

In a few moments the door opened, 'Monsieur le curé has arrived,' Paul announced. 'He is waiting in the private chapel, and wishes to know if you will join him.'

Victor saw the man's gaze rest on his stained shirt. He refused to ask for another one; he had no wish to delay. 'Did he say how long he intended to stay?'

'No, Monsieur, but he told me that he came especially to see you.'

'Then I will join him later.' He turned his back; the servant would know that he was dismissed. Victor clenched his fingers, forcing himself to wait a moment longer. He breathed deeply and tried to compose himself before he walked through the open double doors and along the long passage fronting the house. He passed his father's rooms, at the back of the house, and entered his own suite.

There, with some difficulty, he found a clean shirt, struggling with the buttons until it was secured. He left the stained garment on the floor with his jacket, and descended the stairs in his breeches and a plain white shirt, pleased with the stark simplicity of his appearance.

Paul was waiting for him at the foot of the stairs. Victor waved him aside and put his hand on the doors of the chapel. He felt the servant's eyes still on him, and turned angrily. 'Leave me,' he said. 'I have no need of you.'

The doors, which reached almost to the ceiling, were hewn from single planks of ebony, heavily decorated with gilded acanthus leaves, carved by a master. As a child, Victor had entered the chapel only with his mother. Now he stood outside, knowing that the only true friend he had in the world waited for him there. The harsh metal of the handle imprinted its pattern on the palm of his hand as he gripped it tightly. He turned it, and held his breath. The door opened a crack and he stepped inside.

Standing there, Victor could smell the bitter scent of incense which he recognised from his childhood, as the heavy doors swung shut behind him. He saw the curé standing with his arms raised, facing the altar, his back outlined against a blaze of coloured light from the stained-glass window. Above him, a yellow halo of light surrounded the face of the wounded Christ and shone on the faceless figure below. Victor remembered the warmth and comfort of this man's presence in his youth, and the security of the days he had spent in his study at the vestry. That small room where he had spent so many hours with Colette.

He felt uneasy. His shirt was not quite comfortable; somehow the long tails of fine lawn had failed to tuck fully into his breeches, and Victor slowly became aware of an awkward fold causing an unsightly bulge in the sleek line over his left hip bone, spoiling the cut. He wanted to explain that he had never dressed himself before.

The curé turned around. His face was severe. 'Your clothes are disordered, Victor. Why is that?'

'I spilt some ink. My pen splattered.'

'And your valet failed to satisfy you?'

'I did not call my valet.'

'Why was that?'

'I thought it not worth the trouble.' Victor felt his face burn at the steady gaze of the older man. 'I knew that you were here. I did not wish to keep you waiting.'

'You used not to be so careless with your pen. And look, the ink has stained your skin. Remove your shirt, Victor.'

The curé turned his back and walked quickly to a polished ebony chest which stood against one wall of the chapel. Its ornate lock was normally secured, and Victor had never seen inside the chest, but now he saw that the clasp swung loosely against the dark wood. He watched the curé lift the heavy lid with ease, raising it so that it rested on the carved frame of a large oil-painting above it. The black cassock blocked out his view of the chest's contents, but he could see the curé's dark hands seeming to stroke something inside, before he spoke again. His words shocked Victor. 'You must be punished.'

It had never occurred to Victor that the curé would dare to touch him. No one had ever punished him. He saw the dark figure straighten, but could not see his friend's face. He felt confused as he waited.

'Tell me, Victor, do you believe you have ever done wrong?'

'When, father?'

'In my study, when you and Colette worked at your books, did your thoughts stray to her body?'

Victor thought of the hours he had spent looking at Colette's head bent over her books, while he remembered the naked body he had seen floating in the pool below the rocks. She had seemed like a spirit of the water, with her long black hair floating in the stream and her creamy flesh drifting beneath the surface. He had wanted to touch her intimately, but always the curé had sat on the bank watching them and he had felt ashamed. Afterwards, at their lessons, he had thought of Colette's slim thighs, and the delicate cleft between them, and had ignored his work. She had taken no notice of him, which was why she had benefited from her lessons. As the curé questioned him, he felt the familiar pleasurable stirring of his penis that he had first known then.

'I have always confessed my sins to you willingly.' Victor remembered the dark closet of the confessional, and his shame when he had first confessed his thoughts. He had sat breathlessly on a hard, oak bench while he waited for the priest's absolution. But there had been no punishment. Not for the only son of Gilles de la Trave.

He stepped forward towards the curé, staring at the black ebony lid of the chest resting against the pure white wall of the chapel. Inside the chest Victor seemed to see a mass of black snakes, encased in chains of steel. He gazed, fascinated, until he was aware of the curé's anger. The man's back was rigid as he bent over the chest, and took out chains of heavy, steel links from the tangled heap within. He threw them on to the red velvet cushions of the pew nearest the altar and turned towards Victor. He held a long, black leather whip in his hands. 'You came to me to study, Victor, and it was wrong to spend your time thinking of lustful flesh. It was not the right place for such desires to fill your mind.'

Victor ran his tongue over his dry lips. 'You never punished me.'

'If you believe that it was wrong, Victor, you must pay for it. Would you like me to punish you now?'

Victor looked at the framed painting of St Sebastien, above the open chest. The saint's wounds spread in dark bruises on his ash pale flesh. He looked down at the smooth front of his linen trousers bulging over his swelling erection and felt the heat burn his face in shame. The curé darted forward, and Victor felt the man's fingers twisting the metal pin of the buckle at his waist, pulling the leather belt unbearably tighter until the pin was torn from its clasp and the fine linen fell down over his hips. Victor could not prevent his rigid stem from jutting forward, unmistakably erect.

The curé appeared not to notice, and Victor watched him stride over to the massive doors of the entrance and slam the iron bolts into their rounded clasps. His voice echoed past the stone pillars bordering the cloisters as he walked through the passage. 'Shall I punish you now, Victor?' he repeated. 'Will you do penance for your sin?'

Victor nodded. He liked the feeling of his swollen penis freed from the tight trousers. The curé turned his back, and lifted his arms in front of the altar. Victor could see nothing except the severe black folds of the cassock, scarcely touching the man's body, except over the curve of his buttocks below a broad leather belt. 'Remove your clothes,' the curé said, without turning to face him.

Victor stepped free from their constraint, so that he was quite naked, and grateful for the privacy of the locked doors. He needed to be punished, to atone for his sin of lust. He must have sinned, or his father would not have taken Colette away from him.

'Lie down.' The curé spoke softly, his voice a husky breath on the silent air. 'Down.' Victor felt stiff fingers digging into his shoulder blades, pushing him on to the cold, marble tiles of the nave. He smelt the strong, sharp odour of freshly tanned leather, saw heavy bands being clasped round his wrists and ankles and heard the clank of steel chains as they were locked on to pinions inside the pews. They fitted perfectly, as though the rings had been designed for the purpose.

Victor tried to move, and failed; his body was spread-eagled on the tiles. He felt the thick stem of his erection forced against the cold floor and shuddered. He was unused to pain; no one had ever hurt his body. Now, unyielding steel bit into his wrists and ankles and he felt powerless to resist. He was aware of a strange sense of security, knowing that he was at the mercy of his friend, who would do only what was best for him.

The mud-caked hem of the curé's cassock trailed over his bare buttocks, and he clenched them instinctively, feeling the warmth of the other man's body close to his skin. The chapel was so quiet that he could hear the faint rhythm of the curé's breath, and tried to link his own breathing to the same pattern, but his heart was beating fast; he could feel it fluttering inside his chest, seeming to echo against the stone floor, and his breath quickened uncontrollably. He waited for the harsh stroke of the whip over his back, and the justice of his punishment. He closed his eyes in anticipation.

A warm hand rested for a moment on his shoulder blades, then he felt the knotted, leather thongs of the whip sliding down his spine, as if his tormentor was assessing the precise point to inflict pain. Folds of coarse wool covered his sides, warming him for a moment, before he felt naked flesh sliding over his thighs. He wanted to turn his head to face the other man, but he was unable to move and could see only the dark outline of the curé's head as his legs were pressed beneath the warmth of bare, lean muscles. Over his thighs he felt the weight of a rigid penis gently resting between the cleft of his buttocks, and realised that he was not alone in the excitement which he felt at this moment. It was the most exquisite pleasure he had ever known.

Long, lean fingers stroked his clenched muscles and he closed his eyes to remember the way the curé's hands had rested so calmly on the scarred wood of his study desk, while he gave his orders for the next lesson. Victor could feel those hands trembling now as they touched him so intimately, and he tried to stretch out in response to the gentle pressure above him, but he was powerless to move. He dared not speak in case he might say something which would break into their pleasure. He wanted to lie here, feeling the delicious sensation of firm thumbs stroking his cheeks and gently moistening the cleft between them. Steadily the pressure increased, until he felt the priest raise himself slightly, and the firm heat of his penis push between his parted buttocks.

Victor wanted to cry out and beg the other man to press harder on to him, to thrust his stiffened flesh deep into him. He felt his clenched muscles soften, then heard a gasp as the hot, swollen shaft slid firmly into the path prepared by the eager, sweating fingers. Victor cried out as he felt the rigid flesh surge inside him, thrusting its full length deep into his core. He was aware of the shock of the man's entry, and then a delicious pain as his muscles enclosed the long, slim, pulsing penis. His whole body was racked with a violent climax, and he groaned in ecstasy as he felt the other man's body shudder on top of him and sink heavily down on him.

Victor no longer felt the pain of his tight bonds or the chill of the marble floor. Anything he might suffer added to the joy of his experience. He knew that the curé was free to move, and yet he remained motionless. Victor opened his eyes a fraction, looking through his lashes at the flickering candlelight on the shadowed walls, as he breathed in the heady scent of incense which still burned in the censer. Then the weight of the curé's body crushed him against the cold stone, and covered him completely.

He believed he must have lost consciousness, before he was aware of the chains rattling on the marble floor as the locks were released, and he reached out painfully, stretching his freed limbs. Then he saw the curé pull his black cassock over his shoulders and throw it down on to the carved oak pew. Victor stared, fascinated, through eyes half-closed with exhaustion at the man's lean, bare chest. His gaze dropped to the plain, black trousers which rested loosely on his hips, exposing his limp penis. The curé stood over Victor, his legs apart, his fingers twisting round the shaft of the whip he had held before. He dropped it in front of him and turned, baring his back so that Victor saw his dark skin criss-crossed with raised, rigid scars. 'Now you must punish me,' he demanded. 'Do it now.'

Victor picked up the whip, ran it through his fingers, felt the soft, leather thongs and raised it high in the air. The sight of the scarred flesh excited him. He made a pattern of fresh, red weals across the ancient scars, and felt his erection rise again. He pushed the slim, black shaft of the whip between the clenched buttocks of olive flesh, fumbling for the puckered round hole of the curé's arse, then he plunged it in and shivered as he heard the man's long groan of ecstasy. He threw the whip aside and pressed the swollen head of his penis into the reddened opening. He pushed harder until he had squeezed the full length of his rigid flesh deep inside his friend.

Victor sank exhausted on to the moist flesh of the curé's back. He felt drained but strangely exhilarated. He ran his fingers over the hard calluses of scarred flesh on the dark skin beneath him where fresh weals had risen in vivid streaks of raised flesh. He would bathe them himself later, and soothe the wounds, then he would offer his friend the food and the wine he had selected so carefully.

He raised himself slowly and lay on his back, sated. 'Come with me,' he said 'I have prepared a room for us. Come upstairs.'

He saw the other man stare up at him, and narrow his eyes. 'You want me to stay with you?' the curé asked.

Victor nodded. 'Come with me,' he repeated, and helped his friend up from the floor. There was a small door on one side of the wall, leading up to a gallery surrounding the chapel, and further, through a narrow passage, to the west wing of the château and his mother's apartments. They could make their way to her rooms unseen. Hurriedly, the two men replaced the leather whips in the ebony chest, secured the lid, and climbed up a circular stone staircase. The door to the first floor apartments was open; Victor had unlocked it earlier. When the door closed behind them he saw the curé turn the key in the lock and take it in his hand.

'No one must follow us,' he said. Victor felt a flash of irritation. He didn't want to think about anyone else; he wanted to show his concern and love for his friend. No one was here but the servants, and what did they matter?

The bath had been drawn and left for him as he had ordered. Now he guided the curé into the side bathroom, and washed his wounds in warm water.

He was very gentle with the fresh wounds he had created; he would like to know who had made the others, but did not dare ask. It seemed too personal. Victor had laid loose gowns out for them, both of rich silk, one in purple and the other in black and scarlet. The curé refused either, and held out the dusty cassock which he had carried from the chapel. 'I must wear this,' he said. 'I am a priest.' He shook it out roughly, and slipped it on over his shoulders. Victor watched him fasten the simple column of buttons over his chest, and admired the austerity of the gesture. He took the black and red gown, which he thought suited him best, and tied it loosely round his waist with a wide silk sash, before leading the way down the main staircase. They would take a glass of champagne together and spend the evening enjoying the food he had selected.

When they entered the dining room, the cold dishes were already laid out on the table. Paul poured their champagne and silently left the room. Victor raised his glass. 'To us,' he toasted, 'to the two of us.'

The curé twisted his fingers round the stem of his glass and lifted it to his lips. Victor saw his black eyes glitter as he tipped the chilled wine into his mouth. 'To us,' the curé repeated, replacing his glass on the table. 'To our love, Victor.' He said nothing as the soup was placed in front of him, and as more wine filled his glass, but he ate greedily, and Victor was satisfied that the meal had been chosen well.

His own food scarcely interested him, and he left much of it untasted on his plate. He was more conscious of his body than he had ever imagined.

His back smarted, even though the whip had scarcely touched him, and the blood seemed to be flowing faster through his veins. He felt more alive, more in love with the whole world. He wanted to feel the other man's fingers on him again. Soon. He ran his finger round the sharp edge of an oyster shell on his plate, watching the curé tip back his head and suck up the sea-fresh juices from one deep shell after another. The tongue that licked the last few drops of moisture from the mother of pearl coating had entered his most intimate parts. Victor took an oyster, sucked the soft mollusc into his mouth and let it fall down his throat. A surge of energy gave him appetite, and soon he was eating with as much enthusiasm as the curé.

His father's dog moved to his side as the quail were served. He felt the warmth of the animal's breath on his feet as he watched the curé's long forefingers slicing the bird. The brief moment of appetite had left him. There was only one desire that filled him now. He wanted to feel again the enveloping warmth that had delighted him before.

Yet it gave him pleasure to watch his friend eating. The curé's eyes had brightened. The pallor in his cheeks was less pronounced and his full lips pulsed with blood as the wine stirred his spirits. The long, dark fingers coiled round the gnarled shell of a walnut, then tightened until a sharp crack broke through the silence.

Victor could sit still no longer. He wanted to touch the man again. He rose from his seat, walked round to the other side of the table, and put his hands on the rough wool of the cassock. The curé turned and held out a walnut, shelled ready for Victor to take in his mouth. He bent down, his hands pressing harder on the man's back. Victor felt a warm moisture soak his fingers and stared at his hands. They were covered with blood.

The curé's strong fingers clutched his wrist. 'Suck them clean before your servants come,' he ordered.

'You are in pain.' Victor was immediately concerned.

'I deserve it. The pleasure was worth anything I might have to bear now.'

Victor did as he was told. He had no further interest in food. He wanted to lie in this man's arms, and to feel his naked body next to his in the big bed upstairs. They walked away from the table, up the grand staircase and into the golden suite. Nestled together in the huge bed, the warmth of the other man's body soothed him. Victor felt strong, lean arms circle his chest, holding him firm in his embrace. Across the room the last embers of a dying fire glowed in the grate. He raised his head so that his cheek rested on the other man's face, and closed his eyes.

Their two bodies sank into the soft mattress together. Last night he had lain here alone, letting his fingers trail over the stiff brocade hangings as he used to do when he was a child. Now the scent of incense drifting through the open door from the chapel mingled with his mother's heady perfume. He had everything he wanted.

The curé's lean body was hard and firm against him. Victor curled his hands over the knotted spine and stroked the raised scars with the pads of his thumbs. He heard a sharp intake of breath, and felt the body tense beside him. A delicious sense of power overwhelmed him, stronger than the rich wine that had exhilarated him earlier. He knew that, if he wished, he could arouse his friend beyond control. Already he felt the stirring of the curé's penis against his own, and paused for a moment to experience the pleasure of the response.

His heart pounded as he lay motionless except for the inexorable pulsing of his sex. He lowered his head and pressed his ear against the curé's chest, hearing the rapid throb of a beating heart pound through his brain.

Slowly, he lowered his hands over the clenched muscles of the curé's buttocks and pulled him hard towards him. The heat of their two bodies burned him. The curé was gasping now, trembling more with every movement that Victor made, and soft moans issued from his lips. Victor kissed beads of sweat from his upper lip and slid his hips up and down, pushing hard against the other man. He had no need to pin him down. He could see the man's black eyes glittering feverishly in the faint red glow from the fire, and stroked his cheek gently. He hooked a gold cord from one corner of the bed and trailed the stiffened tassle over the curé's dark, blistered nipples, through the dark mass of soft hair beneath his arms and over a throbbing pulse at the base of his throat. He sat over the curé's taut, lean thighs, letting his erection strut over his belly as his friend's penis nestled against him. His weight forced the man's immobility, and increased his sense of power. He secured both wrists loosely with the gold cord, not even bothering to secure the knots, knowing that the spreadeagled arms had no desire to loosen their bonds. The heat was becoming unbearable; both their bodies gleamed with sweat now, the salty drops mingling on their joined flesh.

Victor lay full length on top of him, his own arms outstretched, palm to palm, hip to hip, and stared into the black eyes. He saw the tip of the curé's tongue emerge to lick his dry lips, and tasted it with the moist point of his own. Slowly, he circled the living flesh, sucking the glistening beads of sweat from the upper lip beneath him, breathing in the air that escaped with the curé's groans.

His nipples rasped against the lean, bony chest beneath him as he let his full weight bear down, and he forced the man's mouth wide open, pushing his tongue deep inside. He cradled the head between his fingers, pushing harder until their teeth clashed together and their mouths bruised from the pressure.

The heat at his groin became unbearable. Gasping for breath, he struggled to raise himself until he was kneeling over the other man and saw the long, slim penis rising from the dark, sweating mass of curls. He let his head drop down until his open mouth curled round the rigid column and his tongue tasted the sweet, salty moistness of the flesh. The body beneath him shuddered as he took the column deeper inside his mouth. Victor wanted to enjoy his power, to force the other man to lose control and climax, and yet he wanted to prolong their pleasure as long as possible. He knew it could not be long, and felt an exquisite pleasure when the sweet drops exploded into his mouth. He felt the curé's body shudder convulsively between him as he rose up on his knees and pressed his penis between the man's open lips, holding his hands down on the bed and straddling his chest with his powerful thighs. He felt an exquisite pleasure as the hot tongue circled the swollen tip of his penis, and let it rest for a moment against the full lips before he pushed further in. He wanted that beautiful mouth to close around him, to take his full length and give him total satisfaction.

The curé's face darkened, becoming discoloured in the firelight as Victor pressed forward. 'Suck me,' Victor ordered, and felt the man's lips tighten around him. He surged forward as he felt the man take him, letting the pleasure come. Sated, Victor fell back on the silk pillows and slept. His body felt smooth and at peace.

He was woken in the night by moonlight shining in through the open curtains. In front of him, outlined against the window, he could see the dark figure of the curé with his arms raised on to the sill. Twisted between the curé's fingers, Victor saw the long shaft of the whip and the moonlight shining on the man's scarred back.

Victor struggled to clear the sleep from his brain. 'Come back to bed,' he muttered drowsily.

The curé shook his head. 'I can't sleep now. Look at the valley. Look how beautiful it is.'

Victor crossed the room and stood behind the man at the window. 'My father has told me I have to marry.'

The curé turned to face him. 'But he has taken the woman you want. Does that pain you?' He spat out the words angrily. 'Do you still desire Colette?'

Victor felt the other man's arms encircling him. He wanted nothing else. Strong, long fingers stroked the length of his spine and he shivered with pleasure. Why should he need a woman? And yet the memory of Colette's body in the river came into his mind at the curé's words. Her limbs were supple, taut and lithe. And she was no doubt now lying in his father's arms. The curé's fingers lowered to curve round the base of his penis and Victor stiffened, closing his eyes again and letting the miracle of his pleasure overwhelm him. The pressure increased deliciously. He wanted nothing but to stay here and experience this delight, but the curé persisted. 'Does it anger you that your father has her now?'

Victor groaned. Why did he have to keep thinking of his father? What they had shared together tonight had put that misery behind him for a time. It was the lean, dark body pressed against him now that filled his mind and overwhelmed all other thoughts. 'Come back to my bed,' he said, reaching out for his friend's hand. 'Come back here and hold me.'

He led him back to their soft nest. Victor had never felt so safe, so comfortable, as he did here, in the cure's arms. They had left the curtains open and the dark shadow of the trees filtered the moonlight into shifting patterns on to the pale gold bedcover.

Victor woke several times in the night, and each time stretched his body luxuriously against the warm chest of the other man. In the morning, late, he woke alone when his valet brought in his coffee and rolls. The table was laid for two. 'Monsieur le curé said that he would join you for breakfast,' Paul said, and Victor looked up to see a dark figure standing in the doorway.

'Why did you leave me?' he demanded, as soon as they were alone.

'I cannot afford to be seen openly with you.'

'By my valet? What does he matter?'

'Nothing to you, but I was born here, one of them. I am not permitted your indulgences.'

'I wanted you in my bed this morning.'

'You had me last night. If you want more than that it is not possible here.'

'Then where can we be free?'

'We could go to Italy. To live with your mother.'

Victor hated the thought of returning to Italy. He had always felt out of place there. He hesitated.

'Your father has poisoned your mind against your mother. Do you understand that?' The curé's voice became shrill. 'She was perfect in every way. It was your father's fault that she left here.'

Victor understood completely. And it was his fault that Colette had gone to Paris; he had been punished now, and she would return to him.

'Your mother was surrounded by beautiful young men. They all wanted to visit her, but your father sent them all away.' Victor could see how angry this had made his friend, whose fingers gripped the thick, gold rope which secured the drapes. Every bone stood out on his knuckles, and his thin lips twisted in an ugly sneer as he continued. 'Your father has taken Colette away from you, as he took everything else. You know how he is able to do that? He spends your mother's money on his mistress.'

It was true. Gilles de la Trave always ensured he had what he wanted, no matter who stood in his way. And the francs poured in from the textile factories belonging to his wife's family in an unceasing flood sufficient to finance any man's desires. Colette's body was lean and firm, and so pale. Victor thought of his father's hard, dark hands paying to touch that creamy skin, and shuddered. She would never be able to resist the lure of money.

The curé moved closer and grasped Victor's arm. 'Do you want Colette, Victor?' he asked. 'I can give her to you. Trust me.'

Chapter Six

Colette woke out of a deep sleep. Her body felt languid and faintly sore, especially between her thighs, where the pressure was now. And Gilles' body felt heavy on hers. Gilles! She opened her eyes and saw him kneeling over her. She smiled. They had made love; she had spent the night in his bed and now he wanted her again. She felt proud and excited, and deliberately parted her legs to let him enter her. She was a woman now. A woman whom men wanted.

Gille's eagerness thrilled her. She had been afraid that after he had first taken her, when she was no longer a virgin, he would not be interested in her any more, and that she would fail to excite him in the same way. It was something she remembered having been told. Now, his heavy male force was thrusting up into her again and he seemed to have even more enthusiasm. He was less gentle, but it was almost more exciting. Half asleep still, she felt the same enchantment as he probed the delicate

106

area which had given her so much pleasure last night. She wanted him again; she wanted him to give her that pleasure once more. The smooth head of Gilles' penis swooped over her still sensitive clitoris, the hot bud that he had brought to life. She felt her whole body respond in a warm flood of joy as he touched her and then, suddenly, with one swift rush, she felt him come and his limp flesh softly withdrew. She lay quietly, wanting him still, unsure what she should do, with a dull ache deep inside, needing the satisfaction he had given her last night.

The door opened and Colette realised that their bedcovers had all fallen to the floor. She lay completely naked and exposed as Jean-Pierre walked in and calmly laid a heavy, silver tray with their coffee on the table beside Gilles. She reached out to pull up the silk sheets, but felt Gilles' hand gripping her wrist and holding her still. Jean-Pierre stared blankly at the two of them, giving no indication that he was aware of her nakedness, or even of her presence in his master's bed. The pressure of Gilles' fingers on her skin left her in no doubt that she was not free to cover herself. He was smiling; Colette saw one corner of his beautiful mouth rise slightly and followed his gaze. Jean-Pierre was fully erect beneath the sleek uniform that he habitually wore.

He poured the coffee and handed it to her without a trace of embarrassment. She felt her face flush, but took her coffee as Gilles released her wrist and sipped from his own cup. It was strong, dark and bitter, and drove the last remnants of sleep from her brain. Neither man seemed to pay any attention to her nakedness. She drained her cup, handed it, empty, to the waiting Jean-Pierre, and sank back on to the pillows. So he could see her bare breasts. So what? They were full and firm and beautiful. She decided that Gilles wanted her to show them off. And there was no doubt that Jean-Pierre had expected her to become Gilles' lover. It would have been more shameful to have failed, and to have returned home to her parents because she was too childish to satisfy a man like Gilles.

He had loved her breasts last night; he had found all of her beautiful, and he had wanted her again this morning. Only it had not been the same for her. There was a dull ache deep inside her that refused to go away. It was stronger now; she would not have thought she could need a man so much. She shifted uncomfortably against the thick lace edge of the pillow and watched Gilles drain his second cup of coffee. She felt ravenously hungry, but there was no sign of any bread to dip into her cup.

'Is there anything else, Monsieur?' Jean-Pierre's eyes did not waiver.

Gilles shook his head. 'Leave us, Jean-Pierre. I will ring when I need you again. We shall spend a little longer in bed.'

Colette blushed. Why did he have to make it so obvious? And yet the thought of staying here with Gilles aroused her. Her nipples were hard and swollen, her thighs moist and throbbing, and she longed to feel again as she had done last night. The doors closed behind Jean-Pierre. Gilles lay back on the bed and let his fingers trail slowly across her belly. She watched his long, brown fingers lightly stroke her skin. His penis lay limp between his thighs, nestling in a dark cloud of black hair that she longed to touch, but did not dare.

'Why did you let Jean-Pierre see me?'

Gilles turned slowly towards her. His black eyebrows were raised slightly. 'Did it worry you? He is only a servant.'

He looked unconcerned and scornful of her, but as she watched she saw him stiffen and his thick column of flesh steadily fill with blood until it was as full and erect as she had felt it once already this morning. His fingers tensed over the slight curve of her belly, lingering on the bare mound of flesh between her thighs that still seemed strange to her. One finger slid between her sex lips and gently parted them. She felt her hips rise towards him at his touch, and moved instinctively, unable to prevent her eagerness. All the longing which his earlier entry had aroused in her awoke now, irrepressibly, and she took him in her arms as he lowered himself on to her.

He stopped with the tip of his penis poised over her eager sex. She closed her eyes for a moment, in expectation, and then opened them again when he made no move. 'Did it excite you to see another man look at you?' he asked.

She closed her eyes again. She did not want to think; she wanted him to enter her and make her forget everything except the pleasure they knew together. She stirred faintly beneath him and felt his stiff shaft rub on her eager flesh. 'You must be proud of your body,' he said as the heat of his penis pressed harder against her. 'Enjoy the pleasure you give to men.' He laughed. 'You want this now, don't you? I was too quick for you this morning, and you lay unsatisfied while he looked at you. If I left you alone for long like that, you would take any man.'

She felt confused. 'Is that what you want from me?' she asked.

'I like women who understand their needs,' he said, 'but I plan to fulfil all yours myself.' His lips were almost touching hers as he spoke softly. She felt the warmth of his lower lip on hers, then he pushed her mouth open and sucked out her breath until her head span. She felt his penis enter her, rising unbearably slowly until he was hard against her swollen bud. Steadily he rode up and down until she was driven mad with her need to come, but he would not let her. There seemed no limit to his control or to his knowledge of her desire. With each thrust she felt a new edge to her experience, expanding all the pleasure she had believed possible.

At last, sated, she lay cocooned by the warmth of Gilles' body, too lazy to do anything except lie here in his arms. She pressed her forehead against his slightly rough jawline, feeling a wave of peace calm her brain. How wonderful this was going to be! She looked through half-closed eyes at the long strand of pearls heaped casually on the table beside her and longed to feel them round her throat again.

'What will we do today?' she asked.

Gilles stirred beside her. He kissed her cheek before he sat up and swung his legs over the side of the bed. Briskly, he rang a bell to summon Jean-Pierre again. 'I have work to do,' he said, 'and so do you. Marie will have arranged appointments that should occupy you all morning. But perhaps I can accompany you to the Bois this afternoon. It would give me pleasure. Shall we say two o'clock?'

She saw him leave the room, wrapped only in his black silk gown, and watched the doors swing shut behind him. She was furious. How dare he leave her like this?

Colette buried her face in the pillow and breathed in Gilles' scent. She felt the weight of her body pressed on to the mattress, and cradled her head in between the soft feathers. What appointments did Gilles mean? She had no desire to have any more gowns fitted today, or to have her hair dressed in another elaborate style. She twisted her finger round one springy curl. She would like to lie here all day, but she wanted Gilles here with her, too. Why did he have to leave her alone now? She heard the door open, rolled over quickly and was disappointed to see Marie standing at the foot of the bed. 'Mademoiselle, we must hurry.'

Marie threw open the curtains, and let the sunlight flood in. It was a beautiful day. Colette turned her face away; the light hurt her eyes and she did not want Marie to see her face. She felt sure it would reveal exactly how she felt. All that Marie had said about Gilles was true. She wished that they were both still lying together in the bed, that she was in his arms, and that he was making love to her.

Marie held out her gown. 'You must hurry, Mademoiselle,' she repeated. 'We have so much to do.'

'What do you mean?'

'Your dressmaker and your hairdresser are already waiting, and there are a hundred appointments for the rest of the week. Do you wish to choose the menus now, and the flowers? What are your favourites?

'My favourites?'

'Of course – the house will be run as you choose

now. Everything will be as you want it. You have only to ask.'

'I can do anything I like?'

'But of course, Mademoiselle. That is usual. But today you may not have time. The morning is almost over; your dressmaker is waiting, and this afternoon Monsieur will accompany you on your drive. It is an honour.'

'My drive?' Colette felt stupid, repeating Marie's words.

'You must be seen in the Bois each afternoon when the weather is fine, but naturally Monsieur will not often have the time to be with you. Now, may I suggest this gown for today? We shall choose something more chic for tomorrow, but at the moment you have so few clothes.'

So few! Colette already had more dresses than she could have imagined. And her day seemed fully planned. So much for choice! 'And after the Bois, Marie. What then?'

'Then Monsieur may wish to spend a little time with you before the opera. Monsieur Worth has brought your gown for tonight. Of course you may choose whatever you wish for next time. But for now . . .'

'For now there is so little choice and so little time?'

'Exactly, Mademoiselle.'

'So I will do everything that Monsieur Gilles desires.' Colette grinned. Her dressmaker, her hair-dresser. And they had waited for her until she was ready. Who would have thought it?

Her dressing-room was crowded. Monsieur Worth had just arrived, accompanied by two assistants laden with gowns. 'I am delighted to learn that you are staying,' he said. 'We will simply try on these few dresses today – this one first. It is for tonight, and then as many of the others as you have time for. They are all almost complete.'

So Gilles had been so confident of her compliance that he had ordered all these clothes for her. They were beautiful, but they were all pale, delicate, and virginal. Colette longed for scarlet satin, for something outrageous. She knew she was no beauty, and she thought these clothes made her look insipid. They were nothing like the gown Gilles had chosen for last night. Monsieur Worth was issuing instructions to his assistants, then he turned to her. 'This is not perfect, but it will do for this afternoon in the park. Claude will return later when we have worked on the gown for the opera. It is a beautiful day, Mademoiselle, enjoy your drive.' With a rustle of silk, he swept out, ahead of the two young men laden with toiles.

Monsieur Alexandre, armed with a brush and an array of combs, nodded to them as they passed in the doorway. She sat on a velvet stool in front of her dressing table, wearing only a sheer lace robe, and let him work on her hair. 'Your style is delightful, of course, Mademoiselle, but I think that today we might try to achieve something a little more chic.' He lifted her long curls, twisted them round his fingers, drove sharp pins close to her scalp and tied the whole creation high up on the back of her head with a narrow band of beaded black velvet. He stepped back. 'It is enchanting, Mademoiselle. Now, for tonight we will add a few pearls. Marie can put these in for you.' He strutted across the room to examine the gown which hung ready for the opera, and held a string of seed pearls in front of it. 'Perfect, perfect,' he muttered. 'Lovely with your dark hair. Marie, come here and let me explain.'

They chattered together as Colette looked into the mirror. Behind her reflection, she saw the two of them bent over her head, arguing about the precise position of each curl. She sat still as though none of this concerned her, a small, pale figure in a white and gold boudoir. Her dressing-room here was larger than any room in her parents' cottage. Their entire home would have fitted into her bedroom, and the cost of one of her gowns was more than they struggled to earn in a whole year. It had all come to her so easily, and for doing something that had given her pleasure. She stared at the outline of her body beneath the light lace robe and tried to decide if she felt different. Did her breasts look fuller, more womanly? Perhaps her lips were swollen from Gilles' kisses? She smiled at her reflection. Her face looked softer and her eyes were large and dreamy. She felt lethargic, content to allow the two gesticulating figures decide precisely how she should wear her hair.

She felt Marie's hands on her shoulders, shaking her slightly. 'We must hurry, Mademoiselle. Monsieur will be waiting!'

Colette stepped into the hooped underskirt that Marie held out for her. A silk petticoat with a frill at the hem was laced on top of the metal hoops. She held out her arms and slipped on a boned bodice with three strong metal hooks below her breasts. Marie bustled round behind her and pulled hard at the laces. 'Breathe in,' she ordered, yanking hard at the strong cord. 'And again.' With

114

a swift movement she tied the final lace and held out an embroidered white piqué gown that she considered suitable for a drive in the Bois.

'And now your pearls.' Deftly, she place them round Colette's neck and held out a lace-trimmed parasol. 'We have done it,' she said with an air of satisfaction. 'You are ready.'

Colette attempted to breathe. She had never felt quite so uncomfortable, and the pressure of the boned bodice, holding in her stomach, reminded her that she had eaten nothing all morning. 'But I am hungry,' she protested, as Marie hurried her out into the corridor. 'Is Monsieur taking me to lunch?'

'Mais non, Mademoiselle, you are going to the Bois. It is late. You were too long in bed this morning.' She giggled. 'Who needs food when you are in love?'

'But I'm starving. Couldn't I have something to eat before I go?'

Marie shook her head. 'I will make sure there is something prepared for you while you dress for this evening. Now please, Mademoiselle, hurry.'

They were almost out on to the landing. Then Colette felt Marie's light touch on her arm, warning her, and she slowed down. The bell of her dress swung out dangerously in front of her, but she restrained it and descended the stairs as Anne had taught her. She was a professional now.

There was hardly room for two of them in the carriage with the skirt. Gilles had driven with her every day in the Bois this week, and yet never had there been so much fuss as today. She was dressed more simply, although this was the most fashionable dress she had worn. Was it more important now that she should not disgrace Gilles?

They passed Anne in her carriage, looking as exquisitely cool and elegant as ever. She nodded, and smiled at Colette, then turned away her head, scarcely looking at Gilles. But the men they passed inspected her quite openly and raised their hats as they passed. The ladies, who refused to acknowledge her, stared hard before they turned pointedly away. It was as though they all knew that she was now Gilles' mistress. But that was impossible. It could not be so obvious. Of course they must know that was why she was here, but she could not look so different from yesterday. They must simply be guessing.

As they neared the tea-rooms, Colette put her hand on Gilles' arm. 'May we stop, please? I am so hungry.'

Gilles looked shocked, and then laughed. 'My darling little girl. Those women are not there because they want tea.'

'No, of course. Everyone is in the Bois to show off their clothes, but I need to eat something.' She could see plates full of tiny gateaux oozing cream which made her mouth water. 'I am a peasant, and we are used to lunch. We didn't even have breakfast,' she reminded him. She half rose from her seat, but felt Gilles' hand on her wrist, restraining her.

'The ladies do not sit there just to show off their clothes.' He raised his hand to the coachman. 'Robert, slow down a little.' As they passed the crowd he loosened his grip on her arm. 'Watch carefully, Colette, but do not let it be seen that you are looking.'

They circled the terrace slowly. Colette saw men and women together at the tables, and several women sitting alone. At the edge on the central area, there were men leaning on their canes, staring at the unaccompanied ladies. She watched, fascinated, as one man languidly left a shady patch beneath the trees, bowed to a lady sitting alone, spoke to her briefly and then sat down at her table. As the carriage moved away, Colette saw another man peel away from a group at the railings, check his welcome, and join a pretty woman in an exquisite, pale-blue ensemble. She barely acknowledged his arrival, but seemed to accept his presence and graciously poured him a cup of tea.

'Do those ladies know the men who joined them?' she asked.

Gilles shook his head and shrugged. 'By sight. They will be aware of their bank balances and their generosity.' She saw his eyes crinkle in amusement as he studied her. 'Yes,' he said. 'You are right. They are here to accept new lovers. Or not. It is of course the lady who decides.'

'Whether the man is rich enough?'

'Do you think that is all that matters, Colette?'

'Not all. But they cannot do it simply for love.' She smoothed down the crisp embroidery on the front of her dress. 'They must think of their futures.'

He seemed amused. Today, everything she said seemed to amuse him. 'You have no need to worry. At the end of our year you will be launched.' He laughed. 'You are a peasant who tells the truth when she is hungry. I shall take you home now and feed you, before I learn something I will not like. *Vite*, Robert.'

In bed, later that afternoon, Gilles gave her liqueur-drenched strawberries, and laughed when the sticky juice dripped over her naked breasts, licking it off with his tongue. He fed her more, and offered her sweet bread filled with chocolate and small cakes dusted with sugar. 'Are you satisfied now, my peasant?' he asked. 'Are you finally satisfied?'

She licked the sugar coating off her lips, and reached up for him. Her voice sounded hoarse in her ears as she pulled him down on top of her. 'Not yet,' she whispered. 'Not yet.'

It took her a whole hour to dress for the opera. Colette sat in front of her mirror, trying to ignore the pressure of the boned corset which bit into her ribs and to be patient while Marie threaded the strands of seed pearls through her hair. A white tulle gown hung on a stand by the armoire, looking like a virgin meringue. Colette hated it. 'Why can't I wear the gown Monsieur chose for me before?' she asked, thinking of the beautiful burgundy silk she had worn last night.

'It is not at all suitable, Mademoiselle, not at all the thing for the Opéra.' Marie deftly tweaked her curls back into the style that the hairdresser had created that morning. 'It would not be suitable in most places,' she mumbled, with a mouthful of hairpins between her lips. She put them down on the dressing-table, and secured the last curl. 'There, Mademoiselle,' she said with pride.

'It's perfect. You are better than Monsieur Alexandre. But I don't want to wear that.'

Marie lifted the gown off its hanger, and held it out. 'Put it on right now,' she ordered. 'You have no choice.'

Reluctantly, Colette put her arms into the tiny, flowered, cap sleeves, and let Marie fasten the row of tiny hooks which secured the bodice. It looked as light as air, but beneath the frothy layers Colette could feel the harsh constraint of her tightly boned corset. 'I look terrible.'

'It is a beautiful gown,' Marie said half-heartedly.

'And half the corps de ballet would look better in it than I do. It doesn't suit me.' She saw that Marie was ignoring her completely, as she deftly lifted the pearl necklace over her hair and wound it around her neck, letting a single, long strand fall between her breasts. Colette suddenly realised why the ladies in the Bois had smiled so knowingly. And the same would be true at the opera – everyone would know. She understood perfectly the significance of her present, and she was not going to give the ladies at the Opéra the pleasure of knowing for certain that she was now Gilles' mistress. Let them guess!

She put her fingers to her throat. It was impossible for her to lift the pearls over her elaborate hairstyle. 'Take them off for me, Marie, please.'

'Mademoiselle!'

'I will not wear them. My neck has been bare all week. It will be bare tonight.'

'No, Mademoiselle. Monsieur will be angry.'

'Either you help me, or my hair will be disarranged.'

She had not noticed Gilles standing in the doorway.

'They do not please you?' he asked.

'It is not that.'

She saw him raise one eyebrow. 'You do not want the rest of the world to know our business.' He nodded to Marie. 'But you will wear them for me in private?'

'Of course.'

'Then come with me.' He took her by the hand and led her across the landing into a dark, oval room lined with books. He opened a small drawer in his desk and took out a red leather box. It was the one which had rested on the table at the Café Anglais on the night she had agreed to become his mistress. The box which he had not given her. Now, he held it in his hand and looked at her carefully.

'I must apologise,' he said. 'It was disgraceful of me to shame you so. I should have understood that you would not wish to be part of such a tradition.' He opened the box and she saw the shimmer of light flashing off dark red rubies. 'These would have been yours had you refused my offer. I chose them for you.'

'You thought they would gladden my peasant heart?'

'I hoped you would not sell them too soon. But they are yours, Colette, to do with as you please. Will you wear them for me now?'

'The ladies will be confused?'

Gilles grinned and put them round her neck. 'The ladies will be shocked. I think we shall both enjoy watching them.'

The rubies felt cold against her skin. Colette looked round for a mirror but there was none in the room. Gilles hurried her away. 'Now let us go. I am beginning to think I shall enjoy your company more and more,' he said.

As they climbed the grand staircase at the Opéra, Colette felt conscious of the weight of the jewels around her neck. She was aware of the interest of the crowd around them, but no one acknowledged her, and she looked straight ahead, longing to see herself in the mirror that walled the landing. Her first sight of the jewels stunned her. It seemed as if a thick, dark collar of flashing blood circled her throat above the bridal white foam of tulle.

She grinned, seeing Gilles smiling behind her. He pressed her arm. 'Don't let them think we are trying to shock them. Behave as though you were wearing a simple strand of pearls.'

As always, the theatre was full of Parisian society watching the audience rather than the stage. Olympe was there with the man Colette had seen before. He raised his champagne glass to her and she was sure he knew why she was not wearing the pearls. She felt a glow of triumph. Tonight she felt sure of herself, and she was having more fun than she had ever had in her life.

Éloise was, as always, accompanied by her dark lover and, as before, he undressed Colette with his eyes. Éloise looked immediately at Colette's neck and stared in amazement at the ruby necklace. Colette was delighted. She deliberately moved her head so that the jewels flashed in the lamplight. Éloise could not hide her fury. Colette laughed out loud and drank her champagne.

'Hush, Colette. I told you to be discreet.' But Gilles' voice was soft, and his eyes were dancing with amusement. And across the crowded auditorium she saw Olympe's companion watching them, and smiling.

Their box was invaded during the interval, but not a word was said about her necklace and Colette regained her composure. She held out her hand to their guests, offered them champagne and accepted their compliments on her gown. The second act had started before they were left alone, and then the door suddenly flew open. Gilles rose angrily to his feet, glaring at the footman, then he smiled. 'Achille, you honour us. Colette, let me introduce you to a great artist.'

She saw a small man, almost insignificant, standing in the doorway. He shook his head at the offer of champagne and pointed to Colette. 'I want to paint her, Gilles,' he said. 'Will you allow it?'

'Ask her yourself. She knows her own mind.'

'So soon?' He laughed. 'Then perhaps that is why I want to paint her.' Achille kept one hand on the open door. 'Well?' he asked.

Colette almost looked at Gilles to check his approval. But no, it was her agreement that Achille sought. She would adore to have her portrait painted.

'Thank you, Monsieur,' she said.

Achille went out into the corridor. 'Two o'clock,' he shouted as he walked rapidly away. 'At my studio.'

Gilles looked amused. 'I hope you approve of his work,' he said. 'He is a fine artist. You should be flattered that he picked you out.'

Colette felt flattered by everything that had happened to her tonight. In the last 24 hours she seemed to have changed from a schoolgirl into a beauty. Apparently no one noticed her coarse, thick hair any more, or the gap between her teeth that Anne found so disturbing. The rubies seemed to increase her value in the eyes of everyone who saw her. And, more importantly, she had fully aroused Gilles' interest.

He took her straight home when the performance was over. After supper, he came upstairs to her bedroom, where Marie waited to help her undress. Colette put her hands around her neck to take off the rubies. She wanted to hold them in her hands, and she intended to keep her promise. In private, and whenever Gilles chose, from now on, she would wear his pearls.

He caught her hand. 'No, keep the rubies on.' He turned to the maid. 'Marie, we don't need you now.'

'Let me take off the rest of your clothes,' he said when the girl had left the room.

Swiftly, expertly, he released each intricate fastening and held out his hand to help her step away from the tangled heap of her clothes on the rug. She wore only the heavy jewels around her throat. Nothing else.

'Now – look at yourself,' he said, turning her towards the mirror.

She saw the glitter of the blood-red stones resting on the ridge of her collar bones. The jewels were huge and vulgar, and she adored them. The three, central, pear-shaped gems fell between the curve of her breasts, echoing the rose-red colour of her swollen nipples, bruised and tender from Gilles' attentions that morning.

She looked hard at herself. A peasant. But she was tall, and her legs were long and slim. Not like her sister's! And her skin was pale. Even her hands now, softened by Anne's creams, were smooth and ladylike. Her body, quite hairless, looked waxen and vulnerable in the half-light of the shadowed bedroom.

In the mirror she could see Gilles moving towards her. Naked, except for a black, silk robe draped loosely across his shoulders, he padded

123

across the blue pile of the carpet until he stood behind her. In the mirror she saw his stiff erection slide between her thighs and rise beneath her bare, shaven mound. She watched the reflection of her body in the glass, pale and feminine, except for the glittering red jewels and the dark head of his penis caught between her legs.

He held her round the waist and pulled her back against him. The black gown fell to the floor and he kicked it aside. As though in a trance, she watched the two reflections of their bodies in the mirror as he pushed her back against the gilded column at the foot of the bed and moved in front of her. Gently he parted her legs until she could feel him guiding his rigid shaft inside her. She shuddered at the sudden entry, and jerked her head back so that her hair caught on the carved, gold wood and escaped from its velvet band. It flowed over Gilles' shoulders, trickling over his tensed muscles as he surged into her.

She watched the reflection of his muscular buttocks powerfully driving into her as he crushed her against the bedpost. She almost fell as she felt her climax come, and heard his cry of ecstasy as he thrust deeply one last time. When he had done, he moved backwards, breathing heavily, and kissed her hard on the lips. Then he turned abruptly away, tied his black gown around him and left the room.

She leaned back against the gilded column, her legs weak and trembling. In the mirror she saw her pale image, like the flickering flame of a candle, and the shimmering glow of the circle of flashing rubies. She clutched at the post for support and fell on to the bed, crawling over the brocade cover until she lay spreadeagled and sleepy on the thick, embroidered silk.

It was exactly how Achille chose to paint her. As instructed, Colette took her clothes off behind a screen in his studio. She stood naked below a vast sweep of sloping window while he examined her. A doctor would have been less clinical, she thought, as he turned away and picked through a pile of canvasses stacked against one wall, muttering to himself. The room was heated by a blazing fire at one end, quite unnecessary for the time of year and, despite her nakedness, she felt too hot. She dared not move, and could only catch glimpses of his paintings as he pulled a few out of the stack he was checking.

They were all of women. Women in the finest couture gowns, or naked. Achille stopped for a moment and spoke to her. 'I make the ladies wear Worth and look as though they were naked. The whores I paint stark naked, and they appear as the *petit bourgeoises* they wish to become. It amuses me.'

Colette looked more closely. He was speaking the truth. One lady, whom she knew to be of the Empress' innermost circle, was dressed in all her jewels and finery and looked on the point of orgasm, while a street prostitute wore an expression of the utmost respectability as she reclined naked on a couch.

'How will you paint me, Monsieur?' she asked, amused.

For the first time he looked into her eyes. 'Tell me,' he said. 'Tell me how you feel, and when you have been most happy. I will paint you at that moment.'

He caught her by surprise. She thought at once of the time in the river with Victor and felt ashamed. She tried to pretend. 'When Gilles made love to me,' she said, 'of course.'

He turned away and examined another painting. 'Do not lie to me, Mademoiselle. It bores me. Go and put your clothes on, and do not waste my time.'

She wanted him to paint her. His work excited her, and she felt privileged that he had chosen her. And she had lied to him. 'No,' she said. 'In a river, naked, with the water swirling round me so that I feel free.'

He nodded, and turned round. 'When you were a child?'

'More than a child.'

'So. A young girl in a river, and perhaps she knows that a man watches her.' He inclined his head to one side. 'Or a boy, a young man no older than herself. And they think they are in love. Yes, I will paint that.' He pointed to a square of bare boards on the floor in front of his easel. 'Lie there if you please. We will begin.'

'Think of that young man,' he said, when she was settled, 'and remember how you felt about him. I want to see that look on your face. And do not worry. I will not tell Gilles the question I asked you. I never worry my friends unnecessarily.'

For her next sitting that area of floor was covered with dark brown velvet. Achille motioned to her to take the same position as she had done before. This time the velvet felt smooth beneath her; it was easier to imagine that she was floating in the water. She could reach out her arms, and then pretend that they were drifting away from her. And above her, poised on a rock, eternally leaping into the water to join her, she imagined Victor's tanned body flying down towards her. What if he reached her lying there? Perhaps she would have let him stroke the limbs that floated so effortlessly in the stream. They might have drifted away together peacefully.

Achille clapped his hands in the air. 'That is it. Hold it like that. Now you believe yourself to be in the river. Now, keep on thinking of your young man, Colette. It is perfect.'

The next day she received an invitation to one of the Princesse Mathilde's weekly soirées. Gilles looked surprised. 'You are honoured. Monsieur Achille must have put your name forward to the princess. You should thank him. It is an honour.'

'And may I accept?'

'Of course.' It seemed that for once she had impressed him, and she felt that she had achieved something of her own. 'You cannot refuse such a command,' he said.

'Will you come with me?'

'Colette, I go there to the princess' soirées every week. Of course I will be there. It gives me great pleasure that you, too, will enjoy the company.'

So this was one of the places where Gilles went without her in the evenings. She was even more delighted with her invitation. Still, it surprised her when she learnt that Gilles expected her to arrive alone. 'I cannot acknowledge you as my mistress in front of the princess. Monsieur Achille has requested your presence. He will look after you.'

But the artist was so strange, and so unreliable. Gilles had told her that the princess did not greet

127

her guests formally on these occasions. Colette felt nervous when her name was announced, and descended the staircase in a panic. What if no one spoke to her?

A group of men surrounded the princess; Colette knew most of them by sight, but she could see no one who would acknowledge her, and she knew that none of the ladies here tonight would speak to her. There was no sign of either Gilles or Achille. She stepped down on to the last stair very slowly, wondering what she should do when she reached the bottom, and wishing that she had not come.

There was a burst of laughter from the princess' group, and the crowd seemed to part before her. One of the men who had been standing beside the princess came over to her. 'Follow me, please, Mademoiselle.'

Relieved, she placed her gloved hand on his arm and moved to the centre of the group.

The princess gave her a charming smile. 'I wanted to see the lady whom my friend, Monsieur Achille, admires so much. I am delighted to make your acquaintance.' She nodded slightly and then waved her hand. Colette felt herself to be dismissed, and a hand at her elbow guided her away from the princess' circle. She thought it was the man who had spoken to her before, but when she looked up, it was Olympe's friend. She had not expected to see him here, yet he seemed quite at home.

'Now that her highness has recognised you, there will be no problem with the others. I am sure you will enjoy your evening,' he said quietly.

'It was kind of Achille to speak to her about me.'

'She admires his work greatly. As do I. It is a pity

128

he is not more recognised by this crowd or he would make his fortune. You should be warned, Mademoiselle, his portrait may not flatter you. Sometimes he sees too clearly.'

'Is that something to be afraid of?'

'Not if you have nothing to hide. But all of us have something we would prefer others not to know. Isn't that so?' He took her into the midst of a crowd of men eager to be introduced, now that she had been shown favour. She wanted to ask him if he had seen her portrait, but he had changed the subject, and the talk was now all about the antics of the latest singer at the Opéra, who seemed to expect that the audience should look at her rather than each other. She amused them greatly.

The salon buzzed with conversation and Colette recognised artists, writers and intellectuals she had heard of before when her companion pointed them out to her. He seemed to know everyone.

'Achille is not coming?' she asked.

'He is already here.' Across the room, Colette recognised the gesticulating figure of the artist. She was angry that he had not come to her assistance before. Now, as she saw him approaching, she had less need of him. It was true that, since the princess had acknowledged her, so would the rest of society; at least the male half, if not the ladies. Only Gilles ignored her, as he had said he would, although he appeared at her side when she was ready to leave, and offered to take her home.

'You have had a success, my dear. Congratulations.'

'Thank you.'

'You were lucky that Edouard Kerouac took an interest in you.'

'Edouard Kerouac?'

Gilles looked surprised. 'The man who arranged your introduction to the princess. I saw you talking to him afterwards.'

'Olympe's friend?' So he had spoken on her behalf. She wished she had thanked him properly. 'Who is he?'

Gilles helped her into his carriage. 'A mystery. No one knows where he came from. But he knows everyone and has influence everywhere. He seems to be Haussman's right hand man, and certainly he has made a fortune rebuilding the city.'

'And Olympe is his mistress?'

'I don't believe so. She is kept by the Baron himself. Edouard Kerouac has never been seen to keep a mistress. Perhaps he works too hard. Do not show your gratitude too far, Colette. He is not likely to offer you his purse next year. But after tonight your services will be in demand. I had to fight off an offer from the Duc de Graine.'

'You spent your evening bargaining about me?' she said coldly.

'I spent my evening listening to your praises, and accepting praise for my excellent choice.' He leant forward and kissed the tips of her fingers. 'I knew you would not let me down when I first saw you, but you have exceeded my expectations. I am proud of you my dear.'

But not proud enough to acknowledge her in public. And she had been made only too aware that no society woman would ever speak to her, no matter how highly she was regarded. The princess was secure enough to please herself. No other woman was. Next time she saw Edouard Kerouac, she would thank him for the trouble he had taken on her behalf.

But she did not see Edouard Kerouac for several months. He seemed to have deserted society, and Olympe sat in her box at the Vaudeville either alone, or with her powerful baron. Colette too, spent a large part of her time alone. Gilles was occupied in his study each morning, and in the afternoons he seemed to have appointments that took precedence over a drive in the Bois with her. Perhaps the ritual bored him.

Colette found it dull, too. She took little interest in the changing pattern of relationships which was paraded so openly amongst the courtesans and, more subtly, in the highest ranks of society. Ladies who thought themselves too fine to do more than glance at her gowns and jewels, took new lovers with each passing month and usually sported at least one new jewel each time they did so.

Monsieur Worth continued to visit her with fresh toiles, and sometimes, for a change, she spent a morning looking at his collection in the Rue de la Paix. Achille had refused to allow anyone to see her portrait, assuring her that her sittings were still essential to its success. When he could no longer justify the hours he spent painting her, she went with him to the Salon des Beaux-Arts, and listened to his explosions of rage against more established and successful artists. She learnt to sketch with a drawing master and to play a few notes on the piano from her music teacher. And she longed to escape the grey streets of a Paris winter and go home to Argnon to see the start of spring.

Of course her life was wonderful. Gilles gave her

everything she wanted, and he treated her with the utmost care. But he spent so long away from her and had so many other interests. She was lonely. Every second of her day was occupied and yet she had no one to talk to. She longed to sit on the end of her sister's bed and gossip late at night. She wanted to show off some of her new clothes to her mother, and tell her that she was happy, that they had advised her well. Gilles was so busy; she was sure he would not mind. In the middle of March, she could bear it no longer. She decided that she would tell him tomorrow that she wanted to visit Argnon.

Chapter Seven

'*O*ne year. Colette, I have given in to you on everything else. Surely you can keep your contract just for one year?'

She had not realised how angry Gilles would be. 'Please let me go. What is wrong with the idea? You are so busy. You would not miss me for a week or so.'

She had intruded on him in his study. He continued working through the papers on his desk, making it clear that she should not have disturbed him. 'It is too soon, Colette. We are still enjoying each other.'

His words chilled her. Still. How much longer would she have before he was bored with her? She did not want to be reminded of the end of her year. But it made her even more determined to see her family. Later, if she was not successful, she might feel too ashamed.

'Gilles, please. I want to see my parents, my home.' I want to understand who I am now, she thought, looking at his back turned against her. I cannot stay here any longer, not like this, with each day planned for me, when I see you only at night and I am no part of your life. You don't talk to me, Gilles. You don't teach me. Yes, you pay for the curator at the Louvre to escort me personally every Wednesday and teach me how to appreciate great works of art. You pay for Alphonse to teach me how to dance and Signor Grapelli to show me how to appreciate music. But I have no ear, and I am too old to learn to play well, although sometimes I pick out a tune on the piano in the salon. I can draw, although I have no natural aptitude for it. So what are my skills? You say I am a wonderful lover, but have you ever had a mistress to whom you have not said that? I wear clothes well. Monsieur Worth is a friend. I surprise you still. And Gilles, I adore you. I had no idea how much pleasure my body could give me. But our year is almost over. And what then? No matter how much I amuse you, you will not extend that period. If you let Anne go, you will not keep me on. In May, you will look for another woman.

But she said none of this.

She gritted her teeth and told him firmly, 'I am a peasant, Gilles, and I need to go home to my roots occasionally.'

'Perhaps you have already come too far away from them.' He replaced his pen in its holder, and laid his file of papers in an open drawer. 'No one else has defied me as you do!'

'But you keep all your women prisoner for the single year of your desire!'

'Don't be ridiculous. You are free to do anything you choose.'

'Except make a visit to Argnon.'

Gilles turned away. 'Go then, Colette. You already have my parting gift.'

She felt chilled. Was this the end? 'If I go, do you not want me back?'

'Oh yes, Colette, I want you back. But you are wrong to leave Paris now. These are dangerous times. The Prussians are gathering their forces.'

'Then it is even more important that I see my parents soon.'

Gilles slammed the drawer shut. 'I have said that you may go,' he snapped. 'But of course you cannot stay with your parents. Look at you – your skirts won't fit through their door.'

'Then I shall dress as I used to.'

'No.' He was quite calm. There was now no anger in his voice. He looked a little sad. 'Colette, while you are with me your behaviour affects my honour. You will return as a fashionable lady, as my protégée. You will select gowns that are suitable for the country. Speak to Monsieur Worth.'

'And I may go next week?'

'If you insist. Your parents of course are aware of our situation. May I ask who else you will choose to enlighten?'

Gilles was right, of course. It would not be so simple as she had thought. What would she say to Gaston, for example? And her friends in the village? How would they ever understand the way she lived now? Not that she had so many female friends. They had resented her special relationship with the curé, and with Victor. 'I shall say I am here for my education, and they can believe what they wish. I shall tell no one the truth.'

Gilles smiled. 'That would be wise. I imagine one

135

week will be sufficient? You must understand that I will never come to Argnon with you. It would embarrass your parents. This way . . .'

This way left everyone free to gossip.

Marie was bristling with indignation. 'Why must we leave Paris now, Mademoiselle, when there are so many balls, so much excitement?'

The packing was completed in a chilly atmosphere. Finally the trunks were ready; two huge pantechnicons filled with clothes. It was all so unnecessary for a week in a small country village.

'Why do I have to take all this, Marie?'

'Monsieur has arranged a compartment on the train, and he has sent a letter asking that the château be prepared for you. Imagine how it would look if you arrived without your accoutrements.'

Marie hated leaving Jean-Pierre behind in Paris, and the thought of a week alone in the country appalled her. 'But if you must go, Mademoiselle, it is better now.' She nodded her head wisely. 'Once your year is over, you must prepare immediately for your launch in society.'

'You mean I must find another man to support me?'

'You will need more than one, Mademoiselle, unless he is very, very rich.'

At the last moment Colette put the ruby necklace into her reticule. It would give her mother pleasure to see it, and it belonged to her. Gilles had said so.

How strange it was to travel through this country again. Sitting with Marie in their private carriage on the train, Colette felt very different from the girl who had left a few months ago.

'Don't you ever miss your family?' she asked.

136

Marie shook her head firmly. 'I would never go back there. I am a Parisian now. How would they understand me?'

Perhaps it was better that Gilles had not come. He had been so adamant. In all her life Colette had only seen him twice in Argnon. Once, when he arranged for her to take lessons with the curé, and the second time when he had returned with Victor. At first, of course, Madame had lived there, too, but she had remained within the boundaries of the château all the time, and she had never been seen in the village, not even in the church.

Their carriage was waiting for them at the station. It was Paul who met them, and the sight of him renewed Marie's anguish. 'What will Jean-Pierre do while I am away?' she demanded. 'He is not a man to do without a woman.' She bit her lip and scowled.

Colette felt sorry. Marie and Jean-Pierre were engaged to be married, but Jean-Pierre gave no sign of deciding on a date. And Marie was impatient. She considered that they had saved almost enough money, and this was no time to leave her man alone in the city. Colette wondered what Gilles would do. The season was building up to a frenzy with the threat of a skirmish with the Prussians, and Paris had never been so gay. Gilles might be too busy to require company in the afternoons, but he would want amusement each evening and at night. She refused to think about it. She had to keep some independence or it would be too painful to part from him. She did not intend to be like Anne, still beautiful, but refusing to take new lovers because she worshipped Gilles.

Marie was questioning Paul about the arrangements at the château. 'You received our message in good time?' she asked. 'Has everything been aired?'

Paul finished piling their trunks at the back of the carriage before he replied. 'There was no need. Monsieur Victor is still here.'

Colette frowned. 'I thought he had returned to Italy to be with his mother.'

Paul steadied the horses as she and Marie clambered inside the carriage. 'Mais non,' he said. 'He will be pleased to see you. It is fortunate, Mademoiselle, is it not?'

Colette was surprised. Why had Gilles not mentioned Victor's presence? Surely he must have known? Was that why he had been so reluctant to let her come home? Because he knew that his son was here?

She forgot her anxiety and felt the excitement burn through her as the carriage climbed the steep route, and she breathed in the fresh mountain air. When she left here, she had thought that Victor would be coming with them. How would it be to see him again? Perhaps this was a mistake after all. She was sure that Gilles did not know that his son was here. He would have told her, wouldn't he?

It was late in the afternoon and daylight was fading when they entered the gates of the Château Maraigne. The drive curved for almost a kilometre through the woods before straightening out into the avenue of chestnuts leading to the main building. Two lights burned between the pillars of the front entrance and Colette could see a faint glimmer through the glass panels above the door; otherwise the château was in darkness. It was only just dusk, and Paul had been occupied collecting them from

138

the station. No doubt Victor kept very few servants here, but it seemed strange that the place should look so gloomy for their arrival. After all, Paul had said that they were expected.

Her legs felt stiff as she climbed out of the carriage, and the sound of her feet crunching on the gravel drive seemed to echo across the bare lawns. Winter was only just over, she thought; perhaps the flower beds would be planted out later in the year, if Victor stayed for the summer. Colette looked up at the fragile beauty of the château outlined against the clear blue of a crisp, spring sky, and walked forwards towards the great sweep of stairs leading to the brass-studded front door.

It opened as she reached the top step, and she saw Victor standing in the wide doorway, holding out one hand to greet her. His fingers felt warm as he touched her, and she thought they trembled slightly as he took her hand. Perhaps it was her own that showed weakness. Or maybe she imagined it.

'I am so glad that you have returned,' he said. 'I have been promised that you would.'

His words puzzled her, but she had no wish to question him now. Who had made that promise? Had Gilles planned to send her back here to Victor when he was finished with her? She did not want to think about it. She was simply happy to see him, and to be home.

Victor seemed to have changed, she thought. He looked happier and more mature. The mouth which had appeared sulky now curved in a full smile, and his amber eyes glowed with a new intensity. No wonder her fingers longed to reach out and touch it! She placed her hands firmly by her side as he led her to her room. She lived with his father now, and she had no intention of cheating on Gilles.

The guest room where she had stayed before had been prepared for her, but Marie still bustled around, rearranging everything to her liking. It did not disturb Colette now to have Marie help her with her clothes and wash and dress her. She was accustomed to it, and grateful for her maid's company.

She chose a simple dress for dinner, careful to keep her thoughts from dwelling on Victor. It would be best to see as little of him as possible. She was beginning to realise that all the old attraction was still there. Then she shook her head as Marie caught a curl in the comb and pulled it painfully. She was simply tired, and this place was too full of memories. It would all seem different in the morning.

The long table was laid for the two of them, but their places were set near the middle, so that they sat opposite each other. A simple meal was served for which Victor apologised.

'But it's delicious,' she protested. 'It makes me feel that I am really home. I have missed country food.'

'After all the wonderful restaurants in Paris?'

'They are superb, of course. But this is perfect.'

'Are you happy to be here?' he asked.

'Of course I am happy,' she answered without thinking. But this did not feel like home any more, however beautiful it was, however much she had missed the hills and the scented air.

She made her excuses as soon as she could.

'Will you forgive me, Victor, if I have an early night?'

'Of course, you must be tired after your journey.'

Tired as she was, she did not sleep. She lay on her bed, stroking the velvet sash which secured the curtain by her pillow. She had lain in this bed, expecting Victor, when she had first come to the château. And then Achille had made her think about it all again so vividly. It did not feel good to be back in Argnon again, whatever she had told Victor; it only reminded her of how far she had come from what she had intended that first night here. Her love for Victor was pure – with Gilles she was no better than a prostitute.

And tomorrow she had to see her parents. Colette wished she had not come. She wanted to see her parents, but she no longer felt able to talk openly to them. The fun of showing off her gorgeous clothes, of telling her sister about the Paris fashions and parties, all seemed to have left her.

She knew that she must wait until the afternoon when they would rest after their work. In the morning she walked alone round the big, empty rooms. It seemed so quiet after Paris. There was no sign of Victor and she was grateful to him for his discretion. This must be as awkward for him as for her. No wonder Gilles had not wanted to come. She wondered what he was doing now.

She looked out past the woods to the hills where she knew her parents' cottage was. She could not see it, but she felt glad that her parents owned the land they worked on, because of her. Through those trees was the farm that Gilles' money had bought for her parents; the farm where she had grown up.

She chose a plain silk gown for her visit, and her narrowest petticoat. Perhaps later she could invite her sister here to see more of her clothes, if Victor did not mind. Beneath the high neck of her dress she wore the rubies. If there was a suitable moment, she would show them to her mother, to reassure her that she was provided for, whatever happened.

Paul drove her in a small, country carriage through the back lanes to the edge of the last field before her parent's cottage. Colette stepped out and asked him to return for her in four hours. As she walked along the rough track, she felt the stones of the path cut through the soles of her soft leather shoes and decided to tell her bootmaker more firmly next time what she needed for the country. Despite the discomfort, her spirits lifted with every step she took. Already, at the end of the path, she could see her family waiting on the doorstep, looking out for her; as soon as they saw her, too, her sister and brother, Jeanne and Pierre, darted out of the small front garden and raced towards her.

Pierre reached her first. He flung his arms round her waist and buried his face in the folds of her dress. Jeanne held back. 'Careful, Pierre. You'll make it dirty,' she said, but then she grinned, and she, too, ran forward. In step, they all marched along the track, bubbling over with the joy of being together again.

There was a little warmth in the spring sunshine, and she sat outside with her parents, sipping a glass of their best wine and breathing in all the familiar smells of the garden herbs and the hens and the woodsmoke from the cottage chimney and the rich odour of her mother's casserole from the open kitchen window.

The gate had been mended, and her mother wore a new dress. Colette said nothing. She was happy that her decision had bought these things for her family, but she did not want them to think about it while she was here. It made her feel awkward.

'How are you all?' she asked. 'Have you been well?'

Her father put down his glass. 'It has been a good winter, thanks to you. We've fixed up the roof on the shed, and there's meat in the pot.'

'Pierre goes to school now,' her mother added, 'but he doesn't work hard. Not like you.'

Pierre hovered beside the table, suddenly shy, as though she was a stranger. She held out her arms and he came to her. Then the cock ran after one of the hens and he chased off, following them. Colette folded her hands in her lap and looked at her younger sister. Jeanne smiled briefly and said nothing, then she went upstairs to her room.

Colette ate a piece of her mother's cake, swallowing carefully. She played with the crumbs on her plate.

'When will she marry?'

She was pleased to see her mother relax. 'In August,' she said.

'May I come?'

Colette looked at her mother. There was a stony reluctance on her face. 'Of course, Colette, you may come. If it had not been for you . . .'

'I may not have time,' she said quickly. 'Perhaps I will have to stay in Paris.' She saw the relief in her mother's face, but she understood all too well. Jeanne's fiancé was well-off. He was a better match than they might have expected without the dowry that Colette had provided. But his family would look down on her if the count's mistress appeared in her illicit Paris finery.

Her mother looked anxious. 'You will be welcome, Colette. Come if it pleases you.' But how could she come if Jeanne did not want her? No, she had been of use. And now they hoped she would not embarrass them. She understood. She had moved into a different world. And who knew where she might be next August?

She wanted to hear all the news of the village, but the afternoon dragged on and she felt her family's embarrassment at her presence. 'How is Gaston?' she asked.

Her mother's face lit up. She had always been fond of Gaston. 'He is married, and there is a baby on the way. They have said nothing yet, you understand, but I can always tell. There is a glow in the girl's cheeks, and that little tell-tale tinge of blue in her eyes. They are so happy, Colette. You do not need to worry about Gaston.'

Colette wondered if they wanted her to stay for supper, but they had not suggested it, although the scent of the meat drifting out of the kitchen aroused her appetite. It would be better if she left now; Victor expected her back at the château, and she was here for a week. There would be plenty of time. It would be easier after their first meeting. Things would be less awkward on her next visit.

When she left, her mother pressed her hand. 'Are you happy, my child? Was it a good choice we made for you?'

'Oh yes, maman. Look at me. You see how well I am.'

* * *

She had some time to wait before she had told Paul to collect her. It was an hour before the evening service in the church, and the curé would be waiting to hear any confessions. It would be quiet there. She had received one brief, expensive absolution in a chic Parisian cathedral. It had meant nothing to her. But now she longed to talk to someone who might know how she felt. She could talk to the curé here. He would understand.

As she walked down the village street, Colette was conscious of the eyes upon her as she tried to step gracefully over the cobbled stones. She knew that Monsieur Worth's gown looked ridiculous here and was glad to reach the shade of the trees in front of the church. It gave her the chance to catch her breath before she entered the familiar aisle.

'Please God, let it be empty,' she breathed. 'Let me have some time alone.' She needed to collect her thoughts.

The church seemed empty when she walked in. She raised her eyes to its dusty ceiling, and breathed in deeply. She looked at the pews, where she had sat as a young girl, fidgeting and flirting with the young men. Now she was grateful for the solitude.

One old woman. Sidonie Dépard, the grocer's wife, sat in a front pew, praying. She wondered if it was before or after her confession? Colette knew there was still some time to go before the evening service. When Sidonie left, would anyone else come in? She watched the old woman rise painfully to her feet and stand in front of the altar, her head bowed. Sidonie turned and walked down the nave towards the door. She raised her eyes to stare at

Colette; her upper lip curled in disgust, and she walked out without a word.

Colette could see that the door of the confessional was closed. She would have to wait. But that gave her a little time to collect her thoughts. When a man came out she kept her head lowered, and remained in her seat until he left the church and the building was empty. She did not want anyone else to see her. She opened the door of the confessional, chilled by the familiar odour of dry wood and fear, and took her place on the hard bench.

'Bless me father, for I have sinned.'

There was no answer. Had she been mistaken? Had the curé changed his hours? Or left because he thought the church was empty? Or worse, had he seen her waiting for him, and knew that her sin was so bad that he could not give her absolution? Then a voice came out of the darkness.

'How have you sinned, my child?'

'I live with a man in Paris.'

'Perhaps he forced you to become his mistress?'

'No father. I gave myself willingly.'

'Then you are right to feel shame. Why did you not come home when you knew you had done wrong?'

She could scarcely speak. 'I could not,' she said.

'Will you go back to this man?'

'Yes.'

'Then how can I give you absolution?'

She heard a soft moan escape her lips in the darkness. He was telling her what she knew to be the truth. She was lost.

'Wait in the church and talk to me, Colette. Maybe I can help you outside the bounds of the confessional.'

146

She stumbled out of the dark, stuffy enclosure to sit in a side pew, hidden from the main aisle of the church. She heard his footsteps and saw his dark figure come round the corner, past the shadowy box of the confessional.

'We must talk,' he said. 'Do you feel you have done wrong? Your parents are happy; you did this for them.'

Colette felt so relieved. He understood.

'Is there anything unresolved? Anything you wish to tell me?'

There was so much, but for the moment she could not find the words. It felt so good to have someone she could talk to. She would come back tomorrow, when she had collected her thoughts.

The curé spoke again. 'But you should not stay in Argnon any longer. It is unnecessarily cruel. Do you realise the hurt, the pain you have caused to another human being?'

Oh, if that was all! He was wrong. Gaston was not unhappy. Her mother had told her that he was happy and looking forward to his child.

'Father, you are mistaken. All is well with him.'

'His soul is in despair. He will die for love of you. You must show your love, reassure him. He never knew how to tell you. He adores you. Show him, Colette. This time you must make it clear.'

He could not mean Gaston. Perhaps the curé understood. Her heart leapt. Was it possible? 'You mean Victor?' she asked.

'But of course. Who else could I mean? You must reconcile yourself with him and free him of the burden he carries, his burden of love for you. God will show you the way. You must pray together in the chapel. Ask God and Victor for forgiveness.'

147

Her heart swelled. She looked up at the stained glass window of the church and saw the light flooding through. This was meant to happen; this was why she had come home. Her heart had told her so. What did it matter that the curé had refused to absolve her? She felt a weight lift from her soul as though she were forgiven. Everything would soon be well. It was what she had always wanted, and thought she had lost.

She felt cleansed in a way that her expensive confession in Paris had not offered her. The curé had shown her what was right. Perhaps it was not too late to make amends. She walked out of the church in a dream; this was the answer to all her problems. Gilles had taken her away from the only man she had ever loved. How could he have been so cruel? If she had known how Victor felt, she would never have gone to Paris without him. And she had believed that Victor would come with them. Sex with Gilles had been wonderful, but it was all they had together. Gilles had taught her well; she would make it up to Victor.

Her carriage was waiting outside in the square. She lifted her skirts and climbed in. It seemed to drive so slowly along the track to the château, and by the time they arrived Colette knew exactly what she must do to show Victor that she understood how he felt.

Somehow she expected him to be waiting for her when she returned, but he was not in the salon or any of the reception rooms where she hoped to find him. It did not matter. She would be with him tonight at dinner, and she would talk with him then.

She went into the private chapel to pray for

guidance. It would take time for Victor to accept her and to understand how she had always felt. He saw her now only as his father's mistress. He would need reassurance but, with the curé's help, he would learn to trust her. The curé, she was sure, would guide her now that he had told her that Victor loved her. And then he would grant her absolution from her sins. She prayed that it would be soon.

She dressed with care, choosing her most simple dress, wishing that she still possessed the old, red dress she had worn when she first came here. Then she caught a glimpse of herself in the mirror and smiled. She now looked like the lady she had so longed to be, for him, and she would show him that she still had the same heart. He could not fail to believe her.

'You are happy to be here, Mademoiselle,' Marie said as she fastened the last hook on her bodice. 'There is colour in your cheeks and your eyes shine. Sit down please while I adjust your hair.'

'Make it simple, please, tonight. This is the country, Marie.'

'You do not have to remind me! I know it only too well.'

Colette felt the brush pushed through her hair with more vigour than was necessary. Poor Marie. She looked pale and unhappy. Argnon did not suit her at all. Colette made up her mind that she would send Marie back to Paris as soon as possible. It was not fair to keep her apart from Jean-Pierre. She wanted everyone to feel as happy as she did.

The curé was with Victor in the salon when she came downstairs, and she smiled at him, to reassure him that she understood what he had said to her earlier. It was kind of him to come to help her tonight. He must have known how difficult it would be for her.

Their dinner was much more elaborate this evening, although plain by Paris standards. Victor had asked if she would prefer to choose the menu herself, treating her like the lady of the house, but she had been happy to leave it to him. Victor had chosen a selection of small fish delicately stewed in their juices, with roasted wild birds to follow and then a dish of lightly baked fruits arranged on a heavy porcelain dish. Some little goat's cheeses, served on a bed of fragrant leaves, were eaten with the last of the heavy, red wine they had drunk throughout the meal. Colette savoured each mouthful with added awareness. She watched Victor closely all evening, noticing how he flushed when he caught her gaze.

She smiled at Victor who remained impassive. He was so innocent. For the first time she felt older than him, and more experienced. How could it be wrong when it was the curé who had shown her what to do? He ate with them now, giving them his blessing. Everything felt so wonderfully right, and it was all so easy.

When their meal was finished, the curé pushed back his chair. 'I will leave you now. Victor, may I rest a while in the chapel here?'

Colette felt him brush against her as he left the room. His breath smelled stale and wine-laden, but he had given her so much relief today that she felt nothing but warmth towards him. And he had left her alone with Victor.

He stared across the table at her. She thought he

was a little drunk. Well, what did it matter? So was she. It was time they made their feelings for each other plain. She stood up and heard her chair crash to the floor behind her. Colette felt slightly unsteady as she walked round the table towards the boy she was sure she loved.

She wondered what he wanted her to do to him. The only man she had ever known was Gilles, and he had taught her everything. But the man at the theatre obviously wanted her. She must be desirable. She must be.

Colette thought of how she had felt lying on the brown velvet in Achilles' studio. It was Victor she thought of then. He had not moved from his place at the table. She stood beside him until he turned to look at her, and then she held out her hand.

She could see dark rings beneath his eyes; a faint blemish on the golden sheen of his skin. She felt ashamed to think that she had been the cause of his misery. She placed one finger on the thick curve of his lower lip and let him suck her soft pad into his mouth. She could feel the rasp of his tongue on the nerves at the end of her finger. He looked up at her, his warm, amber eyes glittering in the candlelight, and she moved closer to him.

'Do you remember, Victor,' she said, 'how we used to swim in the river together?'

She wanted him to loosen the lace over her shoulders, and reach out for the curve of her breast, but he did nothing. She stepped back, worried that she was frightening him. The soft Persian rug lay like a warm caress at her feet. She wanted to drag him down on to it, to hold him close to her in the flickering warmth of the fire and tell him that she loved him. Perhaps it was too late. She had hurt him too much.

Then he rose from his chair, and she thought he would touch her. Oh Victor, Victor, please, this is where we should have started from, she thought. Here, on this deep carpet, she could feel as though she floated in the river, and give herself to her love.

He took her hand. 'I want you to come upstairs with me,' he said, 'to my mother's room.' Trembling, she followed him. He stumbled once or twice, and she felt her own legs weaken with desire. She had never seen this wing of the château, and when he opened the doors she saw a full-length portrait of a beautiful young woman with red-gold hair gazing down at her. Madame de la Trave had been a glorious bride; her pure white gown floated around her with a broad, sky-blue satin ribbon round a tiny waist. A small spaniel nestled in her lap, gazing up at her with adoring eyes. Behind her, artfully draped over fallen forest trees, were the exquisite tapestry hangings which decorated the walls of the dining room downstairs.

Colette felt honoured. This room must be important for Victor, and she felt proud that he wanted to bring her here. She saw the gold drapes of the ornate bed pulled back ready for them, and started to untie the laces on her bodice. She saw Victor staring at her and reached out for the top button of his shirt. He pushed her hand away and roughly pulled it open himself.

Quickly, she fumbled with her skirts and petticoats, watching him strip off his shirt and the plain silk breeches that he wore. He turned down the gaslight, left the curtains open and lit one candle by the window. Colette lay down on the bed, and waited for him. Victor seemed to hesitate, and she reached out for him. He stood at the foot of the bed, with his beautiful body outlined against the single guttering flame of the candle.

Victor climbed slowly on to the bed and crawled towards her. She felt his hands gripping her ankles, and waited for him to reach higher. Every nerve in her body was tingling in expectation. Slowly, he slid his hands up her calves and behind her knees. She could see him now, his golden body flickering in the candlelight, kneeling over her, his penis drooping over the long curve of her thigh.

It did not matter. If she could simply hold him in her arms tonight, she would be happy. She took one of his hands in hers and kissed it, feeling the faint pulse at the base of his thumb throb against her lips. Her breasts were full and swollen already, waiting for him to hold them. She placed the palm of his hand over her taut nipple and stroked his smooth, golden shoulders. Gently, without wishing to hurry him, she reached down over his belly and stretched out her hand to encourage his erection. She thought she saw a shadow fall on him; there was a faint noise, like the creak of a door, but it must be the curtains blowing in the breeze. It had blown out the candle. She thought nothing of it as she felt Victor's penis grow firmer in her fingers, and ached for it to rise into her waiting body.

She felt one of the golden cords fall across her from the drapes at the side of the bed and pushed the stiff, gilt tassle away with her hand. As she did so, she felt Victor's young, soft penis harden and grow rigid. He reared up on top of her, and she felt him plunge deep inside her with one quick thrust.

She gasped out loud and struggled to control his rapid thrusts, but he drove faster into her. He was quick and eager, pushing into her with a force she was unused to, and she felt him climax before she had time to enjoy him.

It was so different from what she had imagined. Next time would be easier. They had waited too long, and naturally they could not expect it to be perfect at once. She could teach him how to cherish a woman. For the moment, all that mattered was that he wanted her.

She felt him fall heavily on to her when he climaxed. She closed her eyes and stroked him gently. Then she felt a cold hand touch hers, over Victor's taut buttocks, and she looked up to see the dark figure of the curé bending over her lover.

Victor groaned and turned over on to his back. He pursed his lips, and the curé kissed him. 'Was that enough, my darling? Now you understand that you do not need her. She means nothing to you. I told you she was a whore. Your father's whore. And you could not even come until I touched you.'

She watched Victor climb awkwardly from the bed, take the curé's hand, and follow him through an opening in the panelled wall. She lay in the bed for a moment, as though paralysed, unable to understand what had happened. Then she thought of the way that Victor had looked as the curé kissed him. What a fool she had been to believe he wanted her. There was no doubt as to his feelings for the other man. She had held a dream in her mind for too long, and had been too easily convinced by her own desires.

She tore a sheet off the bed and covered herself. The room was in total darkness now, and she groped her way blindly to the door. The corridor was empty, but she did not care who saw her. She needed to find the security of her own room.

A jug of cold water stood on a chest beside the window. Colette soaked a cloth and rubbed furiously at the flesh between her thighs, trying to escape from the odour of the two men that seemed to linger around her. She rubbed until she was pink and sore, but the stain seemed deeper than she could cleanse in this way.

Gilles had not deserved this from her. He had treated her honourably, and she had betrayed him with his son. And with his son's lover. And all because of a stupid, childish dream.

The memory of the curé's flushed cheekbones hovered in her mind as she lay, unsleeping, on the bed, haunting her until the first rays of morning sun came in through the open windows.

What was she to do now? She could not return to Gilles. He could never take her back. But how could she live in Argnon and see the curé's face every day, knowing that she had ruined her sister's wedding?

She took the rubies out of their velvet box and ran them through her fingers. She would sell these jewels and start a new life. But she was too tired to think any more until she had slept.

The curé was right. She was a whore – but she was a good one. She would earn her own living and Gilles' rubies would pay for it.

Chapter Eight

Colette walked all the next day through the yew-lined avenues of the garden. She was careful not to go anywhere she might see Victor, and had her meals served in her room. In the evening she climbed the hill behind the château and sat on the steps of the small Greek folly, where she could look down the valley towards her parents' farm. What would they think of her now? They expected her to return to Paris and her glittering future, leaving them to enjoy the prosperity she had brought them. But Gilles would turn her out on the streets as soon as he heard about her night with his son, and he would take away the farm and all the money he had given her family.

She walked in the soft, late summer rain until her clothes were drenched and her hair slicked to her scalp. She could not stay here; her parents would never understand. Gilles had said that the rubies were hers to keep. If she went back to Paris and sold them, she could rent an apartment and find another lover. She had learnt a lot from Gilles, and she was sure that he would let her keep her dresses. Perhaps Olympe would help her. Colette had expected to have to look after herself at the end of the year. Now she would simply have to start a little earlier. She would return to Paris tomorrow.

Marie was beside herself with joy at the news. She had their trunks packed in no time, and Paul was commanded to drive them to the station. Marie was too kind to make any allusion to the reason for Colette's change of plan; only once, unable to ignore her mistress' obvious misery, she laid her soft, plump hand on top of Colette's and murmured, 'We shall soon be in Paris, Mademoiselle. That is where you belong now.'

But Marie did not know what had happened. And how could Colette possibly return to Gilles after what she had experienced with his son? Once again she left Argnon without knowing what to expect, but this time with more fears than she had felt before. The acacias on the hillside were shooting green leaves. Victor would spend the summer days hunting in the hills. And his nights in the château with the curé. She shivered.

Without a private compartment booked for them in the train, Colette found the journey cramped and uncomfortable. She had so quickly become used to luxury. But she was too miserable to care much, and Marie did not mind; she babbled on so happily that Colette had to find tasks for her to do to keep her quiet. In the end, she closed her eyes and pretended to sleep. Her thoughts were so wretched that, after a while, she gave up all attempt and read until the train pulled in to the station.

She had sent Gilles no message to tell him of her

early arrival. There would be no carriage to meet her; she was glad of that now. She did not want him to be kind to her. She would have to leave him soon. Just as soon as she had found someone else to pay her bills.

She took a hackney carriage and drove straight round to Anne's apartment, much to Marie's annoyance, who had to fill in time with Anne's maids when she was longing to see Jean-Pierre. Colette waited in the salon upstairs until Anne entered, as beautifully dressed as always, but icy calm and obviously displeased at this ill-timed visit.

'I need your help.'

Anne raised one beautiful eyebrow, and waited for Colette to continue.

'I have to leave Gilles. Will you help me to find someone else? Please, Anne.'

She saw Anne stiffen in her seat and turn her face away. When she looked around again, Colette saw that Anne's face was pale, and her lips bloodless. She rose to her feet, and took Colette's hand with more warmth than she had ever shown to her before. 'What has happened? Tell me quickly. Is it Antoinette? Has she done anything to you?'

'Antoinette?'

'Madame de la Trave. Gilles' wife. She can be very cruel. You must tell me if it is her.'

Colette shook her head. 'No. I have heard nothing from her. I've never met her.'

'Then I cannot imagine why you are being so foolish.' The momentary warmth had disappeared. The colour had returned to Anne's cheeks, but her eyes were cold.

Colette tried to stay calm. 'I can tell you nothing. But you must help me, for Gilles' sake.'

She saw a flash of real anger in the icy eyes now. 'It is quite impossible for you to leave him before the end of your year,' Anne said. 'You would humiliate him.'

'It would humiliate him more if I stayed and he found out what I have done!'

'Why? What have you done, you little fool? Gone to bed with your peasant lover? So what! Just keep your mouth shut.'

'You don't understand. It is not that. But I can never go back to him.'

'Does Gilles know you are back in Paris?'

Colette shook her head. 'I thought I could find somewhere to stay before I see him.'

'That is quite impossible. Think of your future. You must never leave a man without first finding another. Where would you live? Where would you even stay tonight?'

'I hoped that you would help me.'

'And risk my friendship with Gilles? *Mais non.*'

There was a pause while the maid brought in a bottle of champagne. 'I always have a glass at this time,' Anne said. 'Besides being good for the complexion, it is essential in despair. And you should be in despair, Colette. *Salut!*' Anne emptied the slim tulip. 'Now, I will tell you what I will do. I will go to see Gilles, and try to find out if he has any suspicions about you. Then we will decide. But I warn you. I will do what I think best for Gilles. I care nothing about you. And if you hurt him, do not expect me to be your friend.'

Colette waited for two hours in the blue and silver salon until Anne returned. Anne was very quiet. She stared for a long time out of the window. 'I must ask you again, Colette, and this time you must tell me the truth. Are you sure you have never met Gilles' wife?'

Surprised, Colette shook her head. She remembered the portrait of the beautiful young woman in the boudoir at the Château Maraigne.

'Have you had any contact with her? Has she written to you? Or threatened your family?'

'Nothing. Nothing at all, I promise.'

'And yet you will not tell me what has happened?'

'No, but please believe that I cannot live with Gilles. If I stay, I will hurt him.'

'I believe you. What reason would you have to lie about such a thing?' Anne twisted her beautiful, jewelled fingers round a diamond bracelet on her wrist and paced the room. 'You must anger him so that he thinks that it is he who has finished with you. He will still be angry with himself because for the first time in his life he will have chosen badly. But . . .'

'But you will be there to comfort him.'

Anne turned to Colette. She was pale. For the first time she seemed unsure and vulnerable. 'Do you swear you will never tell him if I help you to leave him?'

'I swear. He needs you, Anne.'

'Of course he needs me.' She paced the room again. 'But this is not the time. Or the right way.'

Colette felt a pain. She had never loved anyone like Anne loved Gilles. She used to think that she loved Victor, but not any longer. Now she hated him. And Gilles needed Anne. What was she supposed to say? He is too old to have a new young woman each year? Paid for with his wife's money.

160

Colette sat on the delicate satin sofa and played with a handkerchief on her lap. It was made of exquisite Brussels lace and, like everything she owned, had been paid for by Gilles. She had made a deal; if she reneged on her contract, he had every right to leave her with nothing. Until she found someone else to support her, she could not afford that.

She watched Anne carefully. Anne had succeeded in making a life for herself. But Anne had always been a lady. She would listen carefully to her advice.

'To be a successful courtesan you must look as if you are already protected – with no need of money or men. You offer a man a favour by considering him.'

Colette nodded. She had seen this.

'So, you cannot leave one protector until you have found another.'

'At the Bois?'

Anne shook her head. 'Not if you want to be the best. At the theatre. Men have noticed you – you must let them know you are available. But not until you have arranged things with Gilles.'

'How do I do that?'

'Bore him? Shock him? He likes you to look innocent. Show him that you are not. Why do you think he chose you in the first place?'

'He enjoyed teaching me things.'

'And if you no longer show an interest? This is up to you, Colette. Now you must go back to the Boulevard Haussmann.'

'I cannot. I cannot see him again.'

Anne gripped her wrist fiercely. 'You will do as I say. Tonight Gilles has an appointment. I did not tell him that you had returned, so you will have at least a little time to prepare yourself. Now leave me. Remember, do not involve me in this. And wait, unless you want him to know that it was someone in Argnon who has affected you so deeply. Behave as if nothing has happened for at least a week. I will play my part. I will prepare him so that when the time comes, he can accept what you are doing.'

And Anne would be there for Gilles when she had gone, Colette was sure of that.

It was fortunate that Gilles was not expecting her. When Colette returned to the house, she learnt that he was out, and not due home until the morning. She remembered what Anne had said to her during her first week in Paris: 'Do you expect him to live like a monk?' Gilles was no monk.

She sat on the terrace, watching the lights of Paris, and wondered where Gilles was tonight, and with whom. Perhaps she should pretend to be jealous. He would hate that. But when she finally went alone to her bed, she still had no idea what she would do. She simply had to hope that Anne would find a way to help her.

The next morning, Gilles came to her bed. He seemed delighted to see her. 'Why did you not tell me you were returning early? Of course I would have been here to welcome you.'

Colette tried to smile and look bright and cheerful, as if everything in Argnon had been wonderful. 'I am sorry, Gilles. I came home because I missed you.'

He stroked her cheek. 'I am pleased, and sorry

that I was not here to welcome you. But you look pale. The country air was not good for you. I thought you would return blooming.'

'The journey was tiring. That is all.'

'Well, you are still beautiful.' He stepped back a pace, and examined her. 'You have an air of fragility now that makes me want to take care of you. Perhaps for longer than we thought at first. I have missed you too, more than anticipated. We must spend some time together and talk about this.'

She felt the pressure of his hand on her fingers. It was gentle and loving. Oh, what had she done? She struggled to appear as though nothing was wrong. 'Will we drive in the Bois today, Gilles?' she asked.

He shook his head regretfully. 'You must go alone,' he said, letting go of her hand. 'My wife is in Paris, and I have promised to see her.'

Colette felt a moment's fear. Was this why Anne had asked her about Madame de la Trave? Was it possible that Gilles' wife knew the truth, and that was why she had returned now? She studied Gilles' face. Did he know what had happened in Argnon? Was he playing with her now?

He gave no sign, and kissed her lovingly. 'I shall be free this evening, Colette,' he said. 'What would you like to do tonight?'

She felt unable to think clearly. He was standing so close to her. At any moment she thought he would want to make love to her, and she did not think she could bear that now. 'Whatever you choose,' she said quietly.

He looked genuinely puzzled. 'Are you still tired after your journey? You must stay here and rest today. Tonight I will take you to the Café Anglais. We have not been there since our first evening.

163

Wear your burgundy gown for me, *ma chère*, and we will repeat that wonderful night.'

The thought filled her with horror, but she could not argue with him, and she was too tired to think of anything else that would not disturb him. Anne had told her to do nothing to raise his suspicions for the first few days. He must never know that her change in mood was a result of anything that had happened in Argnon. 'Is it wise to try to repeat something?' she asked.

'One can never do that. But it would amuse me to take you there again.'

She would have to try to endure the evening. Before he left, she had one question to ask him. He had said that his wife had returned. Would Madame expect to live here? 'What difference will it make, your wife being in Paris?' she asked

'Do not let it worry you. She has her own home here. As you may have heard, she is extremely rich.'

'She does not mind that I live with you?'

He did not answer her directly. 'She will not disturb us. But perhaps we will be seen a little less together. She is not a good woman to anger. Now, forgive me, I have work to do.' He moved towards the door, but stopped before leaving the room. 'Colette,' he said, 'tonight will you leave your throat bare, as you did for me before?'

She nodded, feeling sick at her deceit. She wanted to leave now, not to find Gilles more loving than he had ever been towards her. He belonged to Anne; she wanted him, and Gilles needed her more than he realised. He would be hurt, but there was nothing she could do to prevent it, and when that

164

happened, she would be the one to suffer, the one who was left alone.

Colette dressed carefully, remembering how she had felt when she wore this dress before. Surely she could convince Gilles tonight that all was well. And then again, and again, until a week was over and she dared to create a scene.

He was so kind, so thoughtful and seemed so pleased to have her back that she felt a shiver of guilt. She felt so much older than the young girl who had prepared for dinner at the Café Anglais. Then such a glittering future seemed to open out in front of her. She had not even been able to last a single year.

Her dress was too loose for her now. She had lost weight in the last week. The froth of delicate lace that had barely covered her full breasts now seemed to skim over her. Her stays no longer needed to be pulled in tight to give her a tiny waist, and she stared at her reflection in the mirror with a sense of dejection. She felt dull and lifeless, not at all like herself. She looked like any one of the pale, fashionable women who crowded the boxes at the opera every night, not like Colette, the girl from Argnon whom Gilles had chosen because she was so different.

Reluctantly, she left the rubies in their box. She hated to be parted from them. At any moment she felt that Gilles would discover the truth and throw her out; if that happened, perhaps he would not let her come back here for them. She remembered how excited she had felt when she had worn this dress for the first time, and had planned to seduce Gilles. Now the thought of him touching her was terrifying.

When she walked down the stairs, she saw an expression in his eyes that she had not seen before. At first she thought that, like her, he knew how little this gown suited her now. Then she realised that there was a new tenderness which frightened her almost more. She stretched out her hand and let him help her on with her cloak. Anne was wrong; she could not go through with this any longer. She was beginning to understand just what she had lost.

At the Café Anglais she could not taste her food; she struggled to force it down her throat, worried that Gilles would notice if she ate nothing, and demand to know what was the matter. But he talked with animation all evening, her quietness and lack of vivacity seeming to excite him. She glanced across the room at the curtained alcove. How eager she had been for that obvious seduction the last time they were here. Now the drapes drew her attention as forcibly as they had done before. Her body seemed to exist somewhere far beneath the loose layers of silk and lace. Her breasts were no longer full and lush, but her nipples peaked irrepressibly beneath the light covering, and she felt the lace rub over them each time she moved, until they pained her with a constant ache and seemed to swell harder and larger as the evening progressed.

The last time she was in this room she had not known what it was like to make love with a man, what it felt like to have his hands cupping her breasts, his lips brushing lightly over her nipples, and then the pressure increasing until she longed for the pain of his teeth closing over them. Her body trembled uncontrollably. She was tired, she told herself; she wanted to go home, to sleep.

Home! It could not be her home any longer. Whatever happened to her, she must tell Gilles now. She could not go through with this any longer. Dear God, all she wanted was for Gilles to take her in his arms, to love her and to help her forget what his son had done to her. She put down her knife and fork, pushing the untasted food to one side. 'I have to ask you something,' she began, struggling to find the words. What could she say? What reason could she give?

She saw him rise to his feet and put one hand in his pocket. He walked across the room and stood behind her. She felt the heat of his lips on the back of her neck and trembled with desire for him. What if she said nothing? What if she lived with Gilles as before, knowing now how lucky she was to be loved by such a man? Could she do it? She heard the soft click of a jewel box opening, and Gilles' hands around her throat, circling her neck with cold, hard gems. They weighed down on her. She felt his smooth, dry hands slide round and stroke the sharp outline of her collar bone, his thumbs pressing on to her thin flesh, caressing her softly until she burnt with longing for him. His fingers spread out over the faint swell of her breasts, sliding lower until she felt his sensitive pads reach her stiffened nipples, lifting her breasts until they rose clear from the frothy lace and rested free on the cupped palms of his hands.

She could hardly breathe as he held her. She did not want to move. She wanted to stay here, with his hands on her breasts, and not think about anything except the raging desire that swept through her. She heard a sudden gasp behind her and felt Gilles' fingers tighten on her nipples. He twisted her round towards him, and she saw the same desire in his face. He lifted her to her feet, pulling her towards the curtain. His breath was coming fast now; his movements were rough and uneven as he caught at one side of the velvet drape, and pushed it sharply aside.

Colette saw a couch of buttoned, red velvet, bare and hard, nothing more than a length of board where men took the women they had paid for with their dinners and their jewels. Her own quick breathing matched that of Gilles now, as she put her hands to the crisp, white shirt at his neck and loosened the first stud. She felt his fingers tear at the hooks securing her gown, and shivered as he touched the bones of her spine. Her bodice fell to the floor. She pulled at her petticoats, tearing them off. She wanted to stand naked before him, and start again with him, here in this room where she had first decided she wanted him to make love to her. They could make things right. She knew they could.

Gilles' shirt hung loose, revealing his dark chest and the trail of grizzled hair which led over his flat belly to the thick nest surrounding his penis. She reached out for him, wanting to feel the rigid column that jutted out of his sleek evening trousers. She could not wait for him to take off all his clothes. She wanted him now. She flung herself down on the hard velvet couch, spread her thighs apart, and opened her arms to hold him. 'Gilles,' she called out, reaching up for him as he lowered himself on to her.

She heard him groan as he pushed his thick shaft

between her legs. *'Chérie,'* he moaned. 'I was so frightened when you left me. I thought you had gone back to Victor. I knew how you felt about him when you were a child, and I took you away from him. I know it was wrong of me. But now, darling, that is all over and you want me. You really do.'

He surged forwards and she froze. He had known that Victor was at Argnon, but he had not told her. He had known how she felt about Victor, but he had taken her away to Paris without him. It would not be long before he knew exactly what had happened. She tensed, feeling her thighs tighten so that he could not enter her. She felt his hands grip her arm. 'What is it, Colette? You were on fire a moment ago.' He bent over her so that his hair fell over her breast, and caught her nipple between his lips. She knew that it was soft and limp, and that her desire had gone as rapidly as it had come.

He stared down at her. 'In the past,' he said languidly, 'I have always found that a gift of diamonds increased a woman's ardour. You have succeeded in surprising me once again. But I cannot say that this time it is a pleasure.'

Gilles flicked her soft nipple with the tip of one finger and sat up. He started to button up his shirt. 'I have always thought these places were unromantic,' he said, 'but I had not realised quite how off-putting they could be. What is it, Colette? Your village lover? Don't I match up to him?'

She felt a wave of relief that he had not guessed the truth. He was jealous of Victor, but he did not believe that his son would dare to touch his mistress. She watched Gilles as he fastened the front of his trousers and pulled on his coat. She saw him staring at the gems glittering round her throat, and

169

reached up to take them off. She saw his mouth curl up at one corner. 'Keep them,' he said. 'My wife can afford them. You have no need to worry. Put on your dress,' he ordered, but he made no move to help her. She draped it over her shoulders as best she could and bent to pick up her cloak and wrap it around her. Her hair had fallen down over her shoulders. She pushed it back. She no longer cared if it fell loose.

'A woman of experience learns to hide the fact that she has cheated on her lover,' he said coldly. 'It is a skill I suggest you acquire.'

She sat opposite him in the carriage as they drove home, and she waited for him to tell her that she must leave. He said nothing. When they reached the Boulevard Haussmann, he came into the hall with her and stood for a moment at the foot of the staircase. 'It is March,' he said. 'You will stay with me until May, as we agreed. But you need have no fear that I will ever touch you again.' He moved back towards the door. 'You will take no other lover until I release you in May, Colette, or I will destroy you.'

'Will you take back my parents' farm?'

She shrank back at the scorn in his eyes. 'Your father is a good man,' he said. 'Do you really believe that I would make your family suffer for your shame?'

She heard the door slam shut behind him and slowly climbed the stairs to her room. Marie would wonder what had happened, but she would not ask. She would be on her own until May. It would be a long three months.

* * *

Gilles was out increasingly often, and Colette went alone to her box at the Vaudeville. Always men thronged around her in the interval, waiting for an indication that they might join her. Occasionally she permitted one or two to buy her flowers, or a box of sugar raisins. Never more. Gilles' words were seared into her brain. 'Do not shame either of us, Colette. Do nothing until our year is at an end. My habits are too well known.'

'But if you are seldom with me?' she had asked. 'I am so often alone.'

'The political situation demands my attention. You are fortunate that we live in such times.'

Gilles had used that as an excuse, she was sure. Paris had never been so gay, so vibrant. If the situation was really so serious, would everyone spend so much money on frivolity?

She would simply have to wait until May.

Anne accompanied her sometimes, and they made a show of companionship. Colette would have been happy to have had the older woman as a true friend, but the barrier which had existed from the first was made of steel now. Anne could barely conceal her scorn. But when Anne sat by her side, Gilles came to the theatre more often, and Colette was grateful for that.

One evening, when they were alone, she hinted to Anne that it was Victor who had caused her so much pain. 'And you truly loved him?' Anne asked.

'I thought I did, at first.'

'Then you must forgive me for my harshness towards you. I did not understand. I will do all I can to ensure that Gilles treats you honourably when you go.'

171

It seemed that she had succeeded. When May came, Gilles took her into his study and told her what would happen to her. 'You may keep your jewels, Colette, and all your gowns,' he said. 'I have talked to Anne. She knows of a young man who will provide you with an apartment and everything you could wish. He will meet you in the theatre tonight, and you may make your decision. If you accept him you may leave whenever you choose. It would be best to part now.' She felt his hands run lightly through her hair, drawing her nearer to him. 'Victor was a fool to let you go,' he said abruptly, and pulled back. He walked across to the door and held it open. She crossed the landing to her own apartment, and asked Marie to begin packing her possessions. Later, she would prepare for the evening. So Anne had told Gilles about Victor, but neither of them knew the truth. It was better left that way.

That evening Colette sat alone in her box, without her usual bouquet of white flowers. She worked hard at behaving as if this was a normal occasion, acknowledging the attention she received with the same studied insouciance. But she could not control the beating of her heart. The rent on this box expired at the end of the month; she needed to find somewhere to live, and a man willing to pay for that, and for new dresses and jewels. If, at this moment, her lavish lifestyle faltered, she would sink to the second rank and it would be impossible to rise again to the position she now held so precariously. She glanced at the young man whom Anne had chosen for her. He sat, with a group of male friends, in a box at the other side of the theatre, facing hers. She wondered whether she could ever care for him.

She was aware of a heightened tension in the other men who had already made their desires known. Tonight, she was only interested in taking one lover. Later, she would accept others who could offer her carriages and jewels.

The first act was almost at an end. Colette allowed herself to look directly at the count. He was almost on his feet with eagerness. She hesitated, then lowered her fan and smiled at him.

Her door opened, and a footman brought in flowers. As she had expected, there were bouquets from three young men, and it seemed that she had chosen well; that of Charles Fabris was the most lavish, and his card was enclosed in a slim, gold case set with emeralds. She shook it and heard a satisfactory rattle, as though it contained a key. On the card was an address and a brief note. *If you would do me the honour of viewing this apartment, it would afford me the greatest pleasure. If it pleases you, it is yours.*

She would accept him. She expected him to walk through the door at any moment. But her first visitor was Edouard Kerouac. He came in without waiting for an invitation and stood in front of her, leaning against the balcony of her box. 'You look pale, *chérie*,' he said. 'This life does not suit you. You should leave Paris, and go home to the country.'

'You know very well that I cannot do that.' She saw him turn his head to glance at the young count, before he stared pointedly at the little case on her lap.

He uncrossed his long legs and moved to the

door. 'I see I am in your way,' he said. 'I must leave you. I never interfere with business.'

As he left, she heard a murmur outside in the corridor, an unusual noise, and two footmen struggled in carrying a mountain of white flowers. Her smile deepened. The count was behaving with style. The scarlet plush walls of her box were almost hidden behind a bank of white lilac and apple blossom, and all eyes were fixed on her. The count made a spectacular entrance.

'Sir, you need not have made your intentions so obvious.' She pretended anger, but smiled warmly at him.

For a moment he looked discomforted. Then he languidly waved a hand at the novel arrangement. 'I am not alone in my desires, Mademoiselle. I regret that those are from another admirer.' Then he smiled as he saw his gift in her lap. 'I see you have mine.'

Who could have sent her such a dramatic display, and failed to make his presence known? For a moment she was confused, then she saw the young count's eagerness increased by the rivalry and smiled at him. 'Monsieur?' she queried.

'Would you allow me to accompany you in the Bois tomorrow, Mademoiselle?' he asked.

She nodded. 'It would be a pleasure.'

Their business was done, but it was expected that they would wait for a few days before it was publicly confirmed. Until the count had made a definite offer of at least 100,000 francs, Colette would leave all her options open.

Graciously, she accepted sweets and flowers from her other admirers. Then she dismissed them all, and sat alone in her box until Anne joined her later.

She raised her eyes at the wall of flowers. 'A little vulgar,' she murmured, glancing round at the other offerings. 'But I would say you have had a successful evening. May I ask whom you have chosen?'

Colette clasped the box in her hand. 'The count has offered me the key to an apartment,' she murmured. 'I will inspect it tomorrow.'

'You have made an excellent start.' Anne studied the stage, and then pointed to the mass of country flowers. 'But I would not have thought Charles would have been so blatant.'

'He wasn't. I don't know who sent those.'

'No card? No gift?'

'Nothing.'

'How very interesting. Colette, my sweet, our relationship has not been an easy one.' Anne raised a glass of champagne and saluted her. 'But it has not been dull. To your success, I shall miss you.'

Only because you do not know the truth, she thought. But I can never tell you. 'To your advice,' she said. 'And to Gilles.'

Perhaps she would talk to Anne, now that she was free of Gilles. In a week or two, when she was established, she might tell Anne about the curé, and ask her to warn Gilles however she thought best. Anne and Gilles were closer now, almost as if they intended to renew their relationship. It might have been the problems she had caused. Or perhaps it was the war that Gilles feared so much. He had been wrong; the Assembly had just voted their confidence in the Emperor. In a week or so, all her worries would be over.

It was almost too easy. In the morning, Colette drove to the Rue St Florentin, and failed for the first time to keep her weekly appointment at the

Louvre. In the afternoon, Marie and Jean-Pierre brought everything she owned from the Boulevard Haussmann to her new apartment; Marie moved into the room where she would now live, and said goodbye to Jean-Pierre. They had fixed their wedding day for September; until then, Marie would stay here.

Colette wandered through the spacious rooms. The apartment was all she could have hoped for. And it was hers. She could do exactly what she wanted without Gilles' approval. If the count did not like her behaviour, it would be simple enough to replace him.

She sat at an elegant desk by a window overlooking the square and wrote a note to Charles on a sheet of thick, headed paper. To write from this address was sufficient proof of her acceptance of his offer. Now he deserved his reward.

You may join me for supper tomorrow evening. I shall expect you at eleven o'clock. And she signed her name with a flourish. *Colette.*

Chapter Nine

Colette ordered a fire to be lit in her new salon. The days were warm, and the spring sunshine was pleasant, but there was a chill in the evening air, and she wanted the room to look welcoming. She asked Marie to light one or two candles in the wall brackets and was pleased with the effect. The walls were panelled in white and gold and there was a pretty ceiling, painted with garlands of roses and honeysuckle. In the flickering light of the fire, she could see the lilies that Charles had given her last night arranged in a Bohemian glass vase on a console table between the windows. The strong scent of the tall, white blooms dominated the room. She opened a window and filled her lungs with fresh air. Below her, the streets were brightly lit, and carriages filled the square. She could see the inside of a café crowded with diners who had come for a meal after the theatre.

Charles would be here very soon. She had ignored him earlier at the Vaudeville, but now she would make it up to him. He would know that her indifference was merely a pretence. She went to her bedroom and changed quickly. Marie carried her gown out of the room, and left her in a simple robe of embroidered, white satin, which fastened with a single sash around her waist, beneath which she was completely naked.

The bedroom, in contrast to the restrained elegance of the rest of the apartment, was lined with vermilion silk from floor to ceiling, and a tent of the same fabric was draped over her gold, four-poster bed. It was exactly what she would have chosen for herself. She adored the rich texture of the fabric enclosing her and the lavish gilding on the bedposts. But she did not plan to receive Charles in here.

Colette hurried back to the salon and inspected the light supper which Marie had ordered to be delivered from Sardou's. An array of dishes was laid out on a low table beside the fire. She lifted one of the silver lids, dipped a finger into a smooth artichoke mousse and tasted a little mouthful of its delicate flavour. It was delicious. She peered under more of the silver lids and found a breast of chicken nestling in a creamy lemon sauce, shelled lobster meat surrounded by its coral roe and a pan of cherries placed over a flame on a silver stand, which warmed their brandied juice. She hoped that Charles would feel inclined to eat first.

He was very young. But he was sophisticated and very rich. She wondered if he had a mistress before. She was a fool not to have asked Anne, but she had not wanted to appear so ignorant. There was still so much she had to learn.

She shivered, despite the heat. Apart from the

terrible night with Victor and the curé, she had never been with any man other than Gilles, and she felt unsure of herself now. She took a piece of chocolate from one of the boxes on the table and sank down on the rug in front of the fire. She reached out for a long-handled fork which hung on a stand on the hearth and speared the chocolate on to its prongs. She curled her legs beneath her and toasted the rich, dark confection, until she could lick little scoops of melted cocoa off the warm face of the sweet. She felt its dark stickiness coat her tongue, and swallowed slowly. It was a moment of pure pleasure, reminding her of a rare childhood treat, and a winter afternoon when there had been no work at home because of the snow.

She heard a carriage stop outside, the muffled slam of a door and a few words spoken that she could not distinguish. Then the carriage drove away and she heard the sound of her own front door opening and closing. Marie's voice echoed in the corridor. 'Please go in. Mademoiselle is expecting you.'

Colette knew that she should rise to her feet and walk across the room to greet him, but she stayed where she was, on the floor in front of the fire, and drew her loose gown more closely around her. She should behave as though she was offering nothing more than a favour to a young man whom she admired for himself alone; there must be no hint of the fact that he paid for all this luxury and had every right to enjoy whatever he chose from her. She must believe that she was, for the moment, the most desirable courtesan in Paris, and Charles was fortunate to be able to afford some of her time.

But that was not how she felt. Sitting here, on the

soft rug, she felt very young and inexperienced. When she heard the salon doors open, she hesitated a moment before looking up. She saw Charles's eyes fixed on her. He stepped towards her, then stood waiting for her permission to join her. She smiled up at him, and waved the little brass fork. 'Do you like chocolate, Monsieur?' she asked, and held out a second piece to the fire.

He knelt on the rug beside her and took the fork from her hand. When it was toasted, he checked it carefully before offering it to her, his face flushed with pleasure. She ate half and handed it back to him. He sucked the rest off the fork and swallowed. He kissed the back of her hand, and she gave a small smile. He was gentle, and his lips felt warm and comforting on her skin, but his touch did not thrill her. She wondered if it ever would.

He was a very charming young man; his soft brown hair was caught in a satin band at the nape of his neck, and his eyes were warm and lively. Now they glowed with an excitement she found it hard to share and she toyed nervously with the tasselled end of her sash. Charles lifted her hand again, and now his lips caressed the delicate skin on the inside of her wrist. It was a delicious, very gentle sensation that she knew and enjoyed. Gilles often kissed her there, and was aware that she adored his gentle touch. From her wrist, Gilles' lips would move to the faint pulse at the base of her throat, and instinctively she raised her head, exposing the place she wanted to feel him, but Charles' head remained bent over her arm.

She wondered if he had ever been with a woman, but she knew she could not ask him. There was no point, he must have had every opportunity with the maids at his home. And now he was to move up a level. He had the money to pay for it. Charles was extraordinarily generous. And he was in love with her.

She felt quite cold as she took the last chocolate from the hot prongs of the long-handled fork. Charles gazed up at her with longing eyes. He seemed to find it hard to sit still. She knew that feeling well. But now she felt nothing. She leant forward and stroked his silky hair, letting the loose neck of her robe part slightly, so that he could see the slight curve of the top of her breasts. She could see the flush on his cheeks spread down his throat as he raised his head and stared at her. He moistened his full, red lips. She opened her mouth and touched the swell of his lower lip with the tip of her tongue. He tasted young, fresh and chocolatey. She could feel the warmth of his chest now, through the fine linen of his shirt, pressing against her barely covered breasts.

She held back, reluctant to take the initiative. It seemed that Charles expected her to offer herself to him when she was ready, and he was too polite to hurry her. Or too nervous. Colette reached out for one of the little supper dishes and held out a spoonful of artichoke mousse for him to taste. She let him savour it while she filled two glasses with champagne. He seemed to eat and drink without noticing what he was tasting, and his eyes remained fixed on the careless fastening of her gown and the pale skin which glimmered in the firelight. She wanted to eat one of the lobster claws, but knew that she was being cruel. She pushed the tray of dishes to one side and let him see the full curve of her breasts swelling above the translucent silk. Her nipples gleamed in a rosy haze through the light fabric. She had stroked them into life before his arrival, and her nervousness had stiffened them further, so that she had no need to pretend excitement.

Gilles would take her now; he would know exactly what she wanted. But Charles did not – she would have to show him. She reached down for his hand and brought it up towards her. 'Touch me, Charles,' she said, lowering her eyes. 'Put your hand here.' She held his hand over her breast and pushed it down so that the silk dipped below her nipple to leave it fully exposed. 'Hold me, Charles. I need to feel you.' She felt his fingers touch the little rosy bud and gave a little moan of relief when his lips closed around it. She liked the way his hair fell over her breast as he bent over her. She stroked it, running her fingers over the hard shape of his skull and then pressed the silky strands against her skin. Yes, that felt good.

She let him see how much it pleased her, arching her back slightly so that her body nestled into his. She allowed a soft moan to escape her lips when his kisses became insistent, and felt his fingers slowly twisting the loose sash of her gown so that the soft bow securing it parted and the slippery satin fell to the floor. She enjoyed the glow in his eyes and the barely controlled excitement which obviously swept through him. She reached out for the buttons of his shirt and slowly loosened each one. His breeches strained over the hard line of his erection, and she released him quickly, sliding the fine wool down over his thighs and allowing his penis to rise up towards her.

She wondered how long he could last until he

climaxed. She did not think it would be long. She liked the firelight flickering over them, and felt comfortable in the shadowy darkness of the salon. Her boudoir seemed too crude, too obviously alluring for their first time. She would let him take her here, in front of the fire, with their mouths tasting of chocolate and champagne, and not risk losing the fragile intimacy she had achieved.

She lay back on the rug and held out her arms to him. 'Come here, Charles,' she murmured. She heard his sharp intake of breath, and felt his hot lips cover her naked throat with kisses. She was right, he was fully erect and would not be able to control himself for long. Tonight, she would allow him to climax as soon as he entered her. He was very young and strong. After an hour's rest, she would teach him how to satisfy her.

Colette let Charles have her all to himself for a whole month. She became very fond of him, but even he could not afford all the expenses that were necessary to maintain her position. She had borrowed Gilles' carriage for her drives in the park. Now she needed her own. It seemed a good idea to give a party in her new apartment. She had been to several of the other girls' soirées; always alone, never with Charles. He would not have enjoyed their raucous amusement. But now he was forced to return to his country estate to check its safety. The Prussians were moving into eastern France, and those with property in that region no longer felt so secure. While he was away, she would entertain.

Her dining-room was newly decorated in the same silk as her boudoir, and she kept its rich, vermilion drapes closed at all times. It was a room for the night, and the contrast with her discreet, white and gold salon was intense, providing an additional frisson of interest for any man she invited to her boudoir. It amused her to play with the arrangement of the room like a stage-set, and her first party would be the perfect opportunity to show it off.

When Charles returned from the country, he had promised to take a villa for the two of them outside Paris for the hot month of August. They would be sure to have a peaceful time. Now, Colette wanted some excitement.

On the night of her party, Colette inspected the arrangements. Her dining-room looked beautiful: the room was filled with flowers, and exquisite china and glass were reflected in the huge mirrors that covered the walls from the Persian rugs on the polished rosewood floor to the ceiling, tented in vermilion silk; a colour which exactly matched the tight basque which she wore beneath the clouds of white tulle of her latest gown. Marie was beside herself with excitement and dashed around, checking the menu, irritating the chef and bothering the dancers, who were preparing in the ante-room.

Colette received her guests in her salon. Her dress suited her surroundings perfectly. It was pure white, except for the vermilion satin sash which circled her tiny waist and a faint hint of rose, where the deep tint of her petticoats coloured the flimsy tulle. Tonight she wore her pearls; her favourite rubies set aside. She looked, and behaved, like a delicate young debutante, only her manners were, if anything, more perfect, and her confidence permitted an added graciousness to her behaviour. It was the first time she had held a party in these rooms, and she was conscious of a deep glow of pleasure. She was sure that the evening would be a success.

Olympe came early and admired all the arrangements. Nothing had been left to chance. When all the twenty guests had sipped their champagne, and discussed the latest paintings at the Salon, Colette led them through the double doors to dinner.

'*Magnifique!*' The shock of the vermilion splendour of her dining-room surprised them all after the pure white and gold. A hundred candles blazed on the side-tables and reflected in the mirrors, catching fire on the polished silver and glass. She had spent the count's money well, but she was once more in debt, and in desperate need of more funds. At least one man tonight would have to pay well. She looked round her table, crowded with people she scarcely knew, all eating her perfect food and drinking the finest champagne at her expense. Or Charles'. The money he gave her, although generous, was going out faster than it came in.

Which of these men could best afford her? Colette studied them carefully. Olympe had brought neither the Baron nor her friend Edouard Kerouac. She was prepared to enjoy herself tonight, but the Baron was a jealous man. She was not free to take another permanent lover. Éloise had come with Michel. How very foolish of her, Colette thought with pleasure. Michel had always shown an obvious interest in her. Tonight she had placed him on her right side, and Éloise was far away at the other end of the table, between two lascivious merchants who had approached Colette at the theatre, but in whom she was not interested. The other women were all courtesans, more or less successful, but only one, Françoise, presented any real competition.

The wine was flowing fast. Already the men's faces were flushed, and Colette felt the heat of Michel's body as he sat beside her. She would not let the windows be opened. Tonight she wanted to build up the heady atmosphere of indulgence in this room, and her excitement grew as the heat mounted. She adjusted the frill over her breasts. In her favourite style, the sheer layers above her waist became increasingly transparent as they rose higher, and her tiny, vermilion basque left her breasts completely bare. Demure at first sight, the white tulle made little attempt to cover her nakedness, and Colette made quite sure that Michel could see exactly how little there was between him and the ripe swell of her full breasts. She let one finger slip inside the outer layer of sheer tulle and lowered it an inch, turning towards him as she did so. 'Is the wine to your satisfaction?' she murmured, leaning slightly forward.

He looked straight at her chest and smiled. Then he raised his glass and looked her full in the eyes. 'Everything tonight pleases me, Mademoiselle,' he said. 'You have fulfilled all the promise you showed last spring. I drink to your success.' He drained his glass and lifted the curl of hair over her ear. 'And to my share in that success,' he whispered. 'Do not deny me that pleasure any longer.'

Colette felt her thighs part automatically as a surge of pure lust pulsed through her. Charles was only a boy; this was a man who could satisfy every demand of her body. She wanted him then, but she pressed her legs together and maintained her composure. She was here to arouse him, not to give herself for nothing. But he had already been generous with his flowers; she was sure it was he who sent the extravagant displays which gave her so much pleasure. She thanked him, but was surprised when he denied any knowledge of them. She tried to cover up her mistake by placing her hand lightly on the muscled curve of his thigh. She surprised him with her next words. 'I have arranged a little entertainment,' she said. 'I hope it will amuse you.'

The sound of a gypsy violin drifted in from the corridor. Two black-haired dancers, a man and a woman, stepped out from behind a lacquered screen in a corner of the room. Slowly, twining their bodies together, they began to dance to the rhythm of the music, moving faster as the tempo quickened. The girl was a beauty, with almond-shaped eyes framed by lustrous, dark lashes. She arched her slim back defiantly, bending away from the man as she danced, teasing him, before she writhed provocatively against his body.

Colette could feel her guests responding to the pulsing beat. Michel had ceased to eat the exquisite filet of beef on his plate, and had pushed his chair back so that he could watch the pair twine their bodies together.

The girl had opened the man's shirt so that the dark hair which grew so thickly on his chest was exposed to the watchers. She slipped her long, scarlet nails inside the folds of silk and openly caressed his darkened nipples. Colette saw Michel stir uncomfortably in his seat, and was confident that he was fully aroused. She had no intention of easing his discomfort for some time. Her dancers slowed their rhythm as the girl's head bent over the man's body. Her strong white teeth flashed in the candle-light as she took his tiny, hard nipple between them. The man shuddered as her mouth descended slowly over his belly until she caught the fastening of his skin-tight trousers between her teeth and tore it loose.

His penis jerked forward, a stiff column of dark flesh rising powerfully from a nest of thick, black curls. The girl flashed her teeth again and ran her tongue slowly over her full, red lips. She took the swollen stem between her fingers and stroked it gently. The man groaned and grasped her shoulders, pulling her towards him. Colette saw the gleam of moisture on Michel's upper lip, and allowed her hand to rest on the top of his thigh. He tensed immediately and half rose in his seat, but she pressed gently on the hard muscle and motioned to him to remain where he was.

Olympe was openly caressing Paul, whose eyes were fixed on her ample breasts, and whose attention was now diverted from the couple on the dancefloor. She allowed the top of her gown to slip slightly over one shoulder, so that even more of her creamy skin was exposed. Paul reached out his hand and stroked the full swell of one perfect breast. Olympe never took her eyes from the rigid stem of the male dancer. Colette knew that her friend was aroused by the sight of the writhing couple, as she was herself, but neither she nor Olympe could permit themselves to show too much excitement. Tonight they must allow their chosen amours to believe that all their arousal was due to the powers of their lovers. Michel's erection was obvious beneath the perfectly cut wool of his

188

trousers, and he made no attempt to hide it from her. The linen tablecloth fell in thick folds down to the floor, and Colette knew that she could relieve him without any of her other guests being aware. Their attention was fixed on the couple on the floor. But she wanted Michel to wait for her and had no intention of depriving herself of the pleasure of his pent-up desire.

Suddenly the gypsy man turned towards the centre of the room. His penis rose magnificently in front of him, and his hard lips curved in a triumphant smile. He knew the envy he aroused in the men, and the excitement of the women. He held out his arms to Colette's guests and turned slowly from side to side, letting them see the full extent of his erection. Françoise licked her lips and rose from the table, glancing at Colette, who nodded calmly. Françoise's cheeks were flushed with more than champagne as she walked unsteadily across the silk rugs towards the now motionless dancer. When she reached him, he pulled her hard against him with one swift movement and bent her body sharply backwards so that he was pressing against the full skirt of her gown. Then he lifted the floating layers and placed his hand over the exposed flesh of her sex. She moaned and seemed to melt in his arms. Gently he lowered her on to the silk rug and released the fastenings of her gown so that it slipped to the floor, revealing her lace stockings and her neat triangle of blonde curls. Françoise made no attempt to hide her lust. She reached up for the man and guided his thick stem between her waiting sex lips.

The room was silent now as they watched the gigantic column sink into the rose-pink flower of her sex and withdraw, glistening with beads of creamy juice. Françoise groaned as he pulled out of her, and cupped his taut buttocks with her hands, forcing the massive length of his penis deep inside her again.

The gypsy girl watched impassively, eyeing the men at the table with a steady gaze. Colette had given her strict instructions as to which men she could approach, and now the girl advanced towards one of the merchants who had failed to arouse Olympe. Colette increased her pressure on Michel's thigh and let the tips of her fingers press gently on the hot tip of his erection. Her gown had slipped slightly so that a layer of vermilion lace showed just above the frills of white tulle, hinting at the less than demure style of her undergarments. Michel was already fully aroused; Colette knew that if she waited any longer, he would be unable to control the force of his desire. She lifted her hand from his swollen penis, signalled to him to follow her and rose from the table. No one took any notice of their departure from the room, all eyes were on the girl who now rested her naked buttocks on the merchant's lap. She had opened her blouse to reveal the heavy swell of her dark breasts, with their rich brown nipples and wide expanse of her swollen areolae surrounding them.

Colette led Michel down the panelled corridor to her boudoir. As they passed the second bedroom, they heard Olympe's cries of encouragement to her lover, and Colette felt a shiver of anticipation run through her. She had wanted Michel for months. Now she was sure that he was hers.

He was breathing heavily as he closed the door behind them. 'No more teasing,' he said thickly, as

190

he pulled the fragile bodice down to her waist, and reached out to feel her breasts. He pushed her back on to the bed and lifted her skirts. As always, she was bare beneath her lacy petticoats. She felt him release his engorged penis from the tight barrier of his evening trousers and lower himself over her without troubling to remove his clothes.

She felt the hot, stiff shaft that she had fondled earlier push into her sex, and parted her thighs to take him deeper into her, as impatient as he was to couple with him. 'What do you want?' he gasped as he thrust harder. 'A carriage, a glossy black carriage with a couple of horses?'

She opened her lips as his mouth pressed down on hers, and felt him drive into her as his passion hardened. He jerked up his head and reared over her, staring at her naked breasts above the tight, boned basque. She felt the hard stem of his lust fill her sex, and moaned incoherently as he came faster into her and neared his climax.

'Jewels, Colette,' he panted. 'I can give you jewels.'

She clutched the black wool of his evening suit as she trembled with the first wave of her orgasm. He cried out as he felt her come, and jerked hard into her as he climaxed.

'Jewels,' he muttered as he buried his face between her breasts. 'All the jewels you can wear.'

Charles was away longer than she had expected, and Colette was glad of Michel's attendance on her. The carriage, the horses, and the jewels were all of the highest quality, and she was more than happy to gratify his sexual demands. He accompanied her to the theatre, much to Éloise's irritation, and out to expensive dinners. She enjoyed his company and the intensity of his desire for her.

But she still had no clue as to who sent her the continuous supply of exotic wild flowers that arrived at her apartment and exasperated Michel. Finally, she filled her balconies with them and sat in front of the open doors breathing in their country scent, while the city sweltered in the summer heat around her and the Prussians advanced to the north and to the east.

Colette knew success. She was the sensation of Paris – for the moment. Charles still paid the rent on her apartment, and Michel's generosity was unlimited, but, as Anne had taught her, Colette kept other men firmly by her side. She was in demand, and she intended to take full advantage of it.

Invitations crowded her mantelpiece, all on stiff, gilt-edged, white cardboard, just a little larger, and more flamboyant, than any from the society ladies. Colette and her friends were totally excluded from that rank. But the evenings were fun; she would drop in for an hour or two, drink champagne, consider adding to her waiting list of lovers and leave, without committing herself.

For the first time in her life, she felt truly secure.

And sometimes, driving in the Bois, she saw Anne, happy in Gilles' company. She did not have the heart to ask Anne to risk her happiness by telling Gilles about Victor. It was better left alone, an unfortunate incident that she was lucky to have escaped from so lightly.

In mid-July, when the weather was at its hottest, an invitation arrived for her on a heavy gold card, stamped out in the shape of a fish. In a striking

192

aquamarine script, Antoinette de la Trave requested her company at her house on the Champs Élysées. There was to be a ball, and all guests were required to wear costume and to arrive with their identity concealed behind a mask. Colette stared at the flowing words engraved on the invitation. No respectable woman would invite a courtesan to her home. A masked ball! She was filled with curiosity. The invitation stayed in the drawer of her desk until she decided to accept. Then she placed it on her mantelpiece in front of all the others. Michel would accompany her, but she planned to keep the details of her costume a secret, even from him, although she would arrange for her bill to be sent to him.

Colette longed to see inside the house that was the talk of Paris. And, more than that, she wanted to meet Antoinette de la Trave.

Anne was shocked when she heard that she had been invited. 'My dear, you must decline the invitation. You cannot go to that party. No respectable woman will talk to you.'

'Their husbands are usually delighted to do so!'

Anne gave her a sharp glance. 'You are one of the best-paid courtesans in Paris now, Colette. Your lovers have a position to maintain. Do not go too far.'

'Michel has agreed to take me there.'

'That was not difficult. He does anything you ask. But be careful, Colette. Antoinette de la Trave does nothing without a reason. And she has no cause to love you. You must be very careful of her. And you must not go to her house.'

Colette ran her fingers over the smooth edge of a

gilded card on Anne's mantelpiece. 'And you? Will you be there?'

Anne turned away in some embarrassment. 'I will go with Gilles.'

'And you tell me not to go? Surely it is you who should be careful of Madame de la Trave?' She felt a deep pain which surprised her. Surely she could not be jealous of Anne.

'Antoinette has no cause to be jealous of me. Maybe she resents your youth. One never knows with her. You can be sure she has planned something, Colette, or you would not have received an invitation. I advise you not to go.'

Colette stood up. This time she would not accept Anne's advice. What harm could Madame do to her? And she was by now sure that no one knew of her night in Argnon. It was not the sort of thing a young man would tell his mother. She had been sent an invitation, and her costume was ordered. Anne was worrying unnecessarily.

Chapter Ten

Gold was not her colour. Nor was white. For the past week, Colette had devoted all her energy to arranging a costume that would create a sensation; and one that would keep her identity secret for as long as she chose. Michel wanted to accompany her to the ball, and he had promised to pay Monsieur Worth's account. Colette spent more on one ensemble than she had imagined possible. She promised Monsieur Worth that she would wear it exactly as he suggested; he was the king of Paris couturiers, and she had confidence in his judgement.

Now the outfit hung in her dressing-room, giving her a thrill each time she saw its glittering sliver of silver-spangled gauze. Once again she felt a shiver of fear that this time she might have gone too far. It was daring, but Monsieur Worth had assured her that a costume like this would be perfectly acceptable. 'You must shine, Mademoiselle, you must shine.' Still, she had never worn anything so revealing; the slim-fitting breeches were fashioned so that she could walk and dance with ease, but with her legs together they looked exactly like a fishtail, with gauze frills fanning around her feet. None of her lovers had seen her like this; in public she tried to be demure and ladylike as Anne had trained her to be. Now she longed to shock and besides, the close-fitting skull-cap and mask would prevent anyone from recognising her.

Colette had dismissed Anne's fears from her mind. This was the first invitation she had received to a society occasion. Olympe had been invited by one of her lovers, and Anne would be there herself with Gilles. How could anyone possibly harm her? It would be the perfect opportunity to show all Paris that she was becoming one of the first rank of courtesans. She and Olympe and Éloise. Her only problem was that Charles had returned and expected her to be his guest. How could she refuse? She had seen so little of him lately. On this occasion Michel would have to take second place. It was Charles who paid her rent.

Above all else, Colette wanted to meet Antoinette de la Trave. Until now, she had only caught a glimpse of the lady as she drove through the Bois in the afternoons. The distinctive cream landau passed along the avenues regularly at the same hour each day, but Madame de la Trave was always hidden behind silk blinds which shut out the sun and obscured any sight of its occupant. Her house was the talk of Paris; it was the most new extravagant mansion in the city, second only to that of the great courtesan La Paiva. And because Antoinette de la Trave was Gilles' wife, her place in society was assured, even if she was only the daughter of a Lyons silk-merchant. A very rich silk-merchant.

Tonight there was only one event in Paris to which everyone desired an invitation. The ball was the highlight of the season. Colette waited impatiently for the hours to pass until it was due to start. At eleven o'clock precisely, she was dressed and ready for Charles to collect her. She checked her appearance in a mirror and was satisfied. A stiff gauze cape swirled around her, covering the most revealing part of her costume, and her face and hair were completely hidden. For the moment, she looked both mysterious and discreet.

Charles' carriage took her slowly down the Champs Élysées, following a long line of guests making their way towards the Rond-Point, where Madame's house occupied a prominent position. Colette had seen it from the outside many times during her afternoon drives. Now, from this distance, she could see the light from a thousand luminous balloons illuminating the night sky. They drew nearer, and entered the wide sweep of a curved drive, blocked now with landaus, barouches, snorting horses and footmen who held open the carriage doors and assisted the extravagantly clad guests from their satin-lined interiors.

Colette held Charles' arm and walked up with him to the top of a flight of stone steps and into the great hall of the mansion. The light from a long line of glittering chandeliers dazzled her and flashed on the sparkling jewels of the guests who crowded up to a ballroom at the top of the main staircase. Colette kept her light cloak over her costume, but all around her she saw even more scantily-clad, semi-exposed bodies. She gained one or two admiring glances, and she could sense an interest in uncovering her identity, but at this stage in the evening no one would reveal themselves.

The stairs led up to a massive, glass-walled ballroom built out on to a terrace on the first floor. Inside its transparent walls hundreds of dancers circled the room, their images reflected in the glittering glass as they swayed in time to the music of a string orchestra playing in one corner of the room. Colette longed to dance, and to join the crowd.

Charles had disapproved of her costume. Now he ran his hands over her body beneath the gauze folds of the cloak. In keeping with the theme of the sea, he had come dressed as Neptune, but he presented a distinctly un-godlike figure.

'I am at your command, god of the sea,' Colette murmured, letting her cloak float out behind her to expose her skin-tight sequins.

He looked concerned, and glanced round the room. 'You look very beautiful tonight,' he acknowledged, seeming to gain confidence from the admiring eyes fixed on Colette. 'But I prefer to see your face and your beautiful hair.'

She stared up at him. It was important to her to have his support tonight, and she loved being with him again, but she wanted to keep her identity secret for a while longer. The invitation had been clear on that point. Guests were instructed to conceal their faces. She moved slightly closer, so that her fish scales pressed against his body, and felt his heart beating faster against her chest. She knew that he sensed her to be different tonight; normally with him she was shy and gentle. She had grown wilder while he had been away. Tonight, she felt that everything could be as it had been between them.

She began to tease him gently. 'My face and hair are hidden from everyone here,' she said. 'Later, my Lord Neptune, when we are alone, you may remove each covering layer. I will be yours to use as you wish.' She reached up and kissed him through the thin barrier of her mask, then she moved away. She did not want to make him too eager, so that he would want to leave now. This ball was nothing special for him, but for her it was the most exciting evening of her life. Gilles had never taken her anywhere like this.

At the far end of the ballroom, she noticed someone watching her closely. She pretended not to notice. For the moment she wanted to give all her attention to Charles, and do nothing to embarrass him. But he had drifted away from her side, and before she could look for him, the man who had been studying her caught her arm. 'Mademoiselle, you look enchanting. My son has shown taste.'

The man was tall, like Charles but, unlike him, had features distinguished by decades of authority. He led her to a table and poured a glass of champagne. 'Will you drink with me, Colette?'

So her disguise was useless. Or was it only Charles' father who had seen through her efforts at concealment? She smiled up at him, surprised that he should acknowledge her, let alone offer her wine. 'I would be delighted,' she said.

'My son is in love with you.'

She nodded. There was no point in denying the truth. 'Do you object, Monsieur?'

He shook his head. 'He is a lucky young man. I

199

have checked your history, of course. One can always trust Gilles' taste, and to be the first after such a man is a privilege. But why did you leave Monsieur de la Trave so quickly, Mademoiselle? And why were you so foolish as to accept an invitation tonight from Antoinette?'

She caught her breath. It was a second warning. She felt herself thrown off-balance, and sipped her champagne to allow herself time to think. She had been stupid to come here if the whole world knew that Madame de la Trave wished her harm. She was in danger of making a fool of herself and risking all her future. Suddenly the charmed life which had seemed to open so easily before her felt precarious.

She remembered the girls in the village who had teased her when she was gauche and spent her time reading books. When they had envied her relationship with Victor, she had felt redeemed. Then she had won Gaston, the best catch in the village, and they had shown their jealousy of her. From that moment she had learnt that men would always appreciate her, while women were often sharp towards her. She looked up at the aristocratic father of her lover.

'Monsieur, I live in Paris now. Madame de la Trave's home is in Italy. She invited me here while she visits her house in my city. I thought I should accept.' She stared straight into his eyes and removed her mask. 'Do you think I should be afraid to show my face here?'

The lean features broke into a smile. 'It is possible, Mademoiselle, that for once, Antoinette may have met her match. There are many who would be glad of it. Permit me to add myself to your list of admirers.' He kissed her hand lightly. 'However,' he added, 'please do not expect that my wife will be so delighted to make your acquaintance.' He picked up her silver-sequinned mask from the table. 'Wear this a little longer, Mademoiselle. Entrance us with your mystery. But forgive me if I take my son home early tonight. This may be an evening to remember, but it will be a little strong for him. If all goes well – ' she felt his lips touch her skin again ' – if all goes well, he will be your devoted chevalier once again.'

'If.' The doubt in his words chilled her. She began to realise just how serious Antoinette de la Trave's threat to her position was. Perhaps she, too, should leave early, with Charles. She had come to the ball; she had seen how society entertained, and she knew that she could take her place in it. But not tonight, not with so many warnings hanging over her, from people who seemed to be her friends.

She made her way out on to the landing above the great staircase, looking for Charles. Below her, the hall was thronged with guests arriving. Footmen were scurrying around the vast space, carrying mounds of silk and satin jackets and capes. Only Olympe was clearly recognisable, her plump ivory shoulders almost bare, her golden hair flowing unchecked down to her waist, barely covered by the golden casing of a mermaid's tail which floated to the floor. Beside her was Edouard Kerouac. His concession to costume was slight; he wore a full white shirt, worn fisherman's trousers, and carried a net slung over one broad shoulder. His face was obscured by a plain blue mask, but Colette saw that his dark eyes glittered recognisably and were fixed on her.

She saw him point her out to Olympe as they climbed the staircase. Olympe shrieked with delight, and hugged her. 'I would never have recognised you. What a delicious outfit.'

'Does Charles approve?' the tall man questioned.

She shrugged. 'Michel paid for it. I think he feels his expenditure was justified.'

The man smiled, his full lips revealing strong white teeth, but there was no hint of warmth in the glint of eye visible behind his mask. He was a strange companion for Olympe, Colette thought, and almost immediately the courtesan was surrounded by her usual coterie of rich lovers, and swept away. Colette was left alone with Edouard. 'Don't you mind?' she asked.

'Mind what? That Olympe plies her trade? We are friends, Colette. Little more.'

'You look after her. She has told me how much she values your friendship.'

'I look after all my friends.' He gestured towards a sea-god making its way towards them. 'One of your lovers seems to be returning. It is time I left you. Enjoy your evening, Colette, but take care.'

Apparently everyone was trying to warn her about Antoinette de la Trave! Delighted that Charles had not left as early as his father had suggested, she accepted the flute of champagne which he offered her and savoured the perfection of the vintage golden bubbles. Madame de la Trave was sparing no expense. Colette forgot her doubts; she was thrilled to be part of this world.

'Please dance with me,' she asked.

Charles looked pleased. 'Does the god of the sea dance with a fish?' he asked playfully.

She twisted in his arms and let him see the full

outline of her body beneath the scales. 'He may do anything he pleases,' she said. 'That is what being a god means.'

She felt the eyes of the crowd watching her as she circled the floor together. Her disguise meant nothing now; all Paris knew that she was Charles' lover. The older women took one sly glance out of the corner of their eyes; the men took their time, assessing her body, her charms, and envying the young man. She loved the interest she saw in their eyes, and those of the women. The younger ones had no reason to be jealous of her, not if they were rich and well-bred. Charles would soon be looking for a wife, and however much he was in love with her, however much his father approved of her as his son's mistress, she was no threat to any potential alliance.

And then she would have to look for another protector. This was not the place to let her need be known, but she could not prevent herself studying the room. She saw Edouard, standing alone by the fountain. If only a man like that would offer to support her, she thought she would feel secure; as Olympe said, a man like that had no need to pay for a woman's body.

He had said that he and Olympe were friends. Would he be her friend now? Quickly she turned away, shocked by the intensity of the desire that flooded through her. It seemed that it was not only as a friend that she wanted him!

She clung to Charles' arm. 'I am hungry, darling,' she said. 'Can we eat?'

They reached the dining-room on the ground floor, by leaving the glass ballroom and descending a flight of stone steps down to the garden. In the centre of the paved terrace at the foot of the stairs, a fountain sprayed silver jets of water into an artificial lake where six swans, their feathers tipped with gold leaf, glided gracefully through the ruffled water. In the dining-room, carved ice models of the same birds guarded long tables laden with food. Coral lobsters emerged from frozen ice grottoes and waved their trailing claws helplessly into the air. Red mullet lay filleted on a bed of sea-green samphire and, beside an ornamental stand of empty oyster shells, a heap of pearls glistened between the fresh petals of a full-blown rose. Charles took a pearl between his fingers and laid it on Colette's palm. 'Take it,' he said. 'It's real. Antoinette has a gift for extravagance.'

There was a tiny hole bored through the centre of the pearl, as if it had once been prepared for a necklace. Colette slipped it into the pocket of her cloak and grinned. Was this what Madame de la Trave had done with her gift from Gilles? Her desire to meet Antoinette increased.

Charles was becoming impatient. She could feel his eagerness as they danced, and was sure that he wanted her to leave with him now. She could not bear to go so soon. The ball was only just coming fully to life. The most fashionable guests were arriving, and still she had not met Madame de la Trave.

She felt a hand on her arm and saw the looming figure of a giant hawk tower over her. Startled, she looked round for Charles, but he had gone. It was a relief to hear Michel's deep voice, even if he was angry with her. 'You look magnificent,' she laughed. 'Why didn't you tell me what you would be wearing?'

'Since your own costume was a secret, I saw no reason to do so,' he growled. 'Eventually, I recognised you because of your companion. I'm glad to see that he has finally left you alone for a moment.'

Colette felt guilty. Michel had paid for her silver spangles after all, and she did feel wonderful in the costume now. She slipped the cape off her shoulders, and twirled in front of him. 'What do you think?' she asked. 'Is it good enough?'

He put a taloned claw round her waist. 'That depends on who is going to see most of it,' he said. 'Are you going to dance with me at all tonight?'

'Of course. Let's go up now.' She tried to find Charles, to tell him, but he had disappeared. She followed Michel out into the hall. The crowd was now so thick that she struggled to keep up with him, and it seemed impossible to fight their way up the main staircase. She caught hold of his feathered arm. 'We can go by the stairs from the garden,' she said. 'Come with me.'

Silver horns of light swung from the branches of the trees nearest the house, and were reflected in the water of the lake. The music from the upstairs ballroom could be heard clearly out here, and Michel took her in his arms. She could feel the sharp claws at the end of his fingers pulling at the threads of her costume and kept very still. 'I want to dance with you out here,' he said, 'alone.' He shook his hands out of the harsh talons and stroked the flimsy gauze covering her breasts as he led her further away from the house. He pressed her back against the smooth trunk of a silver birch and lifted her face towards his. She could feel his fingers fumbling with the row of little hooks down her back and pushed him away. She did not want him

205

to make love to her now, and certainly not here! She wished she had not let him come so close or touch her so intimately. She knew that he had aroused her more than she wanted and that her body had quickly responded to him. Now he stood a little away from her, breathing heavily. She was terrified that he would try again. Michel was not a man to give up easily, and he knew the effect he had on her. She moved quickly behind the tree and ran towards the house.

Now this staircase was crowded too, and she could see Michel close to her. She ran back through the trees to the far end of the garden to escape the crush, and rested for a moment in a secluded corner. A barrier of delicate wrought-iron marked the boundary between the dark streets behind and Madame's garden, seeming to present no hindrance, but spiked with cruel knife-edged points barring invaders. The darkness here was oppressive. She felt weary. In a moment, she would go back into the house and hope that Charles had not left, and would take her home. She did not want to go with Michel now, and she could hardly walk the streets in search of a hackney carriage, looking like this.

The house was still a blaze of light and there was a perceptible tension in the air; the musicians were playing at a slower tempo, and the crowd had spilled out on to the terrace and were looking down on to the garden. Beside the stairs, Colette could see two mirrored doors opening to reveal an alcove decorated like a flowing river, with more mirrors lining the walls and floor. At one side a cluster of dancers, with dresses and caps like swans, surrounded a bank of tall willows and one single swan.

They moved apart, and the swan raised its head. There was a flutter of applause, the swan shook off its head-dress and Madame de la Trave acknowledged her guests. So this was Gilles' wife. Colette saw a woman of medium height, with a fine pink and white complexion and glorious golden curls which cascaded down the creamy bare expanse of her beautiful back. Golden sequins, caught on to net so fine that they appeared to float unaided over her flesh, glittered over her shoulders and spilled out over the delicate drift of her tulle skirt. Colette remembered the exquisite portrait at the château. Twenty years after that portrait was painted, Antoinette de la Trave was still a beautiful woman.

Fascinated, Colette lingered in the shadows of the trees. She found herself unwilling to leave; her attention was held fully by Antoinette de la Trave. No longer did she think of her only as Gilles' wife. This was Victor's mother, and every feature of his face was apparent in the woman's lush beauty. Then she turned to go. She could find someone to take her home now. She had seen all she wanted. She scarcely heard the soft footsteps which crossed the lawn towards her – Madame de la Trave was almost beside her before she looked up. She held out a glass of champagne. 'I do not like my guests to be without wine,' she said. 'Won't you stay with us a little longer? I have a small group of friends who are eager to meet you. I had foolishly promised them your presence, and now they feel deprived. You won't deny me the honour of satisfying my guests, will you?'

Colette followed the pale figure through the trees,

faintly lit now by the first rays of dawn, seeming darker nearer the house, where the lanterns still blazed, blocking out the morning light. An elegant curve of stone stairs swept down to the lower regions of the mansion and she blindly followed the glittering figure of Madame. As she lifted her skirts, Colette saw her legs encased in fine black leather boots, reaching high up her legs. The slim ankles, with full calves, delicate knees and long, fine thighs, were outlined by the glove-smooth leather and accentuated by delicate bands which criss-crossed her thighs.

Above them, Colette could see the throng of guests, their glasses glittering in the blaze of lantern light. She needed to know what this woman wanted from her. It interested her more than anything else in her life at this moment. She followed Madame de la Trave through a wide stone arch at the top of the staircase, and entered into the depths of the house.

The area at the foot of the stairs was as brightly lit as the rest of the house, and full of guests. Colette was disappointed. She had hoped to have the opportunity to talk privately. Madame led the way through the throng; men parted on either side of her, but they closed in around Colette and she felt their fingers brushing against her bare arms and stroking the sheer gauze covering her legs. She looked at them angrily. Madame laughed. 'Leave them. They won't hurt you.'

At the far end of the open space, between two marble pillars, there was a narrow door of beaten bronze, exquisitely carved. As Madame approached, she ran her fingers lightly over the carving and the door swung open. She gestured to Colette to follow her, and they both entered a narrow passage. The door closed behind them, shutting out the sound of voices outside. In here there was an eerie silence. They were in a small corridor, quite bare, with a door at the end matching the one through which they had entered. As before, Madame stroked a pattern on the bronze. This time Colette heard a faint metallic sound as it swung open, and a soft hum of low voices. She followed Madame into a dimly lit cavern, shadowed by motionless figures. When her eyes became accustomed to the gloom, she saw that she was deep in the cellars of the mansion, in a room where the walls were of bare stone and the floor of beaten earth. It smelled dank and felt cold after the heat of the glittering rooms above.

The only light came from two blazing torches, held high in the air by a couple of tall, black men, bare to the waist, and covered only by a narrow strip of black leather hiding their sex. They carried their monstrous flames without a flicker of movement, and seemed to ignore the crowd around them.

The room was full of party-goers, all in costume, but it seemed that they had been well-prepared for this particular stage of the evening, for they were all dressed in similar, diaphanous black robes, as if they belonged to some archaic religious order. Colette felt conspicuous in her shimmering, skintight sequinned leotard, as it reflected flashes of light from the blazing torches. She was aware of an absence of sound in the room and an expectancy, as though everyone had been waiting for this moment.

She looked at the beautiful face of her hostess. Madame de la Trave showed no sign of emotion, her face was impassive as she led the way to a raised dais at the end of the room. A hard leather bench, backed against the bare stone of the walls, was piled high with large, thick cushions, and she sank down on to this and motioned to Colette to join her. Above them, hanging from the vaulted ceiling, swung the steel frame of an iron trapeze, moving as though it had recently been in use and had just been abandoned as they entered.

Two women, as nearly naked as the torchbearers, approached them, carrying tall glasses filled with a dark, red liquid. Colette saw Madame take one, and copied her. She sipped. It tasted full and fruity, and heavy after the champagne which was all that she had drunk all night. And she saw that jugs of the wine were being passed around the room, and glasses filled for the cloaked figures surrounding them.

Antoinette laid her glass down on the earth floor and glanced at one of the women, who immediately left the room through an arched doorway at their side. When she returned, she was completely naked and accompanied by three other girls, all tall, black and beautiful. They held out their hands to Antoinette and she rose from the bench and went with them to a space which had been cleared in the centre of the cellar.

Colette saw that beyond the space, a narrow stream seemed to emerge from the ground and flowed for a short distance until it disappeared again into the earth. Some form of glossy jet seemed to form a gunnel to support the stream, and now that she had seen it, she was aware of the continuous sound that had hovered at the back of her mind since she had entered the room. It was the sound of fast running water.

Antoinette de la Trave stood motionless in the centre of the room, her white gown swept aside to reveal the skin-tight, black leather covering her long, slim legs. The red-gold of her hair flashed like a sheet of flame in the torchlight. One of the girls placed her hands on top of Antoinette's head and stroked the golden curls between her fingers, arranging the mass of hair so that it covered her bare shoulders. Antoinette sank to her knees as the other girls bent over her, pulling at the fastenings which secured the front of her gown. Her bodice of white feathers fell to the floor and they carried it out of the room.

Antoinette de la Trave lay naked to the waist on the beaten earth floor of the cellar. Colette stared, fascinated, remembering the haughty young woman of the portrait in her virginal white gown, and the stiff perfection of her formal silks. Two girls returned and knelt beside her. Each one bent over Antoinette's creamy golden breasts, took one rose-red nipple between her teeth and closed her dark lips over it. Colette saw Antoinette stir for the first time, as her leather-clad legs parted.

The black leather gleamed softly in the dim light, and the tight covering seemed to accentuate the voluptuous curve of Madame's thighs. She raised one knee and Colette saw that the division between the top of her thighs had been left open to expose the creamy gold of her naked sex. Above her, between the bench where she sat and the ground where Madame lay spreadeagled, Colette saw the iron trapeze start to move again, and a figure descended on one of the rigid columns as though it were a rope, his feet curled round the metal, his hands moving steadily downwards, one after the other, until he had reached the horizontal bar. Looking up, she saw a circle of light in the ceiling and realised that he must have entered through that hole, before the light was abruptly shut out as the trapdoor closed.

The man sat on the horizontal bar, staring down at Madame, and arrogantly allowed the thick column of his erect penis to thrust out from the metal rod. Colette saw Antoinette raise her knees to her chest and part her legs to expose the full nakedness of her sex. The man smiled and let the trapeze swing softly from side to side.

Now the crowd stirred like a wave running through the sea. Their light, black gowns opened to reveal their nakedness, and they turned to the person immediately beside them and started to fondle the naked flesh in front of them. Colette saw a heaving mass of bodies entwined together, and felt isolated and alone on her hard bench, with the costume which had seemed so indecent before now covering her from head to foot in an armour which seemed to bar her from the pleasures they were experiencing.

Some of the couples were openly having inter-course in front of her. Many of the men, preferring their own sex, rode on top of their partners with increasing vigour. Madame de la Trave, her legs still covered by her tight leather leggings, turned from side to side as the girls sucked more vigor-ously at her nipples. Colette wanted to leave the cellar; she could see the bronze door at the far end of the room and she half-rose from the bench, before feeling the hand of one of the torch-bearers instantly

descend on her shoulder, pressing her back down
on to the cushions and forcing her to remain exactly
where Madame had placed her.

She wondered why she had been brought here.
Was this Madame's punishment? Was she to take
no part in this at all? She watched with increasing
envy as she saw a naked man bend between
Antoinette's thighs and slowly lick the cream from
between her legs. Antoinette was writhing now
with a slow rhythmic movement from side to side
as though she demanded more satisfaction than
they were offering her. Her amber eyes, wide open
and glittering in the torchlight, were fixed on the
man on the iron trapeze.

Colette shifted uncomfortably on her hard bench.
The sight of the erect penis, proudly jutting above
her, made her body rigid with desire. She longed
for the treatment which Antoinette was enjoying.
She, too, wanted to feel lips closing around her
aching nipples, and a tongue darting inside her
eager sex. She alone, of all the seething mass in the
dank cellar, was clothed and untouched. Beneath
her, she saw a frenzied sexual movement and heard
a collective sigh of ecstasy. She turned her head
towards one of the torchbearers and saw that he,
too, was aroused by the sight of the heaving couples. The leather binding his sex was taut with the
force of his erection, but he stood tall and unmoving
and gave no sign other than the straining constraint
that he was eager for release. She looked at the
other man. He also was swollen and struggling for
control. She ran her fingers over the damp beads
moistening her upper lip and tasted her salty sweat,
grateful that her own need was less obvious than
that of the men.

The man whose tongue had so eagerly darted inside Antoinette's sex now stood back behind her. Colette saw the full length of his penis brush over the taut black leather as he guided it between the buttocks of one of the bending girls and slowly entered her. Colette watched the trapeze start to swing and pick up speed. The man leapt off, landing lightly on his feet in front of Antoinette. He stood, legs apart, with the torchlight flickering over his naked body, his massive penis jutting, fully erect, in front of him. He stared at Colette, then turned his back on her and knelt in front of Madame. The golden curls lapped round the base of his stem, moist now with the juices from Antoinette's sex. Colette heard her gasp as he withdrew completely. She saw the glistening tip poised an inch away from the damp curls, saw the dark glitter of his eyes turn on her as his massive tool sought its target and once more plunged in again. She heard Antoinette call out this time as he entered her. Colette saw the muscles clenched on his dark buttocks and Antoinette's body shaken with the force of her climax, but still he plunged until Madame lay limp and drenched with sweat beneath him. Slowly he withdrew, still massively erect, rose to his feet and walked purposefully towards her, the creamy moisture from Antoinette's sex glistening on his penis. She shuddered, sure that he knew exactly how desperate she was to feel him inside her. She moistened her dry lips and waited. He stood in front of her, reaching out one hand towards her. She could smell the scent of Antoinette's orgasm, and see the creamy juice on him. She trembled as she felt his hands at her throat and as his long fingers slid inside the sheer sequinned silk

214

of her costume. Suddenly he pulled sharply down so that it tore to her waist and exposed her breasts, glimmering in the torchlight, her nipples painfully swollen with desire. He ran his fingers lightly over each aching breast before he took the torn fabric in both hands and ripped it sharply again so that it hung in shreds at her feet. She felt his eyes lock on to her bare, smooth mound and watched, helpless, as his dark fingers moved towards the pale flesh surrounding her inner thigh. She shuddered as she felt the tip of one finger part her labia. He slipped it lightly inside her in a tiny, delicate circle before he lifted it to his lips and sucked the taste of her off his finger. She watched the circle of his full lips close round the finger as he raised his other arm high in the air until he grasped the iron bar of the trapeze. Then he bent his arm and slowly raised himself into the air, swung his legs over the bar, and swung gently backwards and forwards. She could see the black eyes still fixed on her, and then the torches were suddenly extinguished and the room was plunged into darkness. Surely he would come now? She waited eagerly for him, longing for more than the tantalising touch of his finger inside her, but there was no sound, no movement in the room, nothing but the faint murmur of the trickling stream.

She stood up, frightened, but could see nothing in the total darkness. There was no sound of breathing; she was alone in the cellar. She felt on the floor at her feet for the costume that had been torn from her body and picked it up. There was nothing left to cover her. She could feel only slivers of fabric, and she could find no way to cover any part of her body with it. She was trapped in this horrible cellar.

How could she walk out of here, naked, even if she could feel her way to the door?

Or was the room still crowded? Were all those people waiting silently to watch her humiliation? Had Antoinette done this because she was Gilles' mistress? Or because she knew about Victor?

She saw a faint glimmer of light at the far end of the room; a glimmer which increased from the outline of a door to a shaft of light that streamed in. She stepped forward, and missed her footing on the step up to the dais, losing her balance and falling to the floor.

She looked up towards the door. As quickly as it had opened, it closed again, but now there was a light in the room. A tall figure in a long cloak held a candle in one hand. He was striding towards her. Instinctively, she cowered back, clutching the shreds of her shattered costume.

He held the candle high. She could not see his face. He called out her name. 'Colette?'

She recognised his voice. She breathed a sigh of relief, then shame. This was the man who had told her she was a fool to come here. Now he must be in no doubt. But she needed his help so badly that she had lost her pride. She scrambled up off the floor and faced him.

He took one look at her and she saw his eyes fall on the shred of fabric in her hand. He put the candle down on the earth floor and took off his cloak. 'Here,' he said. 'Put this on.'

Gratefully, she took the heavy wool cloak and put it round her shoulders. It trailed on the floor, but she was glad of its warmth and protection.

'You can tell me later what happened,' he said. 'Right now we simply need to get you out of here.'

She saw him looking at her, at the damp curls on her head. She no longer cared what she looked like. He bent in front of her and picked up her silver slippers from the floor. 'Put these on.' They were cold and damp, but no one would notice. Edouard held out his hand. 'Give me your costume,' he said. Puzzled, she handed it to him. He examined it in the candle-light, and tore a long strip, which he held up in front of her. 'Bend your head towards me.'

'Please, can we just get out of here,' she begged. Despite the warmth of the cloak, she was shivering. She wanted to be away from here as soon as she could.

'No.' She felt him lift her chin, and swiftly wrap the strip of silver sequins around her head in a turban. 'Very chic,' he said. 'Now, hold up your head. We walk out in style. Take my arm.'

She hesitated. Could she bear to face the crowd upstairs in this condition?

'Your future career will come to an end if you stay here. Is that what you want? I suggest that you leave with me now.' The voice was warm and familiar. Even in her drugged condition she felt secure.

The bright light in the hall hurt her eyes as they walked out of Madame's chamber. The cellar doors closed behind them, and they walked up the marble staircase to the great hall. The party was still in full swing. Colette found it impossible to believe that so much had happened just below this room, where the guests danced on, quite oblivious of their hostess' private pleasures.

She struggled to behave as though nothing had happened, and that she wore a gentleman's cloak for amusement. Her turban was a successful cover for her dripping hair, and the only interested glances came from ladies who wished that they were escorted by Edouard Kerouac and had borrowed his cloak. No one else seemed to pay attention to them, as if their absence had gone unnoticed, and with the extravagant costumes of the guests, it was easy to hide her rather odd ensemble. Colette felt as though she was in a different world as Edouard calmly led her up the marble staircase, through the hall and out into the crisp night air. He wrapped her cloak around her shoulders and raised his hand as one of the carriages started to move towards them. His hand was tight around her wrist. She felt bemused by champagne and desire.

He lifted her into a plain black carriage, and she sank back on to a soft leather banquette. As the horses began to move, Colette turned to look at his tall figure standing motionless at the foot of the steps. She struggled to say something to him. 'Thank you.' It was all she could manage, and her voice was faint.

'You can thank me another time.'

She stared at him. She knew that she should be grateful, but she was conscious of nothing except a deep sense of humiliation and a burning desire for him as a man.

It was nothing to do with Edouard Kerouac himself, she was sure. Any man would have made her feel as he did after her ordeal in the cellar. But another man would have stayed with her, put his arms around her and comforted her. She wanted to feel him holding her, and then she wanted him to take away this desperate ache inside her. Had he not understood how much she wanted him? Or did she disgust him?

She sank into the hot bath which Marie prepared for her. She should feel grateful to Edouard, she knew it, but all she could feel now was shame and anger.

Chapter Eleven

When she woke the next morning, Marie brought in her usual bouquet of lilies from Charles with her cup of breakfast chocolate, as though nothing had happened. Colette opened his note, and read it.

Ma chère, forgive me for leaving so early last night. Family engagements – I hope you will understand – may I see you tonight?
I adore you.   Charles

She threw the flowers on to the floor. Their green silk ribbon caught on the handle of her sugar basin, and scattered white crystals all over the rosewood floor. *Merde*! Her head ached, and the rich smell of the chocolate sickened her. No – she would not see Charles this evening. After last night she could not bear to do so.

She pushed her drink aside, and buried her face in her hands. Edouard had saved her reputation last night, but how long did she have before the truth was known? Perhaps already word had spread about her humiliation. She might even now be the centre of scandal, despite Edouard's intervention.

If Charles learnt about the scene in the cellar, he would have nothing more to do with her. And Michel was already angry. If they ceased to pay her bills, she would be ruined. She was in debt already; her box at the Vaudeville had cost too much, and she had spent far more than she had been given on her gowns. Everyone had been eager to offer her credit. They all thought she had a glittering future. And it had been important to set herself up properly – they had all said so.

Olympe spent far more than she did. But Olympe had a single lover, and the Baron paid all her bills. Colette was not in that position. She knew only too well that while there were other courtesans like Anne, who ended their careers rich and respected, they were few. Most spent every penny they possessed on keeping up appearances, started to borrow when their lovers lost interest and ended up in debt. After last night that prospect seemed all too close. Colette had almost lost everything.

It was the almost the end of July. The rent, which Charles paid every month in advance, would be a problem in a few weeks. She had no money to pay it. Every penny had been spent. And if she sold any of her jewels, the word would soon spread and she would be finished.

Olympe would know all the gossip. Whatever had been said last night, Olympe would know.

She dressed quickly, trying to repair the ravages of the night before. Then she paced her room for half an hour. Olympe would not be up yet; she would sleep even later than usual after last night. Colette thought about what had happened. Would it have been so terrible if Edouard had not rescued her? And then she knew that it would. How could she have left the cellar without his help? She could not have walked out naked into the streets even if she had waited until the ball was at an end. None of Madame's servants would have offered her anything to cover herself with. They would not have dared to disobey their mistress. Antoinette would have humiliated her, just as Victor had done at Argnon.

But how had Edouard understood her danger? And why had he gone to so much trouble to rescue her? Did he want to add himself to her circle of lovers? Or to become an *amant de coeur*? Before he came to see her again, as she was sure he would, she must see Olympe and find out more about Edouard Kerouac.

Colette's impatience grew, and she called her carriage. Anything would be better than waiting here; she would drive round the park and try to sort out her mind. Then she would see Olympe and hear the gossip, no matter how bad it was. There was nothing else she could do.

Even after her drive, she was early. The maid showed her into Olympe's salon and offered her a biscuit and a glass of wine. 'Mademoiselle has a gentleman with her, but she will not be long. Will you wait?' she asked.

The salon was full of sunlight at this early hour in the morning, with the curtains drawn, and the bright light of day shining boldly through. It was a room usually only seen in the evening, with candles blazing, and laughter and music. It seemed bare now, and empty.

Colette wondered who was with Olympe. It was unusual for her lover to stay overnight. At this hour she was normally alone, or asleep. it could only be her *amant de coeur*. Perhaps Edouard Kerouac had returned with her after the ball. Colette felt restless. She did not want to meet him again so soon, especially not now, when she was unprepared, and the situation would be awkward. She needed to find out if he was here.

She could not understand him. He seemed to know exactly what was happening last night, and yet she had no idea why he had gone to so much trouble to help her. He should have looked out of place at the ball: his costume had been so plain; his behaviour so calm and quiet. And yet he had radiated an air of authority: the most influential men had sought him out and deferred to him; women had flocked round him, apparently finding the simplicity of his costume and his bare chest as attractive as she had.

She drew in a deep breath. Yes, she had found him attractive. He had reassured her in the same way that Gaston had done in Argnon. He felt familiar and secure. And now he was probably a few metres away from her, in bed with Olympe. It would be better if she left now and returned when Olympe was alone.

There were two doors out of this room. One led out into the hall. She could walk down the staircase and order her carriage to drive her once more round the park while she waited. Or she could take the other door, creep down the corridor to Olympe's private rooms and find out who was there. Colette knew that she should leave, but the lure was irresistible. She put her hand on the gilt door-knob, twisted it softly, and slipped into the darkened corridor. At its end was a small ante-chamber, outside Olympe's boudoir. Colette stepped into the room, placing her feet softly on the carpet so that she would make no sound. She felt ashamed of her behaviour, but she had to know. The memory of Edouard's hands on her shoulders, as he led her away, made her shiver.

A heavy curtain separated Olympe's bedroom from the rest of the apartment. Colette knew it well; she had often sat in there and talked with Olympe about their lovers. Now she could hear the couple on the bed through the curtain. Unable to prevent herself, she stepped closer until she could just see through the join in the drapes. Olympe lay naked on the bed; a man, half-dressed, was with her, hidden in the shadows. Colette drew back. She could not see who it was.

She wanted to let the heavy fabric fall, to stop looking, but she felt paralysed. She could not move from here. Was it the man whose hands had rested on her shoulders last night? The man who had so calmly covered her with his cloak and led her out of the cellar? What a fool she was to think that he had any interest in her. Colette did not underestimate her charms, but she knew that she was no match for Olympe. The perfect shoulders, the neck like a wounded swan, the golden hazel eyes. And Olympe was always to be seen with Edouard.

She turned and walked out of the room and back to the salon, breathing heavily. She sat down by the window and tried to concentrate, but the same thought kept churning through her mind. She could not leave here until she had learnt what had been said about her last night.

She had almost given up when Olympe walked in, smoothing down her dress and smiling with the flush of perfect health. She is in love, Colette thought, looking at her. She does not just do this for the money. She felt a wave of jealousy, as sickening as the despair that filled her mind. She had only ever wanted the money, and the security. For a while Gilles had made her believe that it was him she wanted. And then Victor. But she recovered. She knew what a fool she had been and had made sure that she would not risk that again.

Olympe flung herself down on the vermilion damask sofa. 'Darling, why are you here so early? Surely you too are tired after last night?' She stifled a yawn, then she grinned. 'No, you are right. It is not the ball which has exhausted me.'

'Have I disturbed you, Olympe? Was this a bad time to come?'

Olympe grinned and shook her head. 'No, it was time the Baron left.'

'I thought Edouard was with you.'

Olympe led her to the sofa. She laughed. 'Edouard is not my lover,' she said. 'He looks after me when the Baron is busy. He merely takes an interest in me, and worries too much.'

Colette looked round the lavish room. Olympe did not look as if anyone need be concerned about her. Rich, gilded mirrors lined the walls, choice bibelots covered every available surface.

'I thought he was your *amant de coeur*? The one you care for enough not to charge?'

'No, no.' Olympe sounded regretful. 'Edouard comes to see me occasionally. We have fun. And then he goes off to make more money. He is too interested in being rich, that one. He has little time for women. Don't think about him, Colette, he is too serious. Especially now.'

Olympe said nothing about the way that Edouard had come to her rescue. It was unlike her to be so discreet. Colette had to know the worst. 'Did you hear anything about me at the ball?' she asked.

Olympe looked surprised. 'Your costume was a success,' she said, sipping a glass of wine. 'Personally I thought something a little less daring would have been better, but you looked lovely,' she added generously. 'Several men asked me if they might have a chance with you. I told them all your time was taken, but that they could always try sending you gifts in case you changed your mind.'

'I hope they took you at your word. I need all the help I can get.'

Olympe stopped sipping. She frowned. 'Why? I thought Charles paid almost all your bills. And Michel picks up the rest. Surely it is too soon to replace either of them?'

'Charles may not want to see me again. And Michel is angry. Are you sure nothing was said about me last night?'

'I didn't see either of them after supper,' Olympe admitted. 'Charles disappeared even earlier than you did. But there was such a crowd that I didn't find it odd. I thought maybe you and Michel had found a private corner.'

'We did,' Colette said bitterly, 'but then he went too far. I tell you, it is all over between us.' She stood up and walked over to the window. 'That is not all,' she said. 'When I left Michel, Madame de

226

la Trave took me to her games room. She had plans for me.'

'I warned you about Antoinette. She is dangerous. What did she do, Colette? Surely it can't have been so very terrible?'

'She intended to humiliate me.'

'You were a fool to go near her! She has tried to hurt all of Gilles' mistresses. Most of them are wise enough to keep out of her way. And, of course, Gilles makes sure she does not hurt them.'

But he had made no effort to help her, Colette thought miserably. Her behaviour had lost her his protection long ago. She wondered if either he or his wife knew about Victor yet.

She questioned Olympe again. 'Are you sure that no one else suspects? There was no gossip?'

'None that I heard. And had there been any it would have been all through that crowd last night. As it was, the only talk was that you were seen leaving in Edouard's carriage. That was enough to make all the women jealous. Then, when he returned alone, he made it clear that you had turned him down.'

It was not true. So why had he spread that rumour? She could see how much it helped her position, but why had he done that for her? 'People will know soon enough what has happened. Olympe, I must find another lover.'

'You mean it is true that you rejected Edouard?' Olympe sounded incredulous.

'He did not offer.'

'Well, perhaps he is right. But maybe you will not need another lover after all.'

'Why not?'

'Edouard says . . .'

227

'I thought Edouard was not interested.'

'Listen to me. He is not. But he thinks we should leave Paris. At least he tells me that I should, and I am sure the same advice applies to you.'

'But why? Where would we go?'

'To Germany. Or England. Anywhere so long as it is out of France. I am sure he is worrying unnecessarily. But,' she added almost casually, 'I have agreed to let him invest some of my money abroad. It is better to be sure.'

'He thinks the Prussians will defeat us? Impossible.'

'Why take the risk? He knows what he is talking about, that one. And I have worked hard for my money.' Olympe stretched luxuriously, and reached out one hand for a sweet biscuit. 'Soon I may retire to the country. But not yet.'

'Perhaps he is trying to cheat you?'

'No, it is not that. I trust him completely, even with money. But he is wrong. Now is not the time to leave Paris.' Olympe yawned. 'Now forgive me, darling, I must rest before my drive. Don't worry about Charles. And replace Michel if he is still angry. Don't worry about anything at all.' She popped another soft madeleine into her mouth. 'Life has never been so good. Enjoy it.'

Colette breathed a sigh of relief. So Madame had said nothing. Was she really safe? Surely Antoinette de la Trave would not be satisfied until she really suffered?

But when she returned home, her apartment was stacked with flowers and attached to a card from Michel was a shimmering diamond and platinum goldfish. It seemed all that remained for her to do was to thank Edouard Kerouac. And she was eager to see him again.

She called on him that afternoon. He received her in his study, and scarcely looked up as she entered. 'I came to thank you for your assistance last night,' she said.

'There was no need.' One of his hands kept a firm grip on the stack of papers on his desk; in the other he held a thick, black pen. He looked as if he hoped she would leave immediately, and not disturb his work.

'If you had not taken me home when you did, I would have been ruined.'

He nodded. 'Quite possibly.'

She tapped her foot impatiently. 'So will you not accept my gratitude, Monsieur?'

'You thanked me last night.'

'Inadequately.'

Now he put down his pen and his papers, and looked her straight in the eye. 'What would you consider adequate, Mademoiselle?'

She blushed. He was making it obvious that he assumed she had come to offer him her body. After all, what else did she have to give?

Well, he was wrong. She had saved a little money, and she had her jewels. If her rent was secure, she could easily sell some of those and send the money abroad. She liked the idea. And it seemed that Michel would buy her as many new ones as she wanted. Her position was not so bad. She stared at Edouard. 'I can give you my business, Monsieur,' she said.

He leant back in his chair and roared with laughter. She had his full attention now. 'Your business?' he spluttered. 'Tell me more.'

She hesitated. Did she really trust this man? 'Olympe told me that you think her money is no longer safe in Paris.'

He nodded.

'Why is that?' she asked.

'We will soon be at war. I do not think we shall win. It is time to make preparations.'

'What would you advise me to do?'

'You trust me that much?'

'You have already helped me once. And Olympe has confidence in you.'

'But she did not believe me when I told her to leave Paris.'

'She is having too good a time.'

Edouard seemed to hesitate. 'You haven't been working long enough to have much worth saving,' he said finally. 'I suggest you leave Paris now with your jewels.'

'But what about my apartment and my clothes?'

'I imagine that your apartment is rented? As for your furniture, you could sell it, or leave it behind.'

'My beautiful furniture? My bibelots?'

'What else can you do? If you sell them you draw too much attention to your plans. Perhaps you have creditors?' He looked knowingly at her. 'It is possible that not everything is yours outright. Take only what you are sure of. Leave the rest. Even Olympe has less money saved than I hoped. She has spent most of what she has received over the years. You all do.'

The words hurt her. This man thought she was worth nothing.

He continued. 'So you can see that your business will not be valuable to me. But there is something else that you could do to show your gratitude.'

She was in his debt. She wondered what his price would be, for she had no doubt that there would be one. In her experience no one did anything for nothing. So he was just like all the others. Only less straightforward. But Olympe was right. He had no need to pay. She wanted him now as much as she had done last night.

She waited.

Edouard put down his pen and crossed the room towards her. 'Go, Colette. Get out while you can. Take your jewels, find a man to escort you and go to London. Try to persuade Olympe to go with you. It would be easier for the two of you together. And she must leave Paris.'

So it was Olympe he was concerned about. She felt a surge of jealousy. 'And will you take your own advice?' she asked. 'Why are you still here?'

'I shall go when I am free to do so. Now, if you believe me, go and persuade Olympe. She may take advice more seriously from you. She admires you.'

Colette returned to her beautiful apartment. So Edouard thought she was worth nothing. How wrong he was. And he was wrong about the Prussians, too. Napoleon III was in no danger. And neither were the Parisians.

Within a week, war was declared. Paris was in a state of euphoria, full of patriots celebrating the news, both in the theatres, where audiences joined in the chorus of the officially banned *Marseillaise*, and in the streets, where coloured lanterns decked the vehicles, and crowds of young men linked arms and marched cheering along the boulevards.

Now all the speculation would be at an end. It

231

was only Edouard, and a few gloomy politicians, who had doubts about the outcome. It was time for the Prussians to be taught a lesson.

In the heat of August, while the Emperor and the young Prince took personal charge of the campaign, Colette and Charles rented a small villa at Bougival, just outside the city walls, and spent a month of peaceful pleasure, content in each other's company.

She forgot the misery of her night at the ball, and the pain of Victor's betrayal. Nothing intruded on her happiness until, at the end of the month, Charles told her that he had to return to his country estate. The Prussians had advanced to within thirty kilometres of his father's land, and he was needed.

'Go back to Paris,' he urged. 'You will be safe there. The city fortifications will never be breached, and soon the Emperor will bring in his troops from the front.' He looked uneasy and his hands trembled as he handed her a small, metal box. 'Take this, Colette,' he said, 'with my love. It will pay for your rent for a year.'

'Will you be so long?' She could not understand. He had assured her that the trouble would all be over soon.

'I shall not come back to Paris,' he said. 'When the Prussians are defeated, I intend to marry. You know that it is necessary. Perhaps later, when the wedding is over, we shall be together again?'

She did not think so. She had grown too fond of him in this month away from the city. It was time she remembered who she was. She took the box, kissed him lightly on the cheeks and drove in the carriage back to Paris. As she neared the barricades surrounding the city, she could see crowds lining the streets, shouting against the Empress Eugénie, but she could make no sense of what was said, and there was no news of the war.

That night, Colette took her place in her box at the Opéra. The rent was paid, and she wanted it to be known that she had returned. And there she was sure to hear the latest news. She felt secure; with the money Charles had given her, she could take her time to find another lover, but she would make sure not to care too much for the next one.

Her new jewels glittered around her neck. The theatre was as full as ever, although she noticed that one or two regulars were not present. Olympe's box was occupied by a chattering crowd she did not recognise, and there was no sign of Gilles or Anne. Colette was not too surprised; maybe like her, they had escaped the summer heat.

But Edouard was here. She saw him across the other side of the theatre, standing behind two women in the latest gowns. She could not see his face; he was deep in conversation with two men in severe, dark frockcoats. So he had not even taken his own advice to leave Paris. When he glanced at her, she gave him a mocking smile, and was surprised to see anger in his eyes. Could he not bear to be wrong? When she looked up again, he had gone.

The door of her box burst open as he marched in without knocking. She was angry. How dare he! She did not invite him to sit down, and then regretted her rudeness as he towered over her. 'Olympe told me you had left Paris,' he said.

'For the summer, yes. Now, as you see, I have returned. It is a pity you did not take the trouble to come to visit me at Bougival. Charles and I had a charming villa there.'

'It's a pity you didn't stay there!'

'If my presence in Paris is so unpleasant for you, I wonder why you bother to come to talk to me.' She flicked her fan provocatively. Why wouldn't this man take more interest in her? She was free now. He was so attractive, and he could not be disinterested or he would not be here. She would make him her target for the season. By Christmas he would be hers, she decided.

He did not answer her for a moment, settling himself on the red plush sofa beside her without waiting for her agreement. 'You wonder,' he repeated, his eyes fixed on the stage. 'Can I take that as a sign that you are at last beginning to think, to use your brain?'

Colette choked on the sugar dragée she was eating, and felt the handle of her ivory fan snap as she gripped it too hard between her fingers. How dare he! She had come a long way from her peasant upbringing. She was a success. Did he think she had done that without using her brain? She had none of Olympe's luscious beauty. She had got where she was by using her wits.

An uneasy thought struck her. Perhaps Olympe had finally taken Edouard's advice. Had she left Paris? Surely she would not have done so without telling her? Colette needed to find out, but she would not give Edouard Kerouac the satisfaction of asking him outright. 'If Paris is so dangerous, Monsieur, why are you still here?'

He put down his opera glasses so slowly that she could have hit him. They looked like toys in his large hands. 'Perhaps I am waiting to persuade you,' he said, and looked away again.

She would have liked his words to be true. 'I am sure your interest is in Olympe.'

'Olympe is in Germany.'

She felt dizzy. Why had Olympe not told her? How could she have left without even sending her a note?

Edouard gestured towards the crowded boxes of the Opéra. 'Look around you, Colette. The theatre is full, but many of the faces you know are missing. Where do you think they are?'

'Away for the summer. I have only just returned myself.'

'There is a war on.'

'So some of the men are there.'

'Do you think it is a picnic?'

'The officers are in no danger.'

He turned to look hard at her. 'No,' he said, 'the officers are not. But our people are. Men like your father, and your brother. Peasants like us. Does that no longer matter to you?'

Colette had never experienced war at first hand. And Pierre was too young for her to have any fears for him. Would anyone else have been taken from her village?

His words hit her in the stomach so that she felt unable to answer for a moment. She would go back to Argnon for their sake, and find out if they needed her, but she would not ask Edouard for his help. 'As you see, Monsieur, I am not afraid. I am sure I will be safe here.'

'Has Charles provided adequately for you?' he asked.

'More than adequately.'

'Then it seems that words cannot persuade you. I thought you were an intelligent woman. Now I believe you are a fool.' He rose to his feet.

235

She wanted him to stay. 'If that is so, why are you still here? Why have you not left Paris?'

'I leave tomorrow.'

She pressed her thumb on the broken spine of her fan. 'It is none of your business. It is obvious that not everyone is of your opinion.' She wanted to throw him out, but could not create a scene on her first night in Paris, when so many potential protectors were watching. She smiled at the young count de Crémy, and was delighted to see his eager response.

She heard Edouard's voice behind her. 'Is money all you value, Colette? Can you not even listen to advice without payment?'

Before she could respond, the door slammed shut behind him. She tried to regain her earlier insouciance, but her pleasure in the evening had gone. She glanced across at his box, but she could no longer see Edouard; his seat was empty. He must have left the theatre. His behaviour was intolerable. He did not understand how much she needed to save. Her expenses until now had cost her more than she had earnt. This year was vital to her future. Some time, later, she would be able to retire. But not now.

She was shaking with anger, but struggled to smile so that no one in the audience should see the effect that man had on her. And they were all looking. It seemed that Edouard Kerouac had become the most interesting man in Paris. At least the attention he had shown her had increased her position in society. Her smile became sincere as she thought about how much that would irritate him.

At home, the beauty of her apartment soothed her. She really had no need to worry for a whole year with all her bills paid, and two carriages at her disposal.

When Marie had prepared her for bed and put away her jewels, Colette sat for a while on the window seat in her boudoir. The glow from a thousand windows lit up the Paris sky. At home in Argnon the sky would be dark, and she would be able to see the stars. There would be the scent of ripening fruit, mingled with sweet-smelling hay and herbs, and the only sounds that disturbed the night were cattle lowing and the distant roar of the river. Here the streets seemed noisier than ever, after the relative peace of Bougival.

But in Argnon there was no time to enjoy the peace and beauty. Her family came home after a day in the fields and fell asleep as soon as they had eaten. Surely they were safe there. The war was taking place far away. Paris itself would be in danger before there was any threat to Argnon. She stretched her arms up in the air and uncurled her cramped legs. It was time she slept. Already the first light of dawn was dimming the glow from the streetlamps, and the first market carts were trundling over the cobbles.

It was Edouard's fault that she was alone. If he had not monopolised her at the theatre, she would have invited a man to spend the night with her.

Damn Edouard Kerouac!

When she woke, her maid brought up a small package. She laid it on her table and opened it while she drank her morning chocolate. Inside the brown paper she found a single, large diamond, and a small piece of white card. *The Bank of England* hold *10,000 louis on deposit in the name of Colette Paquet.*

She laid the jewel in the palm of her hand, a perfect pear-shaped stone. She knew enough about diamonds now to appreciate its value. It was worth more than all her glittering necklaces.

And the letter of credit amounted to the exact sum that she needed to maintain her for a year, 200,000 francs.

There was a second note attached. *Take all your jewels and keep them always with you. E.K.*

So he was concerned for her safety even though Olympe was out of danger. But what was Edouard Kerouac trying to do? Surely he was not so stupid that he did not realise she would have him as her lover without any payment?

Chapter Twelve

*T*here was an eerie silence in the streets the next morning. The crowds Colette had seen yesterday had dispersed, and there was no sound from the streets. She was frightened to go outside until she knew more about what had happened, and hoped that Jean-Pierre would come to tell them the news. Or Edouard. Surely he would come to tell her what he expected in return for his gift?

She felt a shiver of excitement at the thought of his generosity. Now she had money out of the country as he had advised – and he had given it to her. That could only mean that he intended to make her his mistress. There was no man she would rather have as her lover. And to have succeeded in attracting a man who had never paid for a woman before was a triumph. Colette wished that she could talk to Olympe about it.

Her morning passed slowly. She could not decide what to do. Edouard's words in the theatre had struck home. It was her family and people like them who were suffering now. She had felt too secure because the battles had all been fought to the east of Paris, and the danger to her home seemed remote, but she had forgotten that men were being called up from all over France and there would be many in Argnon who would have to leave home. She realised that she could not leave France to go to London with Edouard. She had to return to Argnon and make sure that her family was safe. She would wait today to learn what was happening, and then she would ask Michel to help her, if Edouard left the city without her.

From her window, she could see men gathering in small groups and talking quietly. They lingered on the corners of the square and seemed as aimless as she felt. There was none of the wild exuberance she had seen the day before, and it seemed that there was an inevitable acceptance of imminent defeat. It was a relief when Marie announced that Edouard Kerouac was at the door, demanding to see her.

'Would you like me to say he is too late, Mademoiselle? That you are out?'

'No. Please ask him to come up.'

Now she would know what he wanted from her. But she would have to tell him that she could not accept the jewel, or the money. She hated the thought of parting with them.

She saw that he looked tired when he entered the room, as if he had been up all night. Colette opened her mouth to thank him, but he turned away, and walked quickly over to the window. 'It is worse than I thought,' he said, watching the activity in the streets, 'and we have little time. Will you come with me now?'

She felt confused. If matters were so urgent, perhaps she might need his help simply to leave the city. She wondered what he would say when she told him that she was prepared to leave Paris, but not France. 'Where?' she asked stupidly, playing for time.

He turned to face her, but his back was against the light, and she could not see his expression. 'I am not asking you out for a drive, Colette. For the last time I'm telling you to get out of Paris before it's too late.'

'But why? You were at the theatre last night. You heard the news. We can hold out against the Prussians.'

He beckoned her over to the window, and pointed to one or two figures scurrying beside the walls of the square. 'Look, you can see that the truth is starting to filter through. There was no victory. The rumours were false.'

As she watched, she saw more men gathering outside. They looked anxious, and there was an unnatural silence. Perhaps Edouard was right; there was an air of disaster this morning. She needed time to think. She still could not understand why it was not wiser to stay in Paris. Everyone had told her that it was the safest place in France. 'The theatre was full last night,' she said. 'People are coming back to Paris after the summer.'

'Only the fools are left, Colette, or those who cannot afford to go.'

She flushed. 'Michel is not a fool,' she said icily, 'and he has no plans to leave.' She held out the diamond and the letter of credit. 'Perhaps you should take your generous gifts, Monsieur, since I

241

will not be accepting your offer. Michel will look after me.'

He made no move to take the package she held out to him. Instead, he turned his back and continued to look out of the window. 'When did you last see him?' he asked.

'Before I went to Bougival.'

'And you expected to find him here?'

'He does not come every day.' She felt angry. She did not have to explain her arrangements to this man. He was humiliating her by refusing to take back his gift, as if he knew how reluctant she was to part with the diamond and the money.

'Don't play games with me,' he said. 'This is not the time. Do you know where he is?'

'He may be at the Tuileries.'

She saw Edouard's face change. 'Then I'm sorry, but he will not be back.'

'Don't be ridiculous. He will come tonight, or maybe tomorrow.'

'Did he tell you how long he would be?'

'It isn't like that, Edouard. I'm sure you understand. He will come when he can.' She did not want to explain that she was not sure of Michel's protection. Now that Charles had left her, she felt quite alone.

Edouard took her hand. 'If he is at the Tuileries, he has gone to help the Empress, and he will not leave her for your sake, no matter how much he may wish to do so.'

She could hear noises in the square now, the dull rumble of carts on the cobbles, but still no sound of voices. She crossed to the window and looked out. She felt a chill of fear. Perhaps Edouard was right.

He was standing in the centre of the room, and

now she could see how tired he looked. His voice was low as he spoke. 'Don't you think I have paid enough for your time for you to humour me?'

'It was not necessary.'

'I was aware how much your lovers paid you. I wanted to offer more.'

'What do you want me to do?'

'Take the train to Boulogne. There is a ferry that will take you to England. So far, that western part of France is safe.'

'So far?'

'The Prussians have won the war. Be in no doubt about that.'

She tried to think clearly. If the palace was in trouble, Michel would not return. Edouard was right about that. And, like him, she had little sympathy for the Empress. Edouard beckoned her to the window. 'Look, the news is starting to filter through. We must hurry.'

'Why? You saw the theatre last night. Everyone is staying in the city.'

'Everyone? Olympe has gone. She went because she took my advice. But Gilles and Anne have left for her estate in the country. Gilles is not a fool.'

So Anne had finally agreed to be with Gilles, even if it had taken this to persuade her.

'Where will we go?'

'To London.' He pointed to the package on the table. 'You have money there now. You'll be all right. But I may have to return to Paris. I have work to do. Give me your jewels.'

Numbly, she handed them over. She would let him help her get out of Paris, and then she would tell him that she must stay in France.

'Now ring for Marie.'

When the maid came in, Edouard handed her the diamond and the letter of credit. 'Can you sew these into the hem of a travelling dress for Mademoiselle? And as many of her other jewels as you can manage. Choose something as plain and discreet as possible. And Marie – be quick.'

Marie looked questioningly at Colette. She nodded. The silence in the streets made her nervous. Now she could hear occasional footsteps, walking fast over the cobbles, but no one spoke. It was as though the whole city was waiting for news which did not come.

'And Marie? How can I leave her?'

'She will not leave while Jean-Pierre is in the Garde Nationale. He will take care of her. You have a carriage and horses?'

She nodded.

'Leave them for Jean-Pierre and Marie. Take my carriage.'

'And Marie and Jean-Pierre will arrange the rest of my possessions?'

She saw his mouth harden. 'No, Colette, they will not. They will do everything they can to save their own skins, not your goods. You have your letter of credit. That should cover any losses. And Colette . . .'

'Yes?'

'If I am wrong, you can return next week to reclaim everything. So what have you got to lose? Now come.' He turned away from the window, and gripped her wrist. 'Can't you hear the guns?'

Marie had sewn the jewels into a small bag attached to the waistband of her petticoat. Colette dressed quickly in her plainest gown and came downstairs.

Edouard was waiting in the hall. He took one look at her, and before she could stop him, he lifted her skirt and took hold of her hooped crinoline. With one sharp tug, he pulled it off. 'I'm not sharing a carriage with that,' he announced, as he took her hand and led her into the dark interior. The blinds were down and, when the door was shut, Colette could see nothing.

They moved away immediately. Gradually her eyes became accustomed to the gloom, and there was a little light from one window where Edouard held the blind back slightly and watched as they drove through the streets.

'I think we are in time,' he said. 'We shall make for the Porte de Neuilly, and hope that they will let us through the barricades.'

'They are there to keep the Prussians out, not to keep Parisians in!'

'And they are manned by the troops who blame those in power for our defeat. Make no mistake, Colette. We have two enemies now. The Prussians and our own people.'

There was no trouble at the gate. They passed through unchecked. The Garde seemed neither to notice nor to care about the few carriages leaving the city. They stood as though stunned. 'They are waiting for news, like the rest of us,' Edouard said. 'And they know that the news will not be what they want to hear. They will blame the Emperor.'

'And Eugénie. She is Regent.'

'They will blame her more than anyone. Michel will be lucky if he succeeds in helping her to escape. Do not blame him for deserting you.'

'He would not have taken me out of the city. How could he? Where would we go? To his family home?' She shook her head. 'He was good to me, but he knew that I understood his position. It is the same for all girls of my type.' She felt the hard pouch of jewels at her waist. 'So why are you helping me?'

He did not take his eyes off the road. 'For the same reason as all men. I find you desirable.'

'You never approached me before.'

'I don't like sharing my women. One third of your body would not interest me.'

'So you have paid enough to have me all to yourself.'

He released the blind and let the bright light of day shine through into the carriage. She blinked uncomfortably as it hit her eyes. 'I was aware of the going rate,' he said quietly.

She sank back into her seat. She wished she could have told him he did not have to pay. But it was time he understood that she was not leaving France.

'When we reach Lisieux, I want you to find me some horses, and a carriage. And I must give you back these.' She reached into her pouch for the diamond and her letter.

He leant forward, his dark eyes angry. 'Did I offend you?' he questioned sharply. 'Or are you playing games again? This is not the time for that.'

'It's neither. You were right when you said that it is our sort who will pay the price for this war. I'm going to Argnon, to see my family. They may need me.'

'You won't make it,' he said. 'There is fighting close to there. And where do you think I can find a horse in these times?'

'Then I will find some other way. I still have my other jewels. A horse cannot be worth so very much.' She thought he looked even more tired, and wished she had not had to hurt him. She would very much have liked to stay with him, if he wanted her, but she could not tell him that. It was not what a man wanted to hear from a mistress.

He pushed back the gift she had returned to him. 'Put it away,' he said tiredly. 'I'll see what I can do.'

At Lisieux they stopped to rest the horses. She saw him walk into an inn, and question men who had come from other routes about the Prussian advance. He seemed satisfied with what they said, and came to join her at a table. 'We are safe enough here,' he said, 'and for the moment there is no problem with crossing the channel. I think we have time to make a detour.' He called a waiter to bring them some food. 'There is something I have not told you.'

She waited. Why, if they had moved so fast to leave Paris, was he so willing to delay now?

'Gilles has gone to live with Anne at her property in Bordeaux, but Antoinette has returned to Argnon. She will be very angry that her husband has finally left her, and for some reason she hates you. So tell me, what harm can she do your family? Because I am sure she will try.'

'Gilles gave them their farm. And some money when I agreed to live with him.'

'That was why you went with him?'

'Partly.' She could not tell him about Victor. But she was sure now that was why Antoinette hated her so much.

'Do you know if they have the documents?'

She shook her head. 'They were left with the notary in the town. My father trusted Gilles.'

247

'He was right to do so. But Antoinette is not the same. She will do everything she can to ruin your family. And she could succeed. She owns the land, and all the money came from her family. I will visit the notary in the town while you go to Argnon. You are right that you must see your family. So far we are in no danger from the Prussians in this part of France, but there is rioting in many regions, and that is at least as dangerous. We have the misfortune to look rich now, and that stands against us. Are you ready for that?'

She dreaded the thought of seeing Antoinette again. It seemed a worse prospect than evading the enemy. She tore off a chunk of bread, and ate it with her soup. Edouard was right. It was even more important to see her family now. She could not leave France without being sure that the money she had earnt for them was safe. She nodded her agreement, grateful for his support.

'Then we'll stay here tonight. In the morning, when the horses are fresh, we'll travel on. The roads are safe enough, it seems. But we dare not take the railway.'

She watched him eat ravenously. 'Why are you doing this for me?' she asked.

'I told you. I want you!'

And he planned to stay with her at this inn. 'Tonight?' she asked.

He smiled, his tired eyes crinkling up at the corners. 'No, Colette. I have longer term plans.'

'You mean you don't want to make love to me?'

He roared with laughter. 'I have no doubt about your abilities in bed. Have you ever failed to please a man in that way?'

'Then what do you want from me?'

He shrugged. 'I want a wife who amuses me. And you do. A woman who draws all eyes in public.' He shrugged. 'You do.'

'In clothes that cost more than my parents' farm.'

'And that of my family, too. But it isn't simply the clothes. Achille saw more than that in you. And you carried off your soirée with the Princess better than most society ladies.'

She had forgotten that evening. It seemed a long time ago. 'You know I never saw my portrait,' she said suddenly.

Edouard made a face. 'Achille hoped you wouldn't. He has taken it to America. It is to be the start of his new career over there. I gather his painting of you left little to the imagination.'

She looked down at the table and felt his hand cover hers. 'You see, you can still blush!' His fingers were warm over hers, and comforting. 'Above all else,' he said, 'I want a wife who won't despise my background. You are an independent woman, now, Colette. You are safe, whatever you decide.'

She looked across the table at him. He had made no move to make love to her. He had hardly touched her. So why was she so conscious of him close to her? 'I know nothing about you,' she said.

He hesitated. 'I try to keep my background quiet. It makes my life easier if people cannot place me. But you have a right to know. I come from Marseilles. My father was a fisherman. We lived a poor life, and I decided I would make enough money so that I was never poor again. So, you see, I know what it is to want money.'

How could she marry him? He would always be thinking of the lovers who had paid for her. Just as

249

he proposed to do. 'It wasn't just the money,' she said.

'Not even for your family?'

'My parents wanted me to go with Gilles, but even for them it was not just the money. They thought I would have a better life.'

'They were right.'

'Perhaps.'

'But you had another reason?'

'I was in love with Gilles' son.'

He frowned. 'So you became his father's mistress? Why?'

'So that I could come to Paris. I thought Victor would come, too. But he didn't.'

'And then it was too late?'

She nodded. 'I couldn't go home after Paris. I no longer belonged.' It was so easy to talk to Edouard. She could feel his attention on her all the time they ate, as though no one else was in the room and nothing else mattered. She wanted him to hold her tonight, just to let her lie in his arms.

But when their meal was finished, he gave her a key. 'This is your room. The carriage will be ready early to take you to your parents' farm. I will join you in Argnon as soon as I have the deeds to your parents' farm.' Then he turned, and left her at the foot of the stairs.

She spent the night alone, thinking of the way he had looked at her when they travelled together in the carriage. He had been so close all the time, and yet he had made no move towards her. He said he wanted her and he had paid enough to buy her several times over. When was he going to ask for a return? Would he wait until they reached England

250

and it was too late? Did he think she would run away if he advanced too soon?

She drove the carriage herself up to the village, grateful for her experience in driving the farm cart in her youth. Argnon was quiet. The streets were empty and, although it was late in the season, the harvest was only half in. Her mother explained. 'Most of the men in the village have been drafted into the Garde. Those who are left do what they can, but if they appear too strong and fit, they will be taken away, too. So they must be careful. We are lucky. Your father is too old, and Pierre too young. But Gaston has been forced to join up. He has had to leave his wife, and his young boy.'

So Gaston was fighting, and the war seemed real at last. Not a game that the officers played at with the Emperor. A game the Emperor had lost. If he surrendered soon, the young men might come home alive to their villages.

There was so much to say. She wanted to tell her mother that she was leaving France, but she could see the anxiety in her father's eyes when she asked about the deeds for the farm.

'Do you need the money back? Tell me what is wrong.'

'It is not that. But I understand that Madame de la Trave is here?'

Her father nodded. 'She came two days ago.'

'Has she been to see you?'

'I would not expect her to.'

'But you have the deeds safe?'

Her father shook his head. 'They are with the notary. Monsieur de la Trave would not cheat me. You do not have to worry.'

So Edouard was right to check in the town. Everything seemed to be well with her family. There was little else for her to do. 'The money?' she asked finally. 'Do you have Jeanne's money for her wedding?'

Her father looked satisfied. 'The gold is safe with the curé for your sister. Jeanne's dowry has bought her a fine husband. She is grateful to you.'

Colette felt a chill of fear. 'Why does the curé have the money?' she asked.

'He came for it last week. It seemed normal. The wedding is soon. Why, Colette, is anything wrong?'

'Does the curé talk about me?'

Her mother looked embarrassed. 'You cannot expect him to understand what you did. But we all do. No matter what he says.'

'So he talks badly of me?'

Her mother nodded.

'How long will he keep the money?'

There was the slightest hesitation. 'He will hand it over to her husband after the wedding.'

Colette was sure that they would never see the gold again. What if he denied that it had existed, or told Jeanne's young man how it was earnt? Then what would happen to her sister's wedding? She had to see the curé again, but she must not alarm her parents. She kissed them both, and pretended that it was time for her to leave.

And it was only a small lie. As soon as she had dealt with the curé, she would go.

But at the church they told her that he was at the château with Madame. So the two people who had tried to ruin her were together. She could confront them both at the same time.

She had agreed to meet Edouard in the town this evening. She had plenty of time.

She had been so sure that she would never see the château again, but at her first sight it looked only beautiful, and she felt nothing of the grim despair she had known when she left here. Only the garden seemed neglected. But then Madame had only recently arrived. And Victor had always failed to attend to the property.

Paul announced her arrival. She waited in the long salon where her parents had first told her of Gilles' offer. Antoinette entered almost immediately. Her cheeks were flushed. 'How dare you come here!'

'I won't take long, Madame. I am here to see the curé.'

'You cannot imagine he will want to see you.'

'I am sure he does not. But he has some money which belongs to my parents.'

Madame turned her back. 'The money they sold you for.'

Colette felt angry, not ashamed. 'It was a business arrangement. I kept my part of the bargain.' Well, almost, she thought. But it was the de la Trave family who had prevented her from keeping her word. She continued calmly, 'The curé has said that he is keeping my sister's dowry safe for her. If he is not here, Madame, I shall trouble you no more.'

'He is here. Unlike you, he is a welcome guest.'

'You invited me to your home in Paris.'

'That was before I knew what you had done to my son.'

'I did nothing to your son. It was he who took advantage of me.'

'That is not what the curé says.'

253

'Where is he? Let him say it again in front of me.'

'He is in the chapel. We were praying.'

Was it possible that Madame really did not know the truth? 'Are you sure that is all you were doing in the chapel?'

'What do you mean?'

'Ask your friend the curé. Ask him what he and Victor did in there.'

'We will ask him together, since you seem determined to see him. We will ask him now.'

Colette followed Madame across the sunlit hall, and through the dark corridor leading to the chapel. As the doors opened, she saw a smile vanish from the curé's dark face. No doubt at first he thought Madame had returned alone. He glared at Colette. 'I thought you would be too ashamed to come back to Argnon.'

'Because of the lies you had told about me? I am sure you were careful not to admit your part in the affair.'

Madame had closed the doors behind her, and now she locked them. She advanced towards the priest. 'Tell me everything,' she demanded.

'The girl is lying.'

Colette went to the chest where the leather thongs were concealed. The lid was locked. 'Do you have a key, Madame?'

She held out her hand. Colette took it and flung open the lid.

Antoinette took out a leather whip and ran the blood-stained thongs through her fingers. 'Who put these here?' she asked.

'Perhaps your husband.' The curé was pale.

'Fool. This would hold no pleasure for him. It was you who taught me this. And now you have trained Victor to enjoy your pleasures. Why couldn't you leave my family alone? Hadn't you done enough when you destroyed my marriage?' Madame's lovely face was suffused with rage.

The curé stepped backwards. He snatched one of the thick candles from the wall bracket, and moved swiftly to the side aisle. He pulled at one of the panels on the wall, and a door beside him swung open. He slipped through it and they heard a key turn in the lock. Colette pushed at the panel, but it was useless. She had to try somehow to force him to give back her money. 'Where has he gone?' she asked.

'Come with me,' Antoinette said. 'It is time that man paid for what he has done.'

They ran up the staircase, and along the corridor to Antoinette's suite of rooms. As they opened the door, they saw flames leaping up the curtains and the drapes of the bed. The curé leapt around the room like a madman brandishing the flame. He opened the cupboard doors and lit the hems of the fragile, dry gowns that had been stored here for so many years. And then he placed the candle beneath Antoinette's portrait and stood in front of it, barring their way.

'Come and get your money, Colette. Come if you dare.'

Madame took one look at the burning frame of her youthful image and drew in her breath. 'We will leave him here,' she said, pulling Colette back and locking the door. She ran to the top of the stairs with the key in her hand and threw it down. Colette pushed frantically against the door, but it would not move. She shouted to the footmen, who started to climb the stairs, carrying buckets. Before they could force entry into the room, Victor came towards them with the key in his hand. Antoinette tried to stop him, but he thrust her aside.

As Victor opened the door, they saw a solid sheet of flame, which blazed out through the opening. There was nothing anyone could do to save that room. But Victor stepped forward as if he could not let the curé die there, even if the flames engulfed him too. Colette grabbed his ankle, and pushed him down the long flight of stairs. She ran down, away from the flames, and towards the chapel. 'Perhaps we can reach him from there,' she shouted. But Antoinette was crouched over the motionless body of her son, and already the painted ceiling in the chapel was caving in. There was nothing more that could be done.

Colette followed Madame outside. 'Where is Victor?' she asked.

Madame smiled, and pointed to where he lay on a bed of cushions on the grass. 'He has a broken leg,' she said. 'He will be all right.'

She looked at Colette, and for the first time, there was no hatred in her eyes. 'At first I thought you were trying to kill him,' she said. 'Then I realised that you saved his life. He would have died for that man. I owe you an apology, Mademoiselle.'

Colette felt sick with the smoke and the realisation of how close she had come to killing Victor. At the time it had seemed she had no choice. She looked up at the blazing west wing of the château and thought that she could see the black figure of the curé outlined against the flames, but it was her imagination. There would be nothing left of his body now.

She turned to Antoinette. 'Why did you try to ruin me?' she asked.

'Because my husband wanted you.'

'But he had so many mistresses. You didn't try to harm them all.'

Madame sat down beside Victor. 'You had my husband, and my son,' she said quietly. She pointed to the smoking shell of her apartment. 'That man told me you would take them both away from me. He poisoned my mind against you, as he did against Anne all those years ago.'

'You tried to hurt her, too?'

'I tried to kill her. Gilles sent me away from France. He was probably wise, but I made sure he finished with Anne. It was simple. I made sure there was no more money unless he gave her up.'

The servants had piled some of the paintings on the ground, but they worked slowly now that the smoke was so thick and there were so few of them.

Colette turned towards the drive. Edouard stood by his carriage, holding the horses steady. 'Are you ready to leave now?' he asked.

She walked slowly towards him, feeling a deep sense of relief at his presence. He stood quite still until she was very close to him, and saw him look over to where Victor lay. 'Do you want him?' he asked. 'Do you still love him?'

She shook her head. 'No.'

'I heard what you did. He was not worth risking your life for.'

'I didn't. I would have been down those stairs just as fast without pushing him first. I might have killed him.'

'I'm glad you didn't. If the man you loved had died a hero, it would have been difficult to make

257

you forget him.' He held out his hand and helped her into the carriage. 'Now, will you come with me to England?'

She nodded, almost asleep, as the carriage moved down the avenue.

Edouard called out from the front. 'I have given the deeds to your father. His farm is safe.'

She sat up. 'The curé had my sister's dowry.'

'Well, it has died with him. Give her your rubies, Colette. That will do. And I think I would prefer that you don't wear them any more. I'll buy you something else.'

In four hours they had reached the coast. Several yachts were moored in the harbour. Edouard led her on to one of them. 'I have arranged for us to take this boat,' he said. 'Have you made up your mind, Colette. Are you coming with me?'

She had no reason to stay in France any longer. Suddenly it seemed a good idea to be starting a new life, away from the intricate web of lies which had caused her so much pain. She had made too many mistakes, and now she was being given a second chance. 'I'm coming with you,' she said.

'The weather is bad, but we must leave tonight. We can wait no longer. I want you safely out of here.'

She followed him on to the deck of the boat. She wanted to watch as the coastline of France disappeared behind them. As the boat left the harbour, she realised the strength of the storm. They would be lucky to reach England without danger. Edouard's arm was round her now, protecting her from the full force of the wind as they stood together on the deck of the small boat, but the rain and spray soaked them both. She watched the coastline of France disappear into a haze of mist and rain, and turned away.

She had the clothes she wore now, stained and drenched with travel, a small box of jewels, her diamond and Edouard's letter of credit. It would be more than enough to start a new life.

'What will you do?' she asked.

His arm tightened around her. 'I must return to Paris. But don't worry, Colette. I'll make sure you are established in London.'

Established! 'What as?' she asked. 'Are Englishmen like the French? Can I earn my living?'

'You are tired. When we reach London, I will find you somewhere to live, and you can decide if you want to marry me.'

She felt indescribably tired, and rested her head on his shoulder. How many years would it be before she could feel secure? How long before she could be free? But there was nothing else she could do. She turned to Edouard. 'Are you needed up here?' she said. 'Is there anything you can do to help?'

'I trust my crew. They can manage very well without me.' She saw him look up at the sky, and assess the strength of the wind. 'I used to fish with my father,' he said, 'but that was a long time ago. I'd do more harm than good if I tried to take charge now.'

'Then take me down below, please.' Her voice sounded low amidst the noise of the storm. At first she thought he had not heard her and then she felt his hand grip her as he led her towards the hatchway. He said something that she could not hear, and held the door open for her. Despite his efforts, the wind slammed it shut behind them with brutal force.

She made her way down the narrow staircase in an almost eerie silence, aware only of the muffled roar of the storm and the violent motion of the small boat. She reached out for the handle and opened the door to the lower deck. As the boat lurched more steeply into the wave, she felt her body pressed against his.

All the fear, all the tension of the last days tore through her. She no longer cared what he wanted from her. She needed to feel him close to her.

He turned to her and looked as though he were waiting for an answer. 'What did you say?' she asked. 'I couldn't hear.'

He stopped in the middle of the narrow corridor, bent over her and kissed her damp forehead. 'I said I wanted to make love to you,' he said.

It was what she wanted, too. But she felt suddenly insecure. She had only ever made love for money, and she did not want it to be like that with Edouard. She held back outside the door of her cabin. Last night, at the inn, she had wanted to spend the night in his arms, and he had slept alone. His control frightened her. At least when a man paid for sex, she knew he wanted her. With Edouard, she could not be sure. And he had said that he had to return to Paris. So she would be left alone again. She smiled.

'What's so funny?'

'I was just thinking that if I ever need you, all I have to do is to get myself into some serious trouble, and then you'll come along and help me out. You always seem to be there when I need you.'

'Are you happy with that?'

260

She nodded.

'It would be easier to keep an eye on you if we were closer,' he said, brushing her forehead with his mouth. She swayed against him, rocked by the motion of the waves.

She liked the touch of his lips on her skin. She liked the feeling of his arms around her, holding her steady. She liked it too much.

She tried to move away. And then she knew that she could not do that. He had already paid for her. He was claiming his right. Business had begun again. Automatically, she moved closer and kissed him on the lips. She reached out her hand and opened the door of her cabin. 'Come in,' she murmured.

She felt his fingers tighten on her wrist. 'You have a choice, Colette. I haven't bought you.'

It was hard to stand upright against the movement of the boat. She sat down on the hard bunk. 'It's little enough to offer for a diamond, a letter of credit and safe conduct out of a city at war.'

'And you believe I did all that just to have sex with you.'

'Haven't you? Then why are you doing this for me?'

'Because I want you.'

She shrugged. All men were the same. Then she felt his fingers lift her face towards him. 'Look at me,' he demanded. 'I want you with me. For good. Do you think I am taking you to England to set you up for other men?'

She nodded. 'You said I had a choice.'

'You do. You don't have to marry me. But am I so bad a prospect as a lover? '

'You've been very reluctant until now,' she told

him quietly. She was not going to let him know how much she had wanted him before. So badly that she had spied on her best friend out of jealousy.

'And you, *chérie*, have been extremely busy. I told you, I don't share my women.'

She felt his hands gently resting on her shoulders. She took one of them in hers and looked at it. He had large, peasant hands, like the men she had grown up with, and although his were elegantly manicured, and well cared-for, they would never have the smooth refinement of a Gilles or a Michel. She was very grateful for that fact.

Just being near to him was stirring feelings she thought she had lost. There was a tenderness in the way he touched her that made her feel young again, as if all the scandals of Paris did not touch her any more. She lifted his hand to her lips and pressed a kiss into his palm.

She felt him tremble. The aloof, disciplined Edouard Kerouac was a man after all. A man whose body next to hers was making her aware of every nerve on her skin, longing for his touch. If they made love now, she would never be free of him. She knew that, as well as she knew that she could never leave here without loving him. She let go of his hand and looked into his black eyes. He was waiting for her; nothing she could do would make him lose that iron control.

She reached out for him, and placed her fingers on the open neck of his shirt. She could feel the pulse beating at his throat, and she rested her hand over it, letting its rhythm throb its message into her body. She could see pain in his dark eyes as her fingers slid further down, over his chest, and gently unfastened each button until she could touch the firm, muscled flesh, and rest her burning forehead against him.

Anne had warned her that it was never safe to rely on just one man. But if she married Edouard that would be different. She found it hard to think coherently, while he was so close to her, while her lips were almost touching his body and her hands continued their slow progress over his ribs. She slid them round behind him, holding him in her arms, not wanting to let him go.

His hands had dropped loosely by his side when she released them. Now she felt the tension of his clenched fists bunch the muscles along the length of his arms and his shoulders. She could feel him fighting for control and she wanted him to lose the battle. She pushed his shirt down over his tensed shoulders and let it fall to the cabin floor. She dropped her arms loosely by her side, waiting for him to undress her.

A faint warmth returned to the unfathomable black eyes, and she knew that he had understood exactly what she wanted. Slowly, she felt his hands gently parting the thin silk of her bodice.

'How bad is the storm?'

'I think we shall make it.' His voice was calm, but still she knew that he was worried. She felt his fingers tighten on her waist. Her clothes were drenched through from the salt spray, making it hard for him to unfasten the long row of buttons down the back of her dress. He seemed to be deliberately slow. Perhaps he did not want her after all. She turned to face him, and felt the bodice slide gently apart. Her breasts rested lightly in the lace cups of her stays. Only three hooks in the front held that on. She reached down to undo them.

It had never mattered so much to her that a man should approve of her body. Now she trembled so that the stiff metal clasps refused to part. She felt him gently push her hands away and release the tight stays so that her breasts fell forward.

In the cellar he had seen her completely naked without seeming to take any notice of her. Now he stood in front of her, breathing heavily, and she saw that he was fully aroused.

She reached out for him and slid her hands over his bare chest, feeling the warmth of his body on her cold fingers. She peeled off his damp clothes until he was there in front of her, completely naked and arrogantly male. She raised herself on the balls of her feet, so that she stood inches away from him, swaying as the boat rocked, and keeping her distance from him as an exquisite form of torture, wondering exactly how long she could endure not to feel him part of her, buried inside her body and her soul. As they swayed together, she felt the touch of her raised nipples scrape against the muscles of his chest, and the tip of his penis brush the vulnerable, bare mound at the base of her belly.

She parted her thighs and inched closer until she felt him pressing firmly against her pelvis, her breasts almost crushed between their bodies. Her hands were shaking now as she reached up for his face, pulling him down towards her so that she could press her lips on his and taste the sweet savour of his kisses. She tried to keep her hands steady, but they trembled uncontrollably as she stroked the rough stubble of his unshaven chin and felt him forcing her lips open with his tongue.

He lifted her in his arms then, still with his lips pressed to hers, carried her to the bed and laid her gently out on the hard, narrow mattress. She nestled into the warmth of his chest, his arms circling her, and the strong shelter of his powerful shoulders protecting her. His lips left hers and she felt the soft pad of his thumb pressed on to her mouth, as he softly licked the little ridged circles around her nipples. The sensation sent little shivers of desire trickling down over her belly and deep into the moist centre of her body, where she waited for him, patiently, knowing that each touch of his lips on her skin increased her need and prepared her for him.

Her breasts were swollen now, painfully firm as he teased the sensitive flesh with his mouth until he could bear it no longer and swayed over her, letting his lips suck on the soft lips surrounding her sex and seek out her sweet juices.

The storm was dying now, but the swell of the waves still rocked the small boat. One moment she was in his arms, the next he had fallen heavily across her so that the breath was crushed out of her. 'I'm sorry,' he said. 'I had planned somewhere more romantic, and more peaceful.'

His body felt so good against hers, cramped together on the strip of wooden board. He lifted her on top of him and let her sink down over him until she felt the smooth head of his penis rest against her sex. She trembled as she felt his hands pushing her hips gently down so that he rose inside her. There was a moment when she felt the sweetness of his entry, and then the boat slammed down with the next wave and his whole length was buried deep inside her.

He cried out as she pressed down on him, sucking him into her, letting him feel the soft cushions

265

of her sex lips circling the base of his penis. For the first time she saw him lose control as he writhed beneath her, and she rose on her knees to release him and torment him. Instantly he lifted his hips to enter her again. As he did so, she sank down and felt him climax as her own response overwhelmed her.

She let her head fall on his chest and felt his arms close around her as the creak of a metal chain told them that the anchor was being lowered. The sea was calm. They were in harbour.

Visit the Black Lace website at
www.blacklace-books.co.uk

BLACK
LACE

FIND OUT THE LATEST INFORMATION AND TAKE
ADVANTAGE OF OUR FANTASTIC **FREE** BOOK OFFER!
ALSO VISIT THE SITE FOR . . .

- All Black Lace titles currently available
  and how to order online
- Great new offers
- Writers' guidelines
- Author interviews
- An erotica newsletter
- Features
- Cool links

BLACK LACE – THE LEADING IMPRINT OF WOMEN'S SEXY FICTION

TAKING YOUR EROTIC READING PLEASURE TO NEW HORIZONS